TROUBLE CREEK

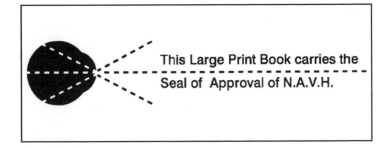

This Large Print Book carries the
Seal of Approval of N.A.V.H.

TROUBLE CREEK

RALPH COTTON

THORNDIKE PRESS

An imprint of Thomson Gale, a part of The Thomson Corporation

THOMSON
TM
GALE

Detroit • New York • San Francisco • New Haven, Conn. • Waterville, Maine • London • Munich

Thorndike Press® Large Print Westerns.

The text of this Large Print edition is unabridged.

Other aspects of the book may vary from the original edition.

Set in 16 pt. Plantin.

LIBRARY OF CONGRESS CATALOGING-IN-PUBLICATION DATA

Cotton, Ralph W.
    Trouble Creek / by Ralph Cotton.
       p. cm. — (Thorndike Press large print westerns)
    ISBN 0-7862-8997-X (alk. paper)
    1. Bank robberies — Fiction. 2. Large type books. I. Title.
PS3553.O766T76 2006
813'.54—dc22   2006019428

Published in 2006 by arrangement with NAL Signet, a division of Penguin Group (USA) Inc.

Printed in the United States of America on permanent paper
10 9 8 7 6 5 4 3 2 1

For Mary Lynn . . . *of course*

And in fond memory of Evan Hunter (Ed McBain), whose inspiration stays with me and keeps me reaching. Long live the boys at the ole 87th.

PART 1

CHAPTER 1

The four riders appeared in the morning sunlight, riding abreast slowly, taking up most of the rutted dirt street. They wore long tan riding dusters with upturned collars. Broad-brimmed hats mantled their foreheads, partially hiding their faces. Bandannas drooped at their chins. Two of them carried sawed-off ten-gauge shotguns across their laps. All four had pulled back the lapels of their dusters, revealing holstered side arms — tools of their trade, their leader, Dick Lowry, would say.

Lowry rode a foot ahead of the others, in a jaunty fashion, liking the way townsfolk along the thoroughfare turned toward him with fear in their eyes. He knew there hadn't been a sheriff in Olsen for quite a while, and he knew the odds were long on anyone here trying to stop him and his men from doing what they came here to do. "We rob banks," Lowry was fond of saying upon cocking his Colt in some hapless bank teller's face. He smiled slightly to himself, thinking about it.

"Looks like this one is going to be as easy as the last one," said Pony Phil Watson, riding next to Lowry. He snickered like a devious child and added, "I don't see why we can't wire ahead and tell them to just *send* the money to us. Save themselves some time and trouble."

"That'd take all the fun out of it, Pony," said Clarence Hawk, riding next to him. "It's always worth more than money, just to see the look on these jay-birds' faces." On the boardwalk a woman grabbed a child by his thin shoulders and yanked him into an open doorway. The door slammed hard behind them.

"Yep, they know why we're here," said Catlan "Black Cat" Thompson, riding on the other side of Dick Lowry. He took a stub of a cigar from his lips, flipped it away and raised the bandanna from beneath his chin to hide his face. "Time to cover up," he said, his voice muffled a bit behind the bandanna.

Having caught a glimpse of Catlan's action Pony Phil snickered again and said, "Look here. The only nigger in the bunch, and he covers his face to keep from being recognized."

"Use that word on me enough, Pony, it'll cost you your tongue," Catlan said evenly, but with a bristle about his broad shoulders.

"I meant *negro*," Pony offered, the snicker gone from his voice.

"I know what you meant," said Catlan, staring straight ahead. "It's your tongue. Use it to suit yourself."

"Jesus," said Pony, "can't a feller have fun with you a little?"

"Shut up, Pony," said Lowry.

"But I was only remarking on him putting on his mask as if somebody —"

"Don't concern yourself with *what* I do or *why* I do it, Pony," Catlan said sharply, cutting him off.

Pony Phil took the hint and pushed the matter no further. Instead he turned his face away, snickered wildly at something unseen, and wiped moisture from the corner of his eye. "I ain't laughing . . . at you, Cat," he said in a wheezing voice, catching his breath and trying to control himself.

"I know it," Black Cat reassured him.

"Damn, is he always this way?" Hawk, the newest member of the gang, asked about Pony Phil.

"It's just nerves," said Lowry, staring ahead at the freshly painted wooden sign

11

that read OLSEN-MORGANFIELD BANK &
LAND TRUST.

"I ain't nervous," Pony Phil said in his
own defense. "I'm just excited is all."

"It's the same thing," said Lowry, without
casting a glance toward him. "Some show it
different ways than others."

"Oh," said Pony Phil, satisfied that no offense had been meant against him.

"Myself," said Lowry, "I never get nervous. Not meaning to brag, but nothing
unsettles me."

"Oh," Pony Phil repeated, staring blankly.

The four veered their horses over to an
iron hitch rail out front of the bank. Clarence Hawk stayed in his saddle, gathered
the reins to the three horses and held them
all in his left hand, his right hand raising
the shotgun, with his thumb over the ham-
mers. Glancing around the now-deserted
street, he said to Lowry, "Damn! I ain't
never seen nothing this easy. To think I was
rustling cattle before you came along. I
ought to be ashamed of myself."

"I told you we never work *too* hard."
Lowry grinned, raising his bandanna, more
out of habit than necessity.

"Yeah, you did, but *gawdamn!* I almost
feel guilty." Hawk chuckled aloud.

Pony Phil raised his own sweat-stained bandanna, following Lowry's lead. So did Clarence Hawk.

"Don't fall asleep waiting for us, Hawk," Pony Phil snickered behind his mask.

"I'll try not to," Hawk laughed in reply.

"Hey, pay attention," said Lowry, partly joking but partly serious. "We don't want to make it look so easy, these loggerheads will start doing it themselves." He moved up across the boardwalk and through the bank door, Pony Phil and Catlan flanking him a step behind.

Inside the bank Lowry stopped in surprise, looking back and forth along the ornate oaken counter, seeing no one behind any of the three bar-enclosed tellers' cages. "Hey!" he called out, drawing his Colt as he did so. "What's a man got to do to get some service here?" But his words drew no attention, only a slight echo. Pony Phil and Black Cat had also drawn their guns. Now they looked at one another above their bandanna masks with puzzled expressions.

"It's empty," Phil muttered.

"Can't be," said Catlan, his eyes growing wary as he scanned the bank.

"Something's not right," said Lowry. "Surely these sonsabitches ain't walked out and forgot they've got a bank full of money sitting here." He advanced forward carefully, his Colt cocked and ready.

"I don't know, Dick," said Pony Phil. "I've seen bankers do some peculiar things, especially if they see some ole boys like us riding in, stoked with scatterguns." He snickered. "They might have run out of here to the nearest jake . . . keep from soiling themselves." He snickered again.

"I don't trust it," said Black Cat, looking all around, stepping carefully along behind Lowry, stopping as Dick Lowry grabbed the bars on a teller's cage and shook it vigorously.

"Neither do I," Lowry said over his shoulder, grinning and jerking his bandanna down from his face. "But if they *are* stupid enough to leave it all laying here for us, I'm obliged to take it."

"Damn right," Pony Phil snickered, also pulling down his bandanna, relaxing a bit, letting his gun slump in his hand. "Fear does some crazy stuff to folks. Don't rule out what I said about running to the —"

A shot rang out, cutting Pony Phil short. He ducked to the side and, crouching, hurried to a front window, his gun hand tightening around the bone handle of his Colt.

"Damn Hawk!" said Lowry, he and Catlan also crouching, swinging the guns

14

toward the closed front door. "I didn't want him shooting up the town!"

Pony pushed a heavy curtain an inch, peeped out the window, then let the curtain fall back into place. Turning to Lowry, he said in a fast, excited tone, "Hell, it ain't Hawk shooting! He's down on his belly in the middle of the boardwalk! There's a gawdamn lawman standing in the middle of the street, holding our horses!"

Before Lowry could respond, a stern voice called out from the middle of the dusty street, "All right, Richard Arnell Lowry, this robbery's over."

"Who?" Pony asked, making a strange bemused face.

"That's me, *damn it,*" said Lowry, clearly shaken. "Shut up!"

"Have your men throw out their guns," the voice continued, "and come out one at a time with your hands raised."

"Who the hell are you?" Lowry shouted, still crouched and hurrying over to the window, Black Cat right behind him.

"I'm Arizona Territory Ranger Sam Burrack," said the voice. "You are all under arrest."

"How the hell do you know my name?" Lowry shouted out the window, careful not to put himself into view.

15

"I know every one of your names," the ranger called out. "You boys have been running wild too long. You've been on a bank-robbing spree across three territories. You should have known somebody was coming for you."

"Bull," said Lowry. "You don't know who the hell else is in here with me."

"The one laying out here gut-shot is Clarence Hawk," said the ranger. "The two in there with you are Catlan Thompson and Phillip Pierpoint Watson."

"Nobody calls me *Pierpoint,* you sons-abitch!" shouted Pony Phil.

Lowry eased upward, took a quick peep out the bottom corner of the window, then ducked back down as realization came upon him. "Jesus!" he said. "That's him! That's the son of a bitch!"

"Who?" Catlan asked, standing hugged against the wall beside the window, his gun up and ready.

"It's that damned ranger who killed Junior Lake and his whole damned gang — that's who!" said Lowry.

"So?" said Catlan. He shrugged. "We rush him, we kill him — that's the end of his string. What's so hard about that?"

"Yeah," said Lowry, giving him a skeptical look, "that sounds *real* easy. Why don't you just jump right out there, shoot him a bunch of times, and we'll finish up here and ride away?"

"Don't think I can't," said Catlan, glowering at Lowry.

"What are we going to do, Dick?" Pony Phil cut in.

"What's it going to be, Lowry?" the ranger called out. "Are you all coming out or do I come in shooting?"

"Damn it!" Under stress, Lowry winced and rubbed his temples, but only for a second, before he blinked hard and turned his attention toward a sound he'd heard on the other side of the bank, behind the counter. "Shhh," he said to Phil and Catlan. His voice dropped to a whisper. "Listen . . . somebody's back there. I hear somebody crawling along the floor."

"I don't hear noth—" Pony Phil's words turned muffled and stopped, cut short by Lowry clasping a gloved hand over his mouth.

"Black Cat, get at the end," Lowry whispered, already hurrying away toward the far end of the counter.

Before Catlan could take position at the other end of the counter, Lowry jammed his gun hand through the bars and pointed his cocked pistol at a bald head that eased up in to sight. "All right, you turd!" Lowry screamed in the frightened man's face. "Open this door or I'll blow your brains all over the wall!"

"Pl-please!" the trembling man said, his thin, pale hands high in the air. "Don't shoot me, mister! I'll give you all the money!" His eyes bulged behind a pair of thick spectacles.

"That's *real* big of you!" Lowry growled. "Now open these bars," he demanded, shaking the bars on the teller's cage. "I want more than the money! You're going to get us out of here."

"Me? How?" The man asked in a shaky voice.

"You'll see," said Lowry. As soon as the frightened banker unlocked the door in the counter and opened it, Lowry snatched him by his suit coat and dragged him out into the bank lobby. "Who are you anyway?"

"I'm Mar-Marvin Albright. I'm the ba-bank president."

From outside came the ranger's voice. "Lowry, your time's up. All three of you come out, or I'm coming in."

"Oh, we're coming right out, Ranger," Lowry called out with a renewed sound of confidence in his voice. He turned his face to Catlan and Phil, nodded toward the open counter door and said in a lowered voice, "Get back there and sack up all the money." Then to the ranger he said, "And I'll be introducing you to Mr. Marvin Albright, my newfound *friend* in the banking business!"

After a tight moment of silence, the ranger called out with equal confidence, "Albright, did you stay in there? After me telling you to hightail it until I arrested these men?"

"Go on and answer him," Lowry said, giving Albright a grin, the barrel of his Colt jammed against the side of the banker's neck. "Tell him I'm about to do to you what no man should do to another." He wet the tip of his gun barrel with his tongue, jammed it against the side of the banker's neck and twisted it back and forth. Albright shuddered.

"I couldn't leave, Ranger!" Albright blurted out. "Money is my whole life!"

Behind the counter Pony Phil snickered as he and Catlan stuffed greenbacks and gold coins into two feed sacks they'd carried under their dusters.

His whole life . . . ? In the middle of the dirt street, Sam shook his head slowly and let out a patient breath, contemplating the banker's words. He looked back and forth along the boardwalk, seeing all the townsfolk safely tucked away into stores and behind cover, watching intently.

Before another second passed, Albright called out in a terror-filled voice, "He-he's making threats on my personage! He's threatening to do things that are . . ." His voice trailed off as his mind searched for a description.

"Vicious and vile," said Lowry, coaching him, still twisting the wet gun barrel.

"Something vicious and vile," Albright repeated to the ranger, his voice sounding more shrill and unsteady. "I fear I'm about to become ill!"

"Turn away from me if you do, you son of a bitch!" Lowry growled, holding him out at arm's length. "Did you hear that, Ranger? You better have! Because we're coming out now. . . . Albright right in front of us. Make a move on us, and I'll open his head like a ripe melon!" To Pony Phil, who had finished loading his bag, he said, "Go check the back door!"

Phil raced to the rear door, unlocked it and tried firmly to open it, but with no success. Turning a look to Lowry he shook his head. "That sonsabitch has put something against it out back!"

"Forget it, then," said Lowry. He shoved Albright ahead of him to the front door, the

Colt now at the base of the banker's skull. Catlan and Pony Phil both rushed in behind Lowry, the bags full of money in their gloved hands. They pressed close behind Dick Lowry.

"He didn't answer," Catlan said, craning his neck a bit to one side, hoping to see something as soon as the door swung open.

"I know," said Lowry, getting tense. "Hey, Ranger! Do you hear me out there? We're coming out. You better not try anything!" He paused for a moment, and when he heard no response he shouted, "Do you hear me? I better have your word that you ain't going to try anything! Else you'll get this man killed!"

The three men and their hostage waited. Still, the ranger offered no reply.

"He's trying to rattle us," Lowry said. "Two can play this game! Banker, open that door. If he starts shooting you can kiss your ass good-bye!"

"Plea-please!" said Albright.

"Please, hell! Open that *gawdamned door!*" Lowry bellowed.

"Oh, God!" said Albright, turning the knob and pulling the door open.

"All the way, banker!" Lowry demanded.

Albright swung the door open wide, revealing the solitary young ranger standing in the middle of the dirt street, their four horses gathered behind him, milling, their reins dangling in the dirt. On the boardwalk, Clarence Hawk lay rolled in a ball, his hands gripping his midsection, blood seeping between his fingers. "Hang on, Hawk," said Catlan, still standing behind Lowry inside the bank. "We'll get you out of here."

"Like hell we will," said Lowry. He took a step onto the boardwalk, hugging Albright to his chest. "Hawk's down! He's no good to us. Forget about him!"

"Drop your guns," the ranger called out to them, his big Colt in hand, hanging at his side.

"Huh-uh, Ranger!" said Lowry. "*You* drop *your* gun! Bring them horses over here, pronto!" He tightened his grip on Albright. "Otherwise he's dead!"

"I start shooting at the count of three, Lowry," said the ranger in a calm, even tone of voice.

Lowry gave a dark chuckle. "Nice try, Ranger, but you ain't taking no chance of hitting an upstanding citizen. If you want to shoot me, you'll have to go through him to do it." Behind him, Lowry heard Catlan and Pony Phil's boots scurrying back away from the open door. "Damn it, boys, he's bluffing!" Lowry called back to them. "You're

22

bluffing, Ranger! But it ain't going to work! What do you say to that?"

"One . . ." the ranger said firmly.

"Yeah, right," said Lowry, in a contemptuous tone. "I suppose you think I'm falling for it." He clenched his teeth and tightened his grip on the terrified banker. "But by God, I ain't! If it's a war of nerves you want, you've got it! Let's let her rip!"

"Two . . ." said the ranger with no difference in his tone or expression. The big Colt had risen and reached out to arm's length, cocked and ready.

"All right, listen, gawdamn it!" said Lowry, his face turning tight and shiny, streaked with sweat. "If you want to kill him just to get me, go ahead! I'm ready to die! I *want* you to kill him! I want the world to see me and you and this bald turd going down together in a blaze of —"

"Thre—"

"Wait!" shouted Lowry. But even as he spoke, he saw the big Colt's barrel leveled toward him, and at that very second the ranger began to squeeze the trigger, Lowry's nerves came unwound. Screaming, he shoved the banker away from him and tried to race away along the boardwalk. But before he'd gone a full step the ranger's Colt exploded. The bullet punched Lowry high in his left shoulder, spun him half around and slammed him against the front of the bank building. He fell to the plank boardwalk, knocked cold. A gasp went up among the townsfolk along the other side of the street. Albright ran, shrieking, in the opposite direction.

Inside the bank Pony Phil said to Catlan, "Damn, Black Cat! He's dead! The ranger's killed him!"

"Huh-uh," said Catlan Thompson, "he ain't dead. He's just down and wounded." He fidgeted with the shotgun in his gloved hands. The bag of money lay on the floor at his feet. "But what about us? Ranger's got our horses! Got us blocked off here!"

"I ain't going to die in prison. What about you?" Pony asked.

"No, not me," said Black Cat. "I'd sooner go down fighting right here than to watch my feet rot away little at a time."

"Jesus," said Pony, thinking about it for a second, before saying with resolve, "all right, then. To hell with it. I'm for charging out there and blasting his ass into a thousand pieces! What say you, my *negro* partner?"

Catlan gave him a look but then said, "I'm with you, my *white* partner. All or nothing." He reached down, grabbed the bag of money and shouted, "Let's go!"

In their frantic run out the front door, neither man realized that the ranger had disappeared from the middle of the street. Now he stood hidden beside the open door, and he stuck out his foot just as Pony Phil came screaming past him.

The shotgun in Pony's hands exploded wildly as he tripped over the ranger's outstretched boot, stumbled outward across the boardwalk and plunged headfirst down onto the iron hitch rail. The rail gave off the sound of a muffled church bell as it vibrated in an aftershock of iron against skull. Pony hit the ground with a thud, facedown, and didn't move. Catlan, who had spilled out through the door behind him, stumbled, lost his footing and his shotgun, then slid across the rough-plank boardwalk, running a splinter into his cheek alongside his nose.

"You are all under arrest," said the ranger, stooping down and snatching Catlan's Colt from his holster before the man could get a grip on the bone handle. A hard swipe of the barrel across Catlan's forehead sent him sprawling backward before the man knew what had hit him.

Three feet away Hawk turned loose of his stomach and fumbled for his Colt with his bloody hands. "I get my . . . hands on you . . . you'll think, *arrest!*"

"Your holster's empty, Hawk," said the ranger, grabbing his hands and pulling them behind his back, causing Hawk to groan long and loud. "But if you're able to make threats I expect it's time we get you cuffed and settled down." He jerked a pair of cuffs from behind his back and quickly snapped them onto Hawk's wrists.

"Oh, *gawdamn,* I'm hurting!" Hawk whined in a strained, raspy voice. "You just as well go on and kill me."

"We'll get you a doctor here in a minute or two," said Sam. He stepped away from Hawk and over to where Black Cat Thompson rose on his palms on the boardwalk and shook his dusty head, trying to clear it.

"Lord . . ." Catlan murmured. He worked his way onto his knees and swayed back and forth, cupping his hands to the long welt on his forehead.

From behind his back Sam came out with another pair of cuffs and snapped them into place before the black outlaw could think of resisting. "All of you who *can* hear me, listen up," he said. "Once Hawk and Lowry are able to ride, we're headed to the badlands outpost. This is your last bank robbery in Arizona Territory. Everybody get used to the fact that you are no longer in business, and it will make the trip easier on you."

"I'll kill you first chance I get," Dick Lowry said through clenched teeth, squeezing a hand to his bloody shoulder wound.

The ranger stepped over to where Dick Lowry sat leaning sidelong against the front of the bank, his nose flat, bruised and bleeding from where he'd smacked the building facefirst. "See? You're starting off with a bad attitude already," Sam said. He jerked Lowry to his feet, spun him around, shoved him against the building and cuffed him quickly. Then he turned him around and shoved him over beside Catlan and Hawk. "I've tried explaining it in a civil manner." He pointed a finger at Lowry. "But now I'll warn you. I won't tolerate any trouble while I'm taking you in." He stepped down to where Pony Phil lay in the dirt, still knocked cold by the iron hitch rail. Pulling Pony's limp arms behind his back, Sam cuffed his hands, still hearing the slightest reverberation of iron.

"Who says you're going to *take us in*, Ranger?" Lowry sneered. "It's a long, hard ways across the desert to the badlands outpost. Anything could happen."

"Yeah," said Hawk, "and I'm betting it will."

27

CHAPTER 2

As soon as the four prisoners had limped and groaned and filed into two dusty cells in the unoccupied sheriff's office, Sam locked the iron doors behind them and dumped the scatterguns, handguns and other assorted weaponry onto a battered oak desk. As he picked up a cushion from an oak desk chair and shook dust from it, the front door opened slowly and Marvin Albright stepped inside, holding a brown bowler hat in his pale, fidgety hands. "Ranger, I-I just want to say thank you on behalf of the town, for what you did out there. We've counted the money, Town Councilman Stewart Nebberly and myself, and I'm happy to report that it's all there."

Sam stared flatly at him and asked quietly, "Where else would it be but *there?*"

Albright looked stunned. "Oh, my! I certainly didn't mean to imply that you —

that is, that anything might — I mean, the money —"

Sam gave him a thin, wry smile. "No offense taken, Mr. Albright. But now that the dust has settled, what made a gentleman like yourself stay inside that bank after me warning you about the Lowry Gang coming?"

Albright looked embarrassed. "I know it came out wrong the way I said it earlier with a gun against my neck, but as trite and incidental as it may sound, protecting this town's money is my *whole life,* Ranger. To me banking is more than a profession. Mine is a position of high trust and integrity. I hold my responsibility seriously. . . . I daresay sacredly. There, that was the way I *should* have said it." He managed a soft, modest smile. "Fear kept me from being able to respond."

"I understand," said Sam. "Fear moves us in its own direction, times like that."

Albright glowed. "Then you forgive me for slipping back into the bank after you telling me to stay out?"

Sam studied the banker's clear, hopeful eyes for a second, seeing almost a childlike innocence there. *No guile, no guise* . . . Sam said to himself. "Hearing you explain it that way, of course I forgive you," he replied.

"Well, ain't this all just sweet and cuddly," Dick Lowry growled from his cell, where he sat on a dusty cot beside Pony Phil.

"That's enough out of you," Sam said, without turning to look toward the cells. Still facing Albright he said, "I'll come by the bank a little later. Right now I need to find these men some grub and get settled in here."

"Oh? You'll be coming by the bank?" said Albright.

"Yes, just to look in, see that everything else is in order," Sam replied.

"Splendid!" said Albright. "I'll have Kaylee Smith, our restaurant owner, bring over some refreshments. . . . I know our townsfolk will want to be there and thank you themselves!"

"Well," said the ranger, his voice turning reluctant, "if it's all the same, maybe I'll put off coming by." He gestured a hand, taking in the neglected sheriff's office. "I best stick here. Keep an eye on these boys and do some cleaning up. Looks like this place has been let go for quite a while."

"That's a pity, then," said Albright, looking disappointed. "I would so love for you to meet our wonderful folks. Perhaps another time?"

"Yes," said Sam, "another time."

Turning the subject back to the sheriff's office, Albright said, "Indeed, it has been a while since we've had a sheriff here in Olsen. Not many people want to come to a place out here . . . off the beaten track, so to speak. The fact is, if it were not for the silver and gold deposits that come down here from the mining companies, Olsen might well become a ghost town. Perish the thought."

Sam only nodded in agreement, having decided to stop talking and see how long it would take Albright to do the same.

"But listen to me." Albright smiled. "I sound just like some old mother hen when it comes to this town. Please don't think me addled, Ranger. It's just that this place has been so special to me, so much a part of my life. I'm afraid I tend to rattle on and on about it."

Sam nodded and smiled flatly.

A tight silence passed. Albright cleared his throat and said, "Right, then, I'll just be off." He turned toward the door, but then stopped and said as if in afterthought, "It just came to me. . . . Why don't I have Miss Kaylee prepare you and your prisoners some good, hot food? I'm sure she'd be delighted to do so. Folks in Olsen are always so happy to be of assistance, especially to an officer of the law."

"Obliged," said Sam, touching his fingertips to the brim of his sombrero.

"Then it's done, sir. . . . And again, I am off," said Albright, beaming. He stepped out the door and closed it soundly behind himself.

Sam looked all around the dirty, disheveled office and shook his head. He rolled up his sleeves and walked to a door leading to a storage room off to the right of the cells.

Watching him step out of sight, Pony Phil, in a pained voice, said to Dick Lowry, "I believe that doctor sewed the skin on my head too tight." He cupped a hand to his bandaged head and turned his face toward Dick Lowry. "Does my one eye look higher than it did?"

Lowry looked at him and seethed for a moment, then said, "You always had one eye higher than the other, so shut up. My shoulder's killing me." He turned and spit on the cell floor in the ranger's direction. "This sonsabitch . . ." he growled under his breath, his left arm in a sling. "Soon as I'm healed, he's dead."

"You keep saying that," Pony Phil whispered, his hand still cupped to his bandaged head.

Lowry gave him a hard stare. "Yeah, I do. So?"

"So nothing," said Pony. "It's just that it keeps him on guard, don't it?"

Lowry had no comeback. He stared at the floor of the cell. "That gawdamned doctor. He should have gave me some dope."

"Yeah, he should have given all of us some," said Pony Phil. "At least you know what happened to you. I don't know what the hell that ranger did to me. It's all a blank. . . . I just as well been in the next town, for all I remember."

Lowry gave him a dark, flat stare and said, "You knocked yourself out, you clumsy bastard. The ranger never had to raise a hand to you."

"Don't fun with me about it, Lowry," said Pony Phil. "This is serious . . . a man getting attacked this way. I might be a criminal, but there's some things even a criminal —"

"I'm not funning with you, Pony," said Lowry, cutting him off. "You bungled everything. . . . You not only knocked the cold living hell out of yourself, you caused Black Cat to fall right behind you."

"Jesus!" said Pony Phil, looking down in shame, still cupping his hand to his bandaged head.

"The doctor had to leave the bullet in

me," said Hawk from the other cell. "Said it was lodged too close to something I didn't even *know I had.*" He sat with his hands folded across his bandaged stomach and said in a strained voice, "Anyhow, you're a no-good shit heel, Pony. If there was any man in you, you'd get yourself a gun and blow your gawdamned brains out."

"That's enough of that," said Lowry, reprimanding Clarence Hawk.

"Enough hell," said Hawk. "I heard what this rotten son of a bitch said out there on that boardwalk when I didn't know if I was to live or die." In a mocking tone of voice he leaned forward, stared over into the other cell and said, *"Hawk's down! He's no good to us. Forget about him!"* With a smoldering stare, he added, "To hell with me, I reckon. Leave me there to die."

"Hawk, I never said nothing like that!" said Pony Phil.

"The hell you didn't. I *heard* you," said Hawk.

"I swear it wasn't me, Hawk," said Pony. "Ask Black Cat!"

Before Catlan could answer, Lowry cut in, saying quickly, "It makes no matter who said what. . . . We were all in a tight spot. What matters is *now.* What matters is how we get out of here. I'll die before I go to prison. Are all of you with me?"

"I am," said Catlan.

"Me too," said Hawk. Still leaning forward, glaring hard at Pony Phil, he added, "I've got scores to settle."

"God almighty," said Pony to Lowry, "I haven't done a gawdamned thing to that asshole! Will you tell him?"

"Shut up, Pony," said Lowry, trying to dismiss the matter. "We got more important things to deal with. Are you with us?"

"Damn right," said Pony. "I always am. You *know* I am."

Both cells fell silent when the ranger walked back in, carrying a broom, some rags and a wooden bucket. Sam stopped in front of Lowry and Pony's cell and said, "Pierpoint, you look to be in better shape than the rest. I'm going to have you sweep this place down real good and give it a dusting."

Pony bolted up from the cot and leaped over to the iron bars, grasping them in a rage, shouting, "Nobody calls me *Pierpoint!*"

Sam looked him up and down. "I'm right — you are doing better than the rest."

"Like hell I am!" said Pony, in a calmer tone, realizing he'd just reacted the way the ranger had wanted him to. "My head feels like I've busted my brain open. You saw the doctor put over forty stitches across my skull."

"It looked bad, all right," said Sam. He shook the broom in his hand. "Sometimes getting up and around helps a cracked skull heal quicker."

"I don't see how the hell it could help," said Pony with defiance.

"It helps by keeping you from getting it busted again," Sam replied in a cool but menacing tone. He leaned the broom against his side, took out the big cell key from his rear pocket and stuck it into the lock. Seeing Lowry start to rise from the cot, Sam said, "You sit still, or I'll shoot you in your other shoulder."

Lowry glared hard at him, but sank back down on the cot; Pony stepped out, took the broom and stood with a slumped, hangdog look on his face while Sam re-locked the cell door. "Ain't there rules about how long a man has to be in jail before he's called upon to do physical labor?"

"Is there?" Sam asked, as if uncertain. "Nobody ever mentioned it to me if there is."

He gestured toward the far corner behind a big potbellied wood stove. "Start over there. Dust every thing down good, then sweep the floors."

"Why don't I sweep first?" Pony asked, being testy. "That way I'll have less dust to sweep up."

"Go ahead. Sweep it first," said Sam. "But then you're going to dust it and sweep it again."

Pony gave him a dark stare. "All right, I'll do it your way — dust it down, *then* sweep it." He walked over behind the stove, turned around, looking back toward the ranger, and said, "I hurt like hell. What did you hit me with anyway, Ranger?"

Before Sam could answer, a knock on the door summoned his attention. He walked over and opened it. "Ranger Burrack?" asked a lovely young woman with blue-violet eyes and hair the color of honey. She held a large tray full of food, covered by a folded-over checkered cloth. Beside her stood a young boy wearing ragged bib overalls and a faded red shirt. He held a wicker basket filled with hot biscuits and covered by a smaller checkered cloth.

"Yes, ma'am," Sam replied, a bit taken aback by her radiant beauty. His eyes left hers, but only for a second as they went to the prisoners, then returned. It occurred to him that this was one of the most beautiful women he'd ever seen in his life.

"I'm Kaylee," she said in a soft, melodious voice. "Mr. Albright asked me to bring you and your prisoners some food."

"Oh yes . . . yes, indeed, ma'am," Sam said, catching himself staring into her eyes like a man entranced. He forced himself to snap out of it. "I didn't expect you so soon," he said, smiling slightly, stepping back and allowing her and the young boy to enter. "I hope we didn't impose."

From the cells, three pair of eyes turned to Kaylee and seemed to lock there. "Lord God . . . !" Pony Phil whispered under his breath, standing behind the stove in a low swirl of dust, his broom in hand.

"No imposition, Ranger Burrack," she said, stepping over to the desk, paying no attention to the staring prisoners. She appeared at ease, accustomed to men staring at her, Sam surmised, watching her closely himself. "As it turned out, I had just prepared roast pork and red beans for the noon meal." Kaylee Smith smiled, sat the tray on the desk and unfolded the checkered cloth, revealing five plates piled high with steaming food. "Robert James here graciously volunteered to assist me in delivering it to you," she said. "Say good day to Ranger Burrack, Robert James."

"Good day, Ranger Burrack," said the boy,

his voice lisping a bit from want of two front teeth.

"And good day to you, young man," said Sam, nodding cordially.

The boy walked over beside Kaylee, sat the basket beside the tray and stepped back as Kaylee unfolded the cloth and let the aroma of fresh-baked biscuits fill the air. As she placed two biscuits on each plate and handed two plates at a time to the ranger, she smiled pleasantly and said, "Mr. Albright also told me that you would like to stop by the bank."

"Yes, ma'am, I would, as soon as I get these prisoners settled in. Do you have someone here who can help watch prisoners?" Sam asked. He stepped over and handed Pony Phil a plate. "Eat while you work." He nodded at the spoon lying on the plate. "Keep that spoon in clear sight at all times," he cautioned.

"Well, we have a blacksmith who will do that when called upon, but I'm afraid he drinks too much to be dependable, Ranger Burrack," Kaylee said. "If all you need is for someone to sit here for a few moments, I will be glad to help out."

"Obliged, ma'am, but I'm afraid that's not a good idea," Sam replied, carrying the other plate to the cell where Lowry stood

39

waiting. "These fellows can get pretty testy, knowing they're going away for an awful long time."

"Not with me, they won't," Kaylee said confidently. "Not if they want to eat well while they're here."

"Still, ma'am," said Sam, "I wouldn't want to burden you." He walked back to the desk and took the other two plates she held out to him.

"Nonsense, Ranger," said Kaylee. "I insist."

Sam returned her smile, looking deep into her eyes as he took the two plates. "In that case, ma'am, I'll take you up on it."

He started to turn toward the door. But Kaylee caught him firmly yet gently by his forearm. "Settle down, Ranger Burrack," she said with a firm smile. "You're not going anywhere until you've eaten and had your coffee. Surely you deserve no less treatment than these prisoners."

Sam relented, took a deep breath and said, "Yes, ma'am. Obliged for your concern."

After his meal and a cup and a half of coffee, Sam left the office and walked to the bank, where he found Marvin Albright standing at his desk, talking to three men in dark business suits. The four turned toward the ranger as he stepped through the front

40

door. Albright's face lit up with a broad smile. "Gentlemen!" he said. "Here is the man of the hour!" He waved the ranger over to them with an exuberant hand. "Please join us, Ranger. We were just discussing you."

"Indeed, we were, Ranger," said a tall thin man who held a straw skimmer hat under his arm. "We owe you a great debt of gratitude for what you did here this morning." He began clapping his hands together in a polite, restrained manner. "Let's hear it for the ranger, gentlemen."

"Thank you, gentlemen," Sam replied modestly, raising a hand to silence their applause. "But I only did my job. Luckily I happened to be in the area and spotted Lowry and his gang headed this way. It's not often I get a chance to foil a robbery in its midst."

"Indeed not!" said Albright, stepping forward with his hand extended. As soon as he'd shaken Sam's hand, he introduced him to the other men. "These are town councilmen Albert Hubert, Dexter Swan, and Stewart Nebberly."

Sam shook hands all around, then said to Nebberly, the man with the skimmer under his arm, "I believe you assisted Mr. Albright in counting the money?"

"Yes, I did." Nebberly beamed. "I was pleased to be of help."

"This town always jumps in and helps out," Albright inserted.

"I would have helped too, had I been in town at that moment," said Dexter Swan, a short, red-faced man.

"Of course you would have, Mr. Swan!" said Albright "That's my point exactly." He spread his hands to take in the entire town. "And that's why we all love this wonderful place."

Albert Hubert, an elderly man with a long white beard, stepped forward toward Sam while Albright spoke. "Do you *feel* well, Ranger?"

Sam realized that weariness had crept over him. He had first felt it on his way across the street, but thought it was only the heat of the noonday sun combined with the hot meal he'd just eaten. Yet upon hearing Hubert's words he realized the feeling had not only stayed with him, but it had in fact grown. But Sam blinked and collected himself, replying to the councilman, "I'm well, thank you. It has been a busy morning." He offered a tired smile.

"Yes, it has, and you must be tired," said Albright. Turning his attention to the councilmen, he said, "Perhaps you gentlemen will excuse us? I believe Ranger Burrack may want to speak to me regarding the robbery." He grinned and cast an admiring glance toward Sam. "I should say the *foiled robbery* owing to the ranger's diligence and courage."

"Of course," said Nebberly "We'll excuse ourselves and allow the two of you to converse." Stepping close to Sam and shaking his hand again, he said, "But let me once more express this town's gratitude."

Sam nodded and shook the men's hands again as they stepped forward before leaving. As the front door closed behind them and Albright locked it and walked back over to his desk, Sam felt another wave of weariness sweep over him, in spite of him demanding himself to stay alert and overcome the feeling. "Ranger Burrack? Are you all right, sir?" Albright asked, looking concerned.

"Yes, I'm fine," Sam said, even though he felt the floor beneath him sway slightly before he could catch himself. He offered a tired smile and heard his own voice sound a bit distant as he said, "A long day . . . like we said."

"Yes, I see," said Albright, stepping forward and taking him by his forearm, as if to keep him from falling. "Perhaps you'd better have a seat here." He helped Sam ease down into a wooden chair. "Let me get you a drink of water."

"Obliged," Sam replied, his voice sounding more distant and foreign to him. He slumped in the wooden chair and watched Albright hurry to a pitcher of water sitting on the counter behind a teller's cage. He saw a worried look on Albright's face as the banker poured a glass full of cool water with a trembling hand. "I'll be all right," Sam called out in a thickening voice, trying to reassure the man. But no sooner had he spoken than Sam felt his head sway forward and bob slightly on his chest, his eyes falling closed against his will.

"My, my," said Albright, "I certainly hope so!" He shook Sam gently by his shoulder and held the glass down to his face. "Should I go get the doctor? I'm afraid you may be coming down with something."

Sam shook his head, forced himself awake and said, "No doctor. I'll be . . ." His words trailed off. That he managed to raise a hand and guide Albright as the banker helped him take a long drink of water.

"There, now, drink it all," said Albright, raising the glass until Sam swallowed the last drop. "You'll feel much better after a nice rest."

A rest . . . ? "No," Sam murmured, knowing he had no time to rest. "Not now. I have to get back to . . ." Again his words trailed off.

"Oh, you don't have to do anything just now, Ranger, but rest and allow yourself to feel better," Albright said, his voice sounding soothing, less concerned.

Sam tried to shake off the heavy weariness that had now completely engulfed him. But he'd become powerless. "I have to get back. . . . The lady is there. . . ."

Soothingly Albright said, "Now, now, don't you worry about the lady." He patted Sam on his slumped shoulder. "I'm certain she's doing just fine."

CHAPTER 3

Kaylee picked up the brass key ring from atop the battered desk and twirled it on her finger. Smiling to herself, she dropped the ring into her apron pocket, realizing the prisoners watched her every move.

From within his cell, Lowry called out, "Hey, ma'am, how about some more of that *gooood* hot coffee?"

Kaylee looked across the room at the outlaw and saw the dark playfulness in his eyes. Ignoring him, she turned to the boy and said, "Robert James, I want you to run along back to the restaurant now." She took a coin from her palm and handed it to him. "You'll need to peel some potatoes for the evening meal and put some wood in the cookstove."

"But, ma'am," said the boy, "you'll be all alone here!"

"Yes, but only for a moment," Kaylee said.

"I'm sure the ranger will be returning shortly."

"Yes, ma'am, but —"

"No buts," Kaylee smiled, cutting him off. "Now run along, before I take back the coin."

Robert James grinned and gripped the coin tightly, stepping backward toward the front door. "Yes, ma'am, I'm gone already."

As soon as the door closed behind the boy, Lowry gave the other men a guarded wink and called out again to Kaylee, "Ma'am, I know you heard me. How's about some more of that *gooood* hot coffee?"

"Of course I heard you. Now shut up, you fool," Kaylee snapped at him. Her demeanor seemed to have changed, suddenly hardened now that the boy had left the office.

"Fool?" said Lowry, giving the others a look and a sly grin. "Lady, you don't know me well enough to call me pet names."

"Don't try my patience," Kaylee warned him. "I know you don't want coffee. You just want me to get back over within reach." She gestured her eyes downward toward her apron pocket. "You're hoping to grab me and force the keys from me."

Lowry looked deflated. "Well, I reckon you can't blame a man for trying, can you?"

"No. Now sit down and keep your stupid

mouth shut," Kaylee demanded.

Lowry couldn't stand for his men to see him bested by a woman. Instead of sitting down or shutting his mouth, he gave the others a look, gripped the bars, and said to Kaylee, "You're right. I didn't want more coffee. I just wanted to see those breasts of yours closer to my face."

Pony Phil snickered loudly.

"Oh, really?" Kaylee gave Lowry a hateful look and began taking short, slow steps closer and closer to the bars. "Why didn't you say so?"

"What the . . . ?" Pony Phil murmured, his snicker halted when he saw Kaylee's fingers reach up and untie the apron string from around her neck.

In the other cell, Black Cat and Hawk stood slowly and eased over to the bars, not believing their eyes as Kaylee's fingers went to the top button on her dress. "She's doing it," Hawk whispered.

"Oh, yeah . . ." Lowry muttered under his breath, seeing her step closer and closer. "Come show me them pretty puppies." His eyes riveted on her fingers and the top of the dress that began to spread open more with each loosened button. Yet he kept himself mindful that only a couple more steps would put her within his grasp. His eyes gleamed with anticipation, a gleam that only faded a little when Kaylee stopped firmly, just short of his reach.

"There," said Kaylee, in a coy teasing voice, revealing only a portion of firm, pale breast. She spread her dress just a bit more in the pretense of closing it, this time revealing her rosy pink nipple before jerking the dress shut. "That's enough for you. I don't want to cause you *problems.*" She looked him up and down suggestively.

"You cold bitch!" Lowry growled, gripping the bars tighter. A low groan rippled across the other men.

As Kaylee began buttoning her dress, the door behind her opened and Albright walked in, carrying a small leather-and-canvas travel bag. He moved quickly over to Kaylee as he said, "Is everything in order here?"

"Oh, yes," Kaylee replied, her eyes still on Lowry. "Everything's in order."

But upon seeing her buttoning her dress, Albright appeared taken aback and said with a stunned expression, "*Indeed?* It doesn't appear to be!"

"Don't worry about me, Marvin," said Kaylee. She jerked the back string on the apron, pulled the grease-stained garment off and pitched it aside. "Are we all set?"

The prisoners stood stunned and confused.

"Yes, and we must hurry," said Albright.

"Is the ranger dead?" Kaylee asked calmly. She stared at Lowry, enjoying the reaction hers and Albright's words elicited from him.

"Yes, he's dead," said Albright. He pitched the bag over onto the desk a few feet behind them.

As if questioning his response, Kaylee asked, "You're certain?"

"I'm certain," Albright said. "Now let's go. The money and the horses are waiting up the alley."

The money, the horses . . . ? Jesus! Lowry felt as if someone had suddenly kicked him below his belt.

"You killed him — finished him off?" Kaylee persisted to Albright, as she saw Lowry start to put things together, his stunned look starting to subside.

"He's dead," said Albright, his countenance turning ashen at the thought of such matters as death and killing. "*Please!* Can we just get going?"

"Whoa!" said Lowry. "Hang on a minute!" He gripped the bars tightly. "How's about throwing us that gawdamned key before you go cutting out of here!"

"You mean, turn you loose?" said Kaylee,

a playful lilt to her voice. "Simply allow desperadoes like you to return to the public?"

"Damn right," said Lowry, still gripping the bars hard. "Lady, don't toy around. This is serious matters. You don't want to leave us locked up here. Not if you want to leave here undetected. We'll commence shouting our damned heads off the minute you close that door! I swear to God we will!"

Keylee asked boldly, "Now would you really do a thing like that?"

"Would we, boys?" Lowry asked sidelong.

"You better know we will," said Hawk in the next cell. Beside him Black Cat nodded vigorously.

"We'll squall out like wildcats!" said Pony Phil.

"If we're going to prison, so are you two," Lowry warned them. "I'll get to see them pretty teats after all . . . maybe get a hand up that dress on the ride to Yuma Penitentiary — the devil's hellhole, they call it." Lowry gave a dark grin. "They keep men and women together there. I can keep you all week and sell you on weekends."

"I see," said Kaylee, as if giving the matter quick but serious consideration. "Then perhaps you're right. I'd better do something." She reached around and jerked a

Colt revolver from under Marvin Albright's suit coat.

"Hey, wait!" Lowry shouted, ducking away to the side. "Can't you tell when a man is only funning? My God, lady! Get yourself a sense of humor! We'd never turn anybody in to the law! Would we boys?"

"Never have, never will!" Pony Phil said, trembling.

"She ain't shooting us," Black Cat said calmly. "She don't want the whole town running in here. . . . Do you, ma'am?"

"Of course not," said Kaylee. "This gun is only in case any of you try anything when we turn you loose."

"Which we've intended to do all along," Albright said, offering a sheepish grin as he walked over and picked up one of the shotguns the ranger had taken from the prisoners. "There are four horses tied right out back here." He broke open the shotgun as he spoke and shoved two loads into the chambers. "Go straight to them and ride away. If we see you on our trail . . ." He clicked the shotgun shut as if for emphasis. "Well, just don't let us see you on our trail."

"Oh, no," said Lowry, shaking his head. "You will not see us on your trail. I *garn-damn-tee* you that! Let us go, and we are out of here!"

"He's lying, isn't he, Kaylee?" Albright asked.

"Yes, he's lying," said Kaylee, giving Lowry a stern look. "They'll be right on our tail, after the money."

"No, ma'am, we won't," Lowry said. "You've got us all wrong! We'll never come near you again. If we even passed you both on the street somewhere —"

"Shut up, fool," Kaylee said, lifting the key ring from her dress pocket. "We've considered the fact that you're greedy and would come after the money. So we've cut you in for a share." She nodded at the bag on the desk and said, "Marvin, show them their share."

Albright quickly stepped over to the desk, opened the bag and held it up for the men to see. "There's five thousand dollars in there for each of you," said Kaylee. "It's payroll money that comes through here, bound for Morganfield's mines, every month. It's not as much as you came here expecting . . . but you can either take it and ride, or follow us and get a load of buckshot in your bellies. Make your choice."

"Hell, money ain't everything." Lowry grinned. "Let us get out of here. We ain't going to try following you."

"That's a wise decision," said Kaylee. She

gave Albright a nod. He stepped over and stood in front of the guns still piled on the corner of the desk, blocking them with the shotgun, up and ready.

"We're all obliged, ma'am," Lowry said, looking her up and down as she unlocked the cell door and swung it open, the Colt still in her right hand. Outside the cell, Pony Phil beside him, Lowry caught the bag Albright picked up and pitched to him. Hefting the bag, Lowry grinned and said with suggestion in his voice, "I only wish we had some time. I always like to thank a woman in a way she'll remember from now on."

But Kaylee paid him no attention. Instead she stepped over, unlocked the other cell and let Hawk and Black Cat hurry past her to join Lowry and Phil. The four went to the back door. They stopped before opening it. "It would be neighborly of you to give us just *one* gun, at least," Lowry said to her in a lowered tone of voice. "Hell, there's rattlesnakes the way we're headed."

"Don't make us change our minds," Kaylee said evenly, holding the Colt menacingly toward him. "And don't let us catch you going any direction but south."

"South it is, then." Lowry continued to grin as he waved adieu. "Like the boy said, ma'am, we're *already gone.*"

Kaylee and Albright watched the four men slip out the back door and close it quietly behind themselves. "Are — are we going to be all right?" Albright asked her, sounding a bit shaky.

She smiled and tossed her long, silken hair back from her face. "We're going to be just fine, Marvin." She looked at the Colt in her hand and asked, "Is this the ranger's gun?"

"Yes," said Albright. "I thought it best I take it."

"I'll hang on to it," Kaylee said, shoving the Colt down into her waist.

Albright only shrugged and went on to say, "I thought our plan had been destroyed when the ranger came and told me these men were headed our way!" said Albright. "If we hadn't made the switch now, it could be months before the mines had this much money coming through here again."

"These men showing up was only a setback," said Kaylee. "Now that it's all over with, I'm glad they did. I don't think anybody will be looking for us for a while. If a posse goes after anybody at all, it'll be those fools, for breaking jail. Lowry and his boys will be lucky if they make it to the border." She gave a crafty smile. "I'm sure some will wonder what the ranger is doing laying dead inside the bank. But as long as no money appears to be missing, you and I are in the clear."

"You planned it well, Kaylee," said Albright. "I daresay I would have never tried anything so bold as this had it not been for you coaxing me along." He moved closer to her, wanting to touch her, perhaps draw her against him for a moment, the excitement of both her and the situation getting to him.

"Not now, Marvin," Kaylee said, keeping his groping hand from sliding down her thigh. "Tonight, somewhere out there under the stars, when we've got all the time in the world. I want to do something special for you."

"You mean . . . something like the French girls do in New Orleans?" Albright said, stepping back and holding the shotgun with both hands.

"Yes," said Kaylee, "over and over, for as long as you want me to." Her voice fell to a soft, creamy whisper. "I'll be all yours."

During the night Sam slid from the chair where Albright left him and lay sprawled on the hard floor beside the polished oak desk. Yet the fall had not awakened him, nor had the roar of thunder and the streaks of lightning that had come and gone outside the bank windows. When Sam did awaken, it was to the feel of a cold morning gloom embracing him and the sound of rain running down the boardwalk overhang and splattering in the muddy street. The sound caused his head to throb like that of a man who'd spent most of the night drinking cheap whiskey. Instinctively in his confusion, his hand reached for the butt of his big Colt, but found only an empty holster. He froze for a moment, his consciousness returning faster upon realizing someone had disarmed him in his sleep.

Sleep . . . ? This was no sleep like any he'd ever known. As he listened to determine who might be in the room with him, he glanced around the floor without raising his head. Names and faces began playing across his mind, attempting to stir and help lift the fog from his memory. He pictured Marvin Albright's beaming face, his outstretched hand, then he saw the concern on Albright's face as he helped him drink water from the glass. *The water . . . ?* Was that it? Albright had slipped him something in the water?

Sam batted his hazy eyes and stared out across the floor, seeing the leg of the desk up close. A fine sheen of dust stretched out across the floor before him like a flatlands desert. He moaned, pushed himself up and sat on the floor, realizing now that there would be no one standing over him with a gun. He had been taken down by a water glass. Yet even as that truth sank in, he began recalling the moments before Albright had brought him water. He'd already been drowsy, barely able to keep his eyes open.

Sam rubbed his temples and pulled himself up the side of the desk to his feet. He'd been drugged before he came to the bank. He stood for a moment against the edge of the desk, picturing Kaylee, the food, the coffee, hearing her insistence that he finish both before doing anything else. He let out a breath as the confusion in his mind began to clear. Kaylee and Albright, working together? He had to press hard to fit those two pieces into the same puzzle and make a fit. *But there it is,* he told himself, forcing his senses to revive themselves and get on with the job at hand.

He walked unsteadily across the floor to the open door of the vault, where the money had been counted and placed after the attempted robbery. Everything appeared to be in place. Stacks of money lay neatly bound, all in a long row, four stacks deep along the vault shelf. Sam batted his eyes again, making no sense of it. Was he wrong? Had this all been some sort of misunderstanding or some strange dream in which he was still entangled?

Behind him, across the floor, he heard the front door of the bank open with a slight creak. He turned to see men step inside cautiously, out of the gray rain, water dripping from their slickers and raincoats. "Marvin?" a voice inquired. Sam recognized Councilman Nebberly's voice and demeanor. "Is that you, Marvin?"

"No," Sam said, his tongue feeling thick and difficult to use. "It's Ranger Sam Burrack."

"Ranger Burrack?" Nebberly asked. "What on earth are you doing here? Where is Mr. Albright?"

"I — I don't know," Sam managed to say, steadying himself against the vault door as he stepped forward.

"What are you doing here?" Nebberly repeated. Behind the councilman Sam heard other voices coaxing him on. "Yes, what are you doing *inside the vault?*" Nebberly asked under the others' prompting.

Sam had no answer. He stepped forward unsteadily, meeting the men halfway across the floor. "I've been here all night, Councilman," he managed to say, knowing it was not nearly enough of an explanation to satisfy either these men or himself. "I think

someone slipped something into my food
. . . or coffee." He realized how uncertain
he sounded, but he could not keep himself
from finishing his thoughts. "Or my drinking water," he concluded.

"Someone slipped you something?" Nebberly looked him up and down, seeing the
empty holster on his hip. "You mean, you've
been drugged?"

"Yes, I have," Sam said, knowing he had
to firm up his answers in order to even get
a better idea of what had happened to him.

As he spoke, two men stepped past him
and over inside the vault. "Looks like the
money's all here," one called out.

"Thank you, Dexter," said Nebberly.
"That's one relief." As he spoke he stared at
Sam, leaving little doubt that he had suspected him of something, but was now feeling swayed otherwise. "And who do you feel
might have done this . . . this *drugging?*" he
asked.

"I have an idea," said Sam, feeling a little
better. "But I don't want to start making
accusations just yet. I have prisoners in the
jail. Let's go check on them. Then we'll see
what we can —"

"The prisoners are gone, Ranger," a voice
tinged with anger cut in from behind Nebberly, "but I suppose you don't know about

60

that either."

"That will be enough, Ed," Nebberly said firmly, without turning to face the man. Keeping his eyes steadily on Sam's, he said, "Before coming here, we went to the sheriff's office."

"Yeah," Ed Thornis cut in again, "and I went by there twice last evening before the storm to see if you needed me to sit watch over the prisoners for you."

"Calm yourself, Ed," said Nebberly. To Sam he said, "We took this off the door moments ago." He held up a DO NOT DISTURB sign for the ranger to see. "At Ed's insistence, we finally decided to force the door open and go inside. The place is empty," he said with finality.

Sam looked past him at the stolid face of Ed Thornis, realization setting in stronger and clearer. "Are you the blacksmith?" he asked.

"Yes, I am," said Thornis grudgingly. "Generally when there are prisoners in the jail, I assist in watching about them." He carried a walnut-handled Remington revolver shoved down in the waist of his trousers.

"I understand," said Sam, taking note of the Remington. "I would have called upon you. But Kaylee Smith told me you were a

61

drunk who couldn't be trusted."

"What?" The blacksmith almost jumped past Nebberly at the ranger. "Why would Kaylee say such a thing as that? I'm not a drinking man, period!"

Seeing that the ranger's hands turned to fists without him backing an inch when the big blacksmith started to lunge forward, Nebberly stood firmly between them and said, "Ed, let's hear him out." He looked back at Sam and asked, "Are you suggesting that Kaylee Smith has some hand in whatever has happened here? If so, I'll send someone to get her this instant. . . . We'll hear what she has to say."

Sam considered things quickly, a clearer picture starting to form in his mind. "Send for her, if it suits you, Councilman," he said. "But don't be surprised if she's gone too."

Nebberly looked all around the bank in the gray morning gloom. Spreading his hands in bewilderment he said, "Meaning what? That Kaylee is involved in . . . what, exactly?" He gestured toward the vault. "The money is here. . . . Nothing seems to be amiss, other than you being in here."

"Where you don't belong," Thornis cut in.

Sam stared past Nebberly at the burly blacksmith as he said, "Let's light a lamp and take a good hard look at that money. I've got a feeling Albright and Kaylee Smith were on the verge of making a money switch and clearing out of here just about the time Lowry and his men came riding in."

"You mean . . ." Nebberly let his words trail.

"I mean all the mining money in that vault just might be counterfeit," Sam said.

"God forbid if it is," said Nebberly, giving a dark glance toward the vault. "I shudder to even think about what Laslow Morganfield will do if it is," Outside lightning licked down as another storm swept closer across the desert floor. Thunder followed, rumbling low and menacing, like an omen of more darkness to come.

CHAPTER 4

Councilman Albert Hubert hurried across the lobby, brought back an oil lamp and lit it. In the glow of the lamplight Sam and the others huddled close together and compared a bill he'd taken from one of the bound packs of cash to another that Nebberly provided from his personal cash clip. "Just as I suspected," Sam said after a moment of tense silence.

"Yes, I see it too," Nebberly conceded, letting out a breath. A sigh went up among the men. "I'm afraid Ranger Burrack is right. This money isn't real."

"How do we *know* he's right?" Thornis said abruptly. "How do we know he didn't just finish switching the money before we came in and caught him?" He stared hard at Sam.

Before Nebberly could answer, Sam cut in, returning the blacksmith's stare, "You don't know. But don't make the mistake of thinking you're going to keep me here, not while I've got four escaped prisoners to round up."

"By thunder, you'll stay if I *say* you're staying," said Thornis, having grown bolder by the minute.

"What about Albright and Kaylee Smith?" asked Nebberly. "We must get our money back!"

Before answering Nebberly, Sam took a step forward and calmly moved the distraught councilman to the side, clearing the way between himself and the big blacksmith as if to address him more clearly. "Just so you understand before this goes any further, Mr. Thornis," Sam said politely, "I will shoot you if you try to interfere with me doing my job."

"*Shoot* me?" Thornis gave him a determined look. Gesturing with his eyes to the ranger's empty holster, he said, "Shoot me *with what?* You haven't done a very good job of holding on to your weapon! If you ask me, the best thing you can do is to shut your mouth and do as I —"

A solid *thud* resounded, followed by a gasp from the rest of the townsmen as the ranger's boot shot upward into the big blacksmith's groin and jack-knifed him forward. Bowed at the waist, his big hands clasped tightly to his testicles, Thornis gagged from deep down in his stomach. He swayed forward unsteadily, almost toppling to the floor had it not been for Sam stepping in, taking him by his broad shoulder and balancing him for a moment.

"Try to breathe deep," Sam said flatly, reaching beneath Thornis' stomach, pulling out the big Remington and checking it as the blacksmith let go a long string of saliva through a strained and painful-sounding groan. Sam reached out his boot toe and dragged the wooden chair up close behind the blacksmith and tipped him backward into it. The blacksmith seated himself, still doubled at the waist. The men stood riveted, aghast.

"*Now* I have a gun," Sam said with resolve. "As far as the bank money and Albright and the woman," he continued as the conversation had not stopped for a moment, "I'll do what I can for you. But escaped prisoners always go to the top of the list." He looked around at the faces. "I know you're without a sheriff here, but is there anyone you trust enough to put on the trail?"

"*Him,*" Dexter Swan said bluntly, pointing a long finger down at Ed Thornis, "except you've kicked his nuts up into his rib cage."

"He'll be all right after a while," said Sam,

keeping the Remington loosely raised, just in case anybody else had any ideas about stopping him. "I'm headed over to the jail to see what things look like. You men are welcome to come with me if it suits you."

"Yes, of course, Ranger Burrack," said Nebberly, "we very much want to come with you." He gestured a hand toward Ed Thornis. "You must excuse Ed." His voice went down a notch. "He has held strong feelings for Miss Kaylee Smith ever since she arrived here."

Hearing Nebberly, Thornis turned a tortured sidelong look up toward him and murmured in a strained voice, "I . . . only . . . befriended her."

"Come now, Ed, we all saw it," said Nebberly. "You had some pretty high expectations for her and yourself. Nobody blames you for it. She did everything to encourage —"

"Which was when?" Sam asked, cutting Nebberly short and ignoring Thornis.

"When *what?*" said Nebberly.

"When did the woman arrive here?" Sam asked, turning toward the door and motioning for Nebberly and the others to accompany him.

"Oh, over a year ago, I estimate," said Nebberly. "She purchased the restaurant

67

from Mabel Reed's estate in Chicago, sight unseen, and arrived by stagecoach with nothing more than a lady's sundry bag . . . which was quite unusual, now that I reflect on it."

"Did anyone have cause to see her ownership title for the restaurant?" Sam asked.

"Yes, I happened to have seen that myself, Ranger." Nebberly smiled, as if having served some sort of purpose. "It was signed and sealed by an attorney of record and *quite* in order."

"I see," said Sam, considering it. Out of the bank and on their way along the rain-blown boardwalk, he said, "Somebody might want to check and see if this Kaylee Smith has any kin back in Chicago. If so, you might want to find out how long it's been since they've heard from her." Sam walked briskly along the boardwalk, turning a scrutinizing look out across the rain-soaked land. In the distance another approaching storm churned and boiled in a black sky.

"Oh, my, then," said Nebberly, hurrying to keep up with the ranger. "Are you suggesting that this *person* might not even be Kaylee Smith?"

Sam didn't answer directly. Instead he said, "If a person knew of Miss Reed's death and wanted to put someone in her restaurant to take over the business, it wouldn't be hard to do, would it?"

"My, my, Ranger Burrack," said Nebberly. "Do you always think the worst of everyone?"

Sam stopped out front of the sheriff's office for a moment and put his hand on the doorknob. "I'm not even sure what's happened here, Mr. Nebberly," Sam replied. "All I know is that somebody drugged me and I woke up on the floor of the town bank. Marvin Albright and Kaylee Smith are two of the nicest folks I've ever met, and so far it appears that they're behind all of this. So for the time being, *yes,* I'm thinking the worst of everybody." He pulled the door open and walked inside.

"Of course, you're right, Ranger," said Nebberly. "I suppose I'm simply stunned by all this. . . . To think that two of our own trusted citizens would do such a thing."

Stepping inside the sheriff's office, Sam looked all around, saw the shotguns and pistols still lying on the edge of the desk where he'd left them, and shook his head, noting one shotgun missing.

Nebberly continued. "Could it be that Lowry and his men overpowered them, forced them to set him and his men free, then perpetrated switching the bank money?"

"I don't think so," said Sam, looking at the empty cells — no sign of a struggle of any sort. His eyes went back to the guns. He nodded toward them. "Lowry and his men would've grabbed the weapons before anything else. I'm thinking that these prisoners were let out under gunpoint and sent out of here to draw me onto their trail instead of Albright and the woman."

"Oh, I see," said Nebberly, seeming only now to have noticed the guns left lying on the desk.

"If that *is* what these two were thinking," said Sam, "they were right. Either one, or both of them, is savvy enough to know that my move will be after the prisoners." A clap of thunder rumbled closer to town. Sam looked back over his shoulder and out the open door toward the encroaching dark cloud. "Even the weather has been in their favor," he said. "By now their trail is washed out. I'll catch Lowry and his bunch, but these other two might never be seen or heard from again."

Having heard the ranger and Nebberly talking, Ed Thornis stepped inside off the boardwalk with a sick look on his face and his hands pressed to his lower belly. Nebberly quickly tried to step in between him and Sam, but Thornis waved him away. "I'm not here looking for trouble, Councilman," he said in a weak voice. Staring at the ranger he said, "I'm going to *see* them again. As God's my witness, they're not getting away with this. I won't stop until I bring them back."

"Ed, you have to settle down first, I beg of you," Nebberly said in a firm tone. "We need you to go after them for the town's sake . . . not because this woman has led you on and shamed you."

"Save your breath, Nebberly," said Thornis. "I'd be lying if I said that has nothing to do with it. But it's for the town's sake I'm going after them. You'll have to trust me on that." He turned his pained expression to Sam and said, "Ranger, I'm asking you to give me back that Remington. . . . I'll soon be needing it, most likely."

Without answering him, Sam picked up one of the outlaws' Colts from the desk, checked it and slid it down into his holster. Staring at Thornis he raised the Remington's barrel toward the ceiling, broke the gun open and let the cartridges fall to the floor.

"Perhaps the ranger will be kind enough to give you some helpful advice about tracking those two, Ed," Nebberly cut in.

"I don't need advice to track a woman and a banker," Thornis said, his pride still stinging a bit from the day's events.

"Good enough," said Sam. He clicked the Remington shut and pitched it to Thornis, butt first. "Here's some *helpful advice* anyway. Keep yourself in front of me until I ride out of here, blacksmith. We've both got plenty to do without killing one another."

On a muddy ridge overlooking a rushing torrent of runoff below, Lowry took off his soaked hat, shook it and slapped it against his wet leg. "Boys, I believe we have finally rode clear through that son of a bitch." He squinted, looking back at the wide black cloud behind them. Gathered around him, the other men shook out their clothes and hats and sat slumped in their saddles.

"One good thing about this weather," said Catlan Thompson, wiping his wet hands on the front of his wet shirt. "We ain't left enough sign for anybody to follow. Rain's washed our tracks plumb over into the next territory." He grinned and patted his wet shirt pocket where his money lay folded against his chest. "Five thousand ain't a fortune, but it sure beats drawing a blank."

"Yeah," Pony Phil agreed, his drenched

head bandage having partly washed away, leaving a long trail of wet, bloodstained gauze hanging down onto his shoulder. "It beats the hell out of Yuma Prison too."

Staring ahead, paying no attention to the conversation, Lowry said, "If my recollection serves me right, two years ago there was a coach stop and trading post on the far side of that stretch of hills." He spit and sat his wet hat back atop his head. "We're going to head over there and see what we have to do to get ourselves armed and get some fresh horses under us."

"You mean Río Frío," said Hawk, sitting low in his saddle, his hand pressed to his side wound.

"Cold River?" said Pony Phil, translating the words.

"Yeah," said Lowry, "Frío Río, or Río Frío." He shrugged. "Some Mexican jargon like that — who gives a damn what it's called? I just want to steal us some horses and guns and get back to the business at hand."

Hawk, Black Cat and Pony Phil all looked at one another. "Jesus, Dick," said Pony Phil, "what do you mean the *business at hand?*"

Lowry stared at him flatly. "The money,

gawdamn it. What other business would I mean?"

"Money?" said Black Cat. "We've got money. . . . Enough to lay up on for a while, go to Mexico City and twirl some senoritas."

"Yeah, what money are you talking about, Dick?" Phil asked.

"The bank money, you slow-witted cur," said Lowry. "Did you think we were going to let those two rank amateurs beat us out of what's rightfully ours?"

"How can we call it rightfully ours?" Hawk asked, his voice strained by the nagging pain in his side. "We stole it. . . . The ranger took it back. The banker and the woman stole it again."

"Ah," said Lowry, raising a finger for emphasis, "but you see, we stole it first. Any way you look at it, that money belongs to us. We're chasing them two down and taking it. Maybe cut a couple of throats while we do so." He ran his extended finger beneath his chin before lowering it. "Anybody don't want to take part in it better clear out now before we get down to cutting meat." He gave each man a harsh stare.

"Hell, I'm in," said Hawk, feeling uncomfortable under Lowry's gaze. "All's I did was ask."

Lowry's eyes snapped over to Catlan

Thompson. "Black Cat?" he asked in a demanding tone.

"Sure. Hell, yes," the big outlaw shrugged. "We got *some* money, but it won't hurt to get some more."

"Pony Phil?" Lowry asked pointedly, giving him the same stare he'd given the other two.

Phil's face reddened a little. "Yes, you know I'm in, Dick," he replied. "I don't know why you think you have to ask every time."

"I ask because I like to keep reminding myself who has enough guts to ride with this bunch and who don't," said Lowry. He jerked his horse back around toward the muddy trail. "Now come on. Let's take what we want from these sonsabitches in Cold River and get on with it!" Giving his horse a hard kick of his boot heels, Lowry took off at a gallop.

"Well, hell," Black Cat growled, "here we go again." He kicked his horse out behind Lowry. The other two followed.

They rode the tired horses hard for the next two hours, looking back over their shoulders, until they topped the stretch of low hills and sat looking down onto the small settlement of Río Frío. In the mid-morning heat, the trading post looked all

75

but deserted, except for three women who stood calf deep with their dresses hiked high, washing clothes in sparkling shallows a hundred yards past the far edge of the settlement, where the cold river revealed itself from within a rocky hillside. On a blanket on the ground lay twin babies in cotton gowns.

Lifting a canteen from his saddle horn, Lowry uncapped it as he eyed the unsuspecting women. He swished a mouthful of water, spit it out in a stream and said, "Guns first . . . everything else after that." He capped the canteen and dropped its strap back around his saddle horn.

"Hell, yes," Pony Phil snickered slightly, eyeing the three women. "The big gal belongs to me," he murmured, staring at the women's half-bared legs from a distance of more than a hundred yards.

"Then you better get to her first and stake your claim deep," Black Cat Thompson warned him. "Once I see some pale legs, something takes over my whole personage."

"Stick to business, gawdamn it," Lowry repeated, turning his horse to a thin path leading down to the settlement.

Pony Phil and Black Cat chuckled as one, staring down as they stepped their horses in behind Lowry, single file. Behind them

Hawk rode slumped in his saddle, a pained expression on his face, his left hand holding his wounded side. Looking back at him, Pony Phil snickered and said, "Damn, Hawk, you're starting to look like something that's laid around too long and gone bad."

"Man," Hawk groaned, "I have never hurt this bad in my life. I think my guts are infected."

"Well, we don't want that, now, do we?" Pony snickered.

"We need to get you some good snake-head whiskey," said Black Cat. "That'll fix you up real fast." He grinned to himself and stared straight ahead.

"Dirty sonsabitches," Hawk murmured to himself. "I knew better than to ever fall around this bunch of buzzards."

From the river's edge, the three women watched the riders move down slowly. Feeling the men's eyes on them even from such a distance, June Cardell, a large middle-aged woman, said to her daughter and her daughter-in-law, "Dears, both of you leave the rest of the wash for now, take the little ones and go find Mr. Cardell for me. He should be making up livery for the afternoon stage. Tell him we've got riders coming down off the high desert."

"Mother," said Dory Cardell, squinting

up at the four riders descending from out of the harsh sunlight, "does this mean trouble?"

"It might," said June. "No good ever rides in from that inferno — only rogues and killers on the run. Now get going, both of you. Tell your father I'm *stalling* them. He'll know what I mean."

"But, Mother June, we can't leave you out here!" said Mary Carver Cardell, gathering the twins quickly.

"Never you mind about me," June replied. "I'll be all right. Get along quickly, now. Find Mr. Cardell and Jamison." She'd been staring closely at the four riders, their worn-out horses, their dark, desperate demeanor. She had seen more than her share of this type of men. "Then the two of you hide yourselves and the little ones," she added quickly, seeing her daughter-in-law pass one of the twins to young Dory.

As she'd spoken, June Cardell's voice had taken on an urgency. The younger women took note of it and hurried away with the twins, without questioning her any further. June waited for a moment until the two young women were out of sight. Seeing the riders nudge their horses out onto the flatter land and form abreast of one another, she walked out of the water and behind a cottonwood tree. Once out of sight, she unbuttoned the top three buttons of her dress and pulled the small .36-caliber pistol from her bosom. She felt her breath become hastened and shallow as she hurriedly raised her dress, stepped out of her summer undergarments, folded them neatly and laid them aside.

Before coming out from behind the cottonwood, she spread the bodice of her dress open a bit, exposing the cleavage of her large, pale breasts. In the pocket of her dress she carried the small pistol. "Well, good God, looky here," said Lowry over his shoulder, seeing the woman step out into view. "Second time in two days I've had teats pointed at me." He chuckled, gigging his horse forward. "Makes me feel like a young suckling pig."

As the four rode closer, June Cardell called out, "We have no fresh animals, if that's what you came for." Eyeing their empty saddle boots and holsters, she almost breathed easier for a moment. But then Dick Lowry looked toward the settlement and back at her, his eyes taking on the gleam of a prowling wolf.

"I bet we can find everything we want around here somewhere if we just ask real polite-like," Lowry said, giving her a harsh, mirthless grin. "Where did those two *young* fillies take off to?" he asked.

"What fillies are you talking about?" June asked, playing dumb.

Lowry's eyes hardened instantly. "Am I going to have to backhand you a few good licks? We saw two young women down here, both as pretty as fresh flowers. Where'd they run off to?"

"She sent them to warn somebody, I expect," said Pony Phil.

Lowry stepped his horse closer. "Aw, is that right? You sent them away. That's damn inhospitable of you — *warning* somebody about us. Now you've gone and hurt our feelings. What are you going to do to make up for that?"

June stood firm and took on a strong, brazen tone. "You can all satisfy yourselves right here if you'll just ride off afterwards." She raised her dress, exposing her pale nakedness to them.

"All this just to stall us?" Lowry chuckled.

"Yes," June admitted freely. "Do you want some or not?"

"You must have something awful valuable in that settlement," he pried, "offering yourself right up this way."

"No, we don't," said June, holding his gaze. "I just want all of you out of here.

80

We've got little ones. We don't want any trouble."

"Then you better hope to hell there's some guns and fresh horses waiting for us afterwards," Lowry said coldly. "Get the dress off. Spread yourself beneath that tree."

Hawk protested. "Dick, we should get what we came here for while we can. We ought not fool around out here."

"Easy for you to say, Hawk," Pony Phil snickered. "You can't do nothing anyways with your belly shot up."

"She's told yas she's only stalling you," said Hawk. "Don't let them get set up enough that they can send us away empty-handed."

"Damn, Hawk," said Lowry, stepping down from his saddle and taking off his gun belt as he walked toward the tree. "When have we ever left anywhere empty-handed?" Smiling, he added, "Since you ain't able to take your share in this, you ride on in there, tell whoever's in charge to send us out four horses and some shooting iron . . . less they want us to wear this woman out and ride in and spend some time visiting with them."

Beneath the cottonwood tree, June Cardell pulled her dress off over her head, folded it and lay back, using it for a pillow, reminding herself that in its pocket the small pistol

81

lay close at hand. But she would only reach
for it as a last resort.

CHAPTER 5

Inside Río Frío, Matson Cardell paced back and forth rigidly, trying to contain his rage. He held his left hand clenched into a tight fist at his side. In his right fist he gripped a double-barreled shotgun. His large knuckles turned white as he watched Clarence Hawk ride in slowly from the direction of the shallows. From the time his daughter and daughter-in-law had run into the livery barn with the babies and told him of the approaching riders, Cardell and his son, Jamison, had barely had time to gather their animals inside the barn and drop all of the wooden shutters down over the windows of the thick-walled adobe. Had his wife, June, not stayed behind, these men would have been upon them by surprise.

"All right, Jamison," Cardell said in a lowered voice to his son, who sat in the bed of an aging Conestoga wagon, "a rider's coming. Looks like he's alone."

"I see him, Pa," the young man replied, peeping through the hole in the wagon's ragged canvas top. Jamison Cardell held a Henry rifle in his capable hands. "Looks like he's about rode that horse into the ground."

"And I expect horses will be what they've come looking for," said Cardell. He stood still, his feet planted shoulder width apart, his jaw clenched tight.

When Hawk had ridden in close enough to see the anger in Matson Cardell's eyes, he brought his tired horse to a halt and raised a hand as if in a show of peace. "They sent me to tell you what they want," he called out across a distance of forty feet.

"They?" said Cardell. "Are you one of them or not?"

"I am," said Hawk, sitting a bit bowed in his saddle, "but as you can see, I'm in no shape to cause you or your family any harm." He gestured toward the large blood-stain on his side.

Cardell looked at the wound, then stared past him for a moment toward the shallows. "All right, what do they want?"

"Four good horses, guns and ammunition, some food and whiskey, and whatever doctoring goods you have on hand."

"Then you'll ride on?" Cardell asked.

84

"We will," said Hawk.

"Once you're armed how do I know you won't attack us?" Cardell asked, keeping the gun stock tight in his hands.

Hawk gave a glance toward the Conestoga, then toward the adobe-and-wood structure that served as business and home for the Cardell family. "Hell, mister, we're on the run. We've got no time to put you people under siege. The sooner I return with the guns and horses, the sooner my pards will turn your woman loose and we'll cut out of here. That's all I've got for you."

"Jamison," Cardell called out, without taking his enraged eyes off of Hawk, "you heard him. Bring four horses, a bag of food and a dozen rounds of ammunition." To Hawk he said, "We've no whiskey or medical supplies. The last band of men riding down from the high desert took all we had."

"We'll need more ammunition than a dozen rounds," Hawk said, showing no concern for what the last riders had wanted from the small trading post.

"A dozen rounds is all you'll get," said Cardell. "I'll see to it you have to save your bullets for whoever's chasing you, instead of my family. You can get bullets at your next stop."

"You best consider your woman, mister,"

Hawk cautioned him, giving him a hard stare.

"I'm considering my wife as much as I can," said Cardell. "But I'm looking out for the rest of this family as well. Take it or leave it." He stood firm and offered nothing more on the matter.

After a tense second, Hawk winced at the pain in his side and said, "All right, mister, let's get this swapping done. I don't want to be in this shit hole no more than you want me here."

"Go get my wife and bring her here," said Cardell. "We'll make the swap right here where we're standing. If she's harmed, we'll have nothing but a fight on our hands."

"She ain't harmed," said Hawk, "unless you call *stalling* us harm." He gave Cardell a knowing stare. "You did have it worked out between the two of yas for her to *stall* folks, didn't you?"

Without answering Hawk's question Cardell clenched his teeth and tasted the bitter bile in the back of his mouth. "Go bring her," he said, seething with hatred. "You'll get your horses and guns."

Hawk backed his horse a few careful steps, then turned it and rode away, back to the shallows, where he saw June Cardell stand up naked, bits of grass and earth stuck to her, and hurry to the river, holding her folded-up dress to her bosom. Seeing Hawk approach, Lowry walked forward to meet him. Behind him, Black Cat Thompson stood buttoning his fly. Pony Phil lay back against the tree, a look of satisfaction on his sweaty face.

"He said she'd better not be harmed," Hawk said to Lowry, stopping his horse three feet from him.

"*Harmed,* hell! That woman would take on an army and not bat an eye. What about the horses, guns and supplies?" Lowry asked, sounding impatient with him.

"No whiskey or medical supplies," said Hawk. "The guns and horses will be waiting for us. We just got to bring her in unharmed."

"Hear that, June honey?" Lowry called out to the woman as she pulled her dress down over her and tried straightening it. "Your husband wants you brought in *unharmed.*" He grinned widely and winked at Thompson and Pony Phil. "Are you *harmed* any? If you are, I can't see it."

"I'm all right," June replied, forcing her voice to remain strong and calm. She ran her fingers back through her tangled hair and let her hand fall reassuringly to the feel of the small gun in her dress pocket. "Can I go home now?"

"Hell, why not?" Lowry said with a dark chuckle. "Unless you want to do it all over again."

"I want to leave now," June said flatly.

"All right, then," said Lowry. "Looks like you've *stalled* us about as long as you're going to. Get on over here."

"They're pretty well prepared in there," Hawk warned him, casting a backward nod toward the trading post. "There was two guns pointed at me that I can swear to. Probably more inside the adobe."

"Yeah?" said Lowry, seeming unconcerned. He swung up into his saddle. "We're pretty well prepared ourselves, long as I've got a hand around this woman's throat." He called out to the woman in an overfamiliar manner as she limped over to him, "June dearest, step up here into the saddle in front of me." He scooted back over the saddle cantle, making room for her. "I know you're anxious to get back to your husband, tell him about the nice time we all had." Reaching down, he took her dirty hand and gave her a pull upward across his lap.

"He knows what happened to me," June said in a defeated tone. She shoved her disheveled hair from her dirt-streaked face and sat slumped in the saddle, powerless to do anything about being in Lowry's arms.

Inside the big Conestoga wagon, Jamison Cardell sat staring intently in the direction of the shallows, where the trail disappeared over a slight rise. So focused was his attention, he did not hear his wife, Mary, walk from the front door of the big adobe building to the rear wagon gate until she said quietly beside him, "Jamison?"

Startled, Jamison almost swung his rifle barrel around toward her in reflex. "For goodness' sakes, Mary!" he said, loosening his grip a bit and letting the rifle barrel down in his hands. "Don't ever sneak up on a man with a loaded gun that way."

"I-I'm sorry," Mary replied, stunned by her young husband's sudden violent response. "I didn't think I was *sneaking* up on you."

"I know you didn't mean to, Mary," Jamison said softly, letting down his tense demeanor. He offered a slight smile of apology. "What are you doing coming out here anyway?" He glanced toward his father, who stood thirty feet in front of him behind a stack of oaken barrels, facing the trail to the shallows. Ten feet in front of his father stood four horses, saddled and ready, their reins tied to a hitch post. On the ground at their hooves lay two pistols, an older brush-scarred rifle, a long single-barreled shotgun and a canvas bag with the dozen bullets in it.

"You're out here," Mary said in a bit of a child-like tone.

"Just to keep close watch on the trail and on the horses," said Jamison. "As soon as we see them coming, we're hightailing it inside. Pa gave strict orders for you and Dory to keep the door bolted until him and me come running."

"I know," said Mary Cardell, "but I couldn't just stand there, peeping out the rifle slot, waiting."

"Waiting is all we can do right now," said Jamison. "If we want my ma back alive, we have to wait for them to make the next move."

"This is so terrible, poor Mother June being held by those men," Mary said, her eyes becoming moist. "This all happened so fast. All we were doing is peaceably washing clothes in the river. We saw these men, and all of a sudden Mother June sent Dory and me running back to the post. She knew these men were trouble the minute she laid eyes upon them." Mary paused in reflection. "Living here in this place is just one long, terrible nightmare."

Jamison looked away, unable to face his young wife as he said, "Ma'll be back with us shortly. They'll take the guns and horses and leave."

"But that's this time, Jamison," said Mary. "What about the next time? There will be other men like these — there always are. What about when it's young Dory they're holding until their demands are met?"

"Ma won't let that happen," Jamison said flatly, still avoiding her eyes. "Neither will Pa or me. Dory is too young. She has nothing to worry about."

"Oh," said Mary, as if coming to a realization, "then what about me? Will I be expected to stall them?"

"No, Mary, I would never let something like that happen," said Jamison, shaking his head vigorously. "Times are changing fast out here. The law is getting better and better at keeping men like these from harming innocent people. We just have to be patient a little while longer —"

"A little while longer?" Mary Cardell said as if in disbelief. "The law will never be able to keep men like these from hurting innocent people, Jamison," she said, cutting him off. "The Bible says the poor will always be with us. It should mention that these monsters will always be with us too."

Jamison took a deep breath. "I'm sure it does, Mary, in some place or other. Now *please* go back inside," he added, catching a glimpse of a horse ride up into view on the trail to the shallows.

From behind the stack of barrels, Matson Cardell called out over his shoulder to his son, "Fall back inside the post, Jamison. Here they come."

"I'm right behind you, Pa," Jamison called out in reply.

"No!" said Matson. "You get inside this minute. I'll be right along, as soon as I see your ma is all right."

Turning to Mary, Jamison said quietly, "Hurry, Mary. Get inside and get to the rifle slot. Don't shoot unless you have to."

"Can't I do more to help?" Mary asked, backing away, ready to turn and run to the shelter of the thick adobe walls.

"No," Jamison said. "Just pray things go the way they should." He called out to his father, "We'll both go inside together, Pa. I want to see that she's all right too."

Under his breath, Matson Cardell muttered, "Damn hardheaded youngster." But he said, without looking back at Jamison, "All right. Then stay calm, son. That's the most important thing."

Riding slowly into full sight of the trading

post, Lowry said to the others as he spotted the horses and guns awaiting them, "Everybody spread out a little and pay close attention. I'm keeping June here against my chest until Pony Phil picks up that six-shooter and sticks it in my hand." His eyes went to the rifle barrel sticking out from under the canvas on the covered wagon. The canvas stirred on a warm breeze. Then his gaze went to Matson Cardell, as the man ventured around the oaken barrels for a better look at his wife's face.

"June, can you speak to me?" Matson called out. "Are you hurt?"

"Yes, Mr. Cardell," June called out, keeping her voice strong and steady in spite of all she'd been through, "I'm as well as can be ex—"

"Hell, she's rosy as a new bride," Lowry called out with a grim chuckle. "This is one fine chunk of woman you've got here, trader. You ought to close this flea trap and put her to working."

"There are your horses and guns," Cardell said, his voice hoarse with rage. "Let her go, and clear out of here."

While Cardell spoke, Pony Phil dropped from his saddle and hurried forward, leaving his tired horse behind. He quickly untied the four fresh horses' reins, snatched up one of the revolvers and the bag of ammunition from the ground and led the horses over to where Lowry still held the woman firmly against him.

"Not so fast, trader," said Lowry, taking the pistol from Pony Phil's hand, checking it, seeing that it was empty. "I'm the one says how this goes, not you." He opened the bag and looked down in it. "Well, well, only five revolver cartridges out of a dozen. You sure cut a hard swap, don't you, now?"

"I told you men, it's all I'm doing!" Cardell called out. "Any more bullets than that, I know you're apt to turn those guns on us!"

Lowry looked all around the cluttered yard at broken shipping crates, shipping barrels and livery items. As he loaded the revolver he asked matter-of-factly, "What is it you think I might want from a place like this?" He grinned, adding cruelly, "Except a good, long taste of ole June here."

Cardell clenched his teeth, trying to keep from flying into a killing rage. "There's nothing else here for you! You've got your horses and guns — now go!"

"Huh-uh," said Lowry, "not with only *five* bullets for this revolver. I take that as a deliberate slight. And after all we've done for your woman."

Hearing the conversation and knowing his father had just about reached his breaking point, Jamison called out, "For God's sake, give him some more bullets, Pa. Get them out of here!"

"Yeah, Pa," said Lowry in a mocking voice, "give us more bullets and get us out of here. June here has satisfied all our appetites. . . . But you never know when red-blooded men like us will get hungry all over again." Grinning broadly, Lowry reached a gloved hand up and squeezed one of June Cardell's large breasts.

"You gawdamned son of a bitch!" Matson Cardell raged, losing all sense of judgment and jumping from behind the barrels, his rifle clenched tightly in his hands. "Turn her loose. I'll kill you!" Even in his rage he knew he could shoot without hitting his helpless wife.

But Lowry only grinned, mocking him. The six-shooter bucked and exploded once in his hand, sending a bullet slicing through Matson's heart. "Damn!" said Lowry, looking at the gun in his hand as if delightfully surprised. "This thing shoots straight enough."

From the covered wagon, a shot came whistling past Pony Phil's head. A second shot thumped into the ground at the hooves of Hawk's tired horse. Lowry held June screaming and fighting against his chest, knowing that no shots were going to be aimed at him as long as he held her.

"Damn it to hell!" Pony Phil shouted at Lowry in a tight, worried voice. "He's going to shoot us all to pieces!"

"Well, kill him, then!" Lowry shouted, laughing loudly, knowing he held a winning hand with June on his lap. "Hell, kill them all, for that matter. I'm not stopping you!"

"You heard him, boys!" shouted Pony Phil. "They started it. Let's finish it!"

CHAPTER 6

The second storm had not yet spent itself and moved on when the ranger rode out of Olsen. But he knew that Lowry and his men had a good ten-to-twelve-hour head start on him. Neither Lowry nor any of his men had impressed Sam as being anything more than a second-rate gang of bank robbers. They were not the brightest men he'd ever come across, and Lowry himself was by no means a great leader. But that was one more good reason why Sam needed to get on their trail and catch up to them as quick as possible. Something about being free and back on the run after hearing the finality of an iron door clanging shut between themselves and the rest of the world caused some men like these to grow wilder, bolder, and in most cases more ruthless, the ranger had observed.

He'd thought about Lowry and his men all the while as he pressed on through the raging storm, his big Appaloosa stallion shying a bit at the sight of glittering lightning, and the roar of thunder rumbling like cannon fire from the belly of the dark heavens. Had he considered Lowry a stronger, smarter leader, Sam would not have been nearly as concerned, he'd told himself, pushing on against the howling wind and sheets of sideways rain. But more than once he'd seen circumstances such as these lead men to make that short jump from second-rate thieves to first-rate killers. Tapping his heels to the big stallion's sides, he rode on, examining the dark possibilities of what Lowry's gang might be up to at that very moment.

Keeping to a high mud-slick path that snaked south along a hillside above the rush of runoff, Sam rode on until the rain began to slacken and the thunder and lightning fell away into the distance. With the brunt of the storm having passed, Sam stopped at the edge of a cliff beneath a sheltering overhang. "Good work, Black Pot," he murmured to the wet stallion, stepping down from his saddle, rubbing the horse's withers with his soaked gloved hand. Leading the stallion beneath the overhang he found scraps of pine kindling in a dry corner, and within moments sat stooped beside a small fire.

He took the small coffeepot and some coffee beans from his saddlebags. He crushed the beans on a flat rock with his pistol butt and put water on to boil. While he waited, he stepped out to the edge of the trail and looked down across the flatlands. Below he watched a hard-rushing creek that had left its banks and spread wide across the rocky terrain. Scanning the widening body of raging water he spotted Ed Thornis having a hard time staying in his saddle atop a struggling bay, twelve feet out from the water's edge.

"You're in trouble, blacksmith," Sam murmured, watching both horse and rider begin to weaken quickly against the sweeping current.

Looking up toward the ranger through the gray falling rain, Thornis called out for help just as the bay lost its footing and the two went sliding away on a brown swirling broth filled with islands of brush, downfall and debris from the desert floor. "Help me!" the blacksmith cried aloud, his hat gone, his yellow rain slicker spread out around him on the roiling surface. He slipped past the horse and groped for its reins as the animal caught footing and quickly pulled itself upright and splashed out of the rushing water.

"Oh, my God," Thornis said, spluttering water from his lips. Above him he saw the ranger suddenly appear atop the Appaloosa, racing down the steep, muddy trail. But from Thornis' position he saw little chance of the ranger reaching him in time to keep him from drowning or being pummeled to death by deadfall or countless upthrusts of rock.

The big blacksmith thrashed and fought, struggling toward the shoreline in water no more than waist deep. Yet the grip of the wild, violent current offered no reprieve. Thornis caught a glimpse of his horse standing safely at the creek's edge, shaking itself off. The big blacksmith struggled harder, but only for a moment; then, almost mercifully, the water rolled him over and over until it pressed him downward and struck his head soundly against a wall of solid rock.

Thornis stopped struggling and rose limply atop the swift brown water, sliding along effortlessly now on his back, as if traveling on a swift, endless sheet of air. Along the water's edge, Sam raced against the current, his stallion splashing through dangerous rock and mud until they had gained enough ground for Sam to leap from his saddle, having dogged one end of a lariat to his saddle horn and throwing the other end around his waist and tying it fast as he ran out into the raging water.

As if timed perfectly by the hand of fate, Sam leaped toward Thornis just as he felt the powerful flow of water sweep him off his feet. As the water overpowered him, Sam hooked his arm across the knocked-out man and held tight, feeling them both caught in the current's grip and speeding downstream. But Sam knew that rope would soon come into play. He readied himself for it, tightening his grip around Thornis just as the rope ran out of slack and made a twanging sound as it stretched taut above the muddy water.

"Hold on, Black Pot!" Sam said to himself, feeling only the slightest give on the big stallion's part. As if having heard the ranger's plea, Black Pot braced himself against the weight of his task.

With much effort Sam scraped his boot soles back and forth until he finally felt them take purchase on the rough, rocky ground. Grappling with the unconscious blacksmith, Sam put his weight against the rope and let the current walk him ever closer to the shore.

He dragged Thornis an extra few feet once he felt the water grudgingly turn them both loose. "Oh, God . . . !" he heard Thornis murmur, strangling on the words and coughing them out.

Out of breath, Sam dropped the blacksmith in water three inches deep, knowing that even this spot might only be safe for the moment, the way the run-off continued racing down from the hillsides and spilling out of rocky ravines. "Come on . . . let's get out . . . of here." He gasped, grabbing Thornis by his wet shirt and dragging him farther out of the water.

Coughing up muddy water, the big blacksmith nodded his agreement, trying hard to stand on his own and stagger forward. "I — I . . . knew better than to do that," he said. "I must . . . not have been . . . thinking straight."

"You were following me," Sam said, catching his breath, untying the rope from around his waist. He whistled for Black Pot and gathered the rope as the big stallion came running to him.

"No, I wasn't," Thornis said between coughs.

Sam gave him a look.

"Okay, I was . . . but only through the storm," Thornis admitted.

"Not because of our disagreement earlier?" Sam asked, still gathering the rope as Black Pot loped up and stopped beside him.

"No," said Thornis, "I've gotten over the kick in the groin. There's no hard feelings there." He looked a little embarrassed. "The truth is, I guess I asked for it, jumping on you the way I did." He spit and coughed again. "You just saved my life. Now I'm ashamed of how I acted in Olsen." He paused, then said, "I just let things get the better of me, the way you didn't ask for my help watching the prisoners."

"I told you why," Sam said, hanging the rope from his saddle horn and rubbing Black Pot's muzzle. "Good work," he whispered again to the stallion.

"I know," said Thornis, "but I expect my pride had already been too badly wounded by then." He reached a hand up to Sam, who took it and pulled him to his feet. "I cared more for that woman than I like to admit, even to myself." He offered a thin, apologetic smile. "I hope you'll forgive me."

"It's done." Sam dismissed the matter. "Then why *were* you following me?" he asked immediately, in a polite tone, not allowing them to get too far off the subject until he heard a satisfactory answer.

Thornis gave him a flat stare for a second. But then he seemed to let something go and said, "All right, I'll tell you. I had no idea which way to go. I hoped maybe following you for a while I'd get some direction, figure a way to get on to Kaylee and Albright's trail. The storms have washed out everything. Turns out this is a damned impossible task."

"I see," said Sam, recalling without mentioning what Thornis had said about not needing any help tracking a woman and a banker. "But if you're following me, it's almost a cinch you're headed in the wrong direction."

"Huh? I don't get it." Thornis looked confused. He wiped his wet coat sleeve across his lips.

"I told everybody back in Olsen that the woman and Albright won't be traveling with Lowry's men. They used these thieves as a diversion. They knew I'd have to go after them for breaking jail." Sam gave him a skeptical look. "Didn't you listen to anything I said to Nebberly and the others?"

"I listened," said Thornis, looking a little embarrassed again, "but to tell the truth, I didn't believe you. I figured you would head out after Kaylee and Albright anyways. That's why I followed you."

"Why did you think I would track the woman and the banker instead?" Sam asked him bluntly. "Because of the money?"

Thornis let out a breath, looking ashamed. "Yes, the money," he said. "I just figured with that kind of money involved . . ."

Sam shook his head and turned to Black Pot as he spoke to Thornis. "Your horse is standing up there alongside the water. You best go get him and dry him out up on the hillside. The rain's stopping. You can rest under an overhang, have some coffee with me and dry out before you head back to Olsen."

"You — you're offering?" asked Thornis, sounding surprised.

"Yes, I'm offering," said Sam.

"Even after me thinking you might —"

"I'm offering you a fire and hot coffee," Sam said, cutting him off. "You want it or not?"

"I'm in no position to turn down help anymore, Ranger Burrack," Thornis said, affably, running his fingers back through his wet hair. "Lead the way."

Sam nodded and gestured toward the big bay standing dripping and spent by the encroaching water's edge. "Gather your horse." He gestured a nod upward toward the cliff overhang. "The coffee's up there waiting for you."

Sipping coffee from a battered extra cup the ranger carried in his supplies, Thornis sat close to the small fire, drying himself, his yellow slicker lying spread on the ground nearby. "How did you know which direction to take, Ranger?"

"I didn't know," Sam replied, "I still don't." He sipped from his own steaming cup of coffee. After a moment of reflection, he said, "They broke jail. They're on the run, no guns. They know I'm on their trail, and they know I won't stop until they're behind bars or dead." He shrugged. "South across the border is my best bet for now, until something tells me otherwise."

"But if you're wrong," Thornis deduced, "you could ride a hundred miles, lose a week's time, before you find out you're headed the wrong direction."

"That's true," Sam replied, "but if I'm in this hunt till it's over, wrong starts are just one more risk I have to take." He gave the blacksmith a pointed stare and asked, "How much time are you prepared to put into hunting Kaylee and Albright?"

Thornis considered it. "When I left Olsen this morning, I was determined to stay after those two until I run them down." He offered a slight shrug of his own. "But that was before I started following you." He gave a tired smile, his hair drying tangled and unattended against his forehead. "Now look at me. I've ridden nonstop, straight through one hell of a storm, almost gotten myself drowned . . . and this day ain't even over yet."

"So now you're not sure how far to take it," Sam said, as if having heard the same story countless times.

"That's right. I'm not," said Thornis. "I've got a business to run. I can't throw it to the wind, not for Kaylee, not for any of this."

"And the town of Olsen?" Sam asked. "What about your neighbors' money? What about letting everybody down?"

Thornis winced. "I didn't say I'm turning back. It's just that I can't give this as long as I first thought I could. Besides, most of the money belonged to Morganfield. I'm certain he'll sic some of his own hired guns onto their trail."

Sam listened to the blacksmith justify the situation to suit himself. "So just how long have you decided you can put into this hunt?"

"A week? Maybe two?" Thornis said, as if asking the ranger if that amount of time should be sufficient.

Sam shook his head. "Go home, black-smith. Run your business and put all this behind you."

Thornis looked stunned. "Why? What did I say? I'm *going on* with the hunt. I just have to be practical and put a time limit on it."

"Putting a *time limit* on hunting criminals out across these badlands is just a way of going back in two weeks and telling the town that at least you tried. If that's all you're wanting, do yourself a favor. Go back now and tell them you nearly drowned and couldn't go no farther. They'll be disappointed, but they'll understand. You'll be back to doing the thing that you do best — shoeing horses and bending iron. Everybody will be the better for it."

Ed Thornis bristled a bit. "Ranger, I'm going on after Kaylee and Albright. I might not be able to put the whole rest of my life into it. But if I —"

"Putting the whole rest of your life might be exactly what you are doing," Sam said, cutting his words short. "That's what I'm trying to tell you. A week tells me your heart is not in it. Two weeks tells me the same thing, except that you want to add an extra week to make it look good. Go back to Olsen now. Quit while *quitting* is a choice still open to you."

"I'm going after them, Ranger," Thornis insisted, "on my terms and on my time. If I catch them, that'll be best. If I don't —" He stopped as if searching for another way to say it. But unable to find one he continued. "Well, then, it's true. I will have *at least tried.*"

Sam took another sip of coffee and seemed to relent a little. "All right, then." He stood and dusted the seat of his trousers. "As soon as you finish your coffee, let's get back on the trail. See if we can get across this flooding basin before nightfall."

"Hunh?" Thornis looked even more surprised and stunned. "You mean, ride with you? The two of us?"

"Yep, if that suits you," said Sam. "Just until we figure who went which way. Once we get some clearer bearings we'll split up and go our own ways. How does that sound to you?"

Thornis got excited and stood up quickly, also dusting his trousers. "Ranger, that sounds danged good to me!" He took a quick sip of his coffee and started to toss the rest of it out.

"Hold it," said Sam, stopping him. "I'd never rush a man through his noonday sit-down." He tipped his cup to him. "We've got time to finish our coffee."

Thornis calmed down but hurriedly finished his coffee, shook out his rain slicker, folded it loosely and draped it across his horse's rump. By the time Sam had finished his coffee, put out the fire and readied himself and Black Pot for the trail, the blacksmith had already led his horse from beneath the overhang and looked off to the west, where sunlight had begun piercing the scattered gray sky. "Maybe this break in the weather will reveal something to us," he said, wanting to sound like a seasoned man hunter.

"We'll see," said Sam, leading Black Pot from beneath the overhang before tightening the stallion's cinch and stepping up into the saddle. "I hope you've got something to cover your head, blacksmith. The sun will be boiling the rest of the afternoon."

"I know," said Thornis, raising a hand to his bare head, then down to the damp bandanna around his throat. "Maybe this will do until we find a place that'll sell me a hat."

Sam only nodded and turned Black Pot to the rambling trail along the hillsides. The two rode away.

Thornis took off his bandanna, shook it out and used it as a skullcap, tying it snug at the back of his neck. Sam led the way in silence for the next few miles until he stopped at a downward trail leading onto the muddy flatlands. He gestured a nod toward a tower of black smoke drifting upward and sidelong toward the patchy sky. "It's not the kind of sign I wanted to see, but it just might tell which way Lowry and his gang are headed."

"What lays beyond those hills?" Thornis asked.

"A trading post, the last time I passed through there," Sam answered. "That's part of the reason I headed this way. Lowry knows this country as well as the next. A trading post is the place for him and his men to get the guns and fresh horses they'd be needing by now." Sam's eyes searched the dark, dissipating smoke for a moment. His expression turned grim. He turned Black Pot back onto the trail and rode on in silence.

CHAPTER 7

When Jamison Cardell first heard the sound of horses' hooves clicking softly on the hard rock trail, he ducked down behind the hot, smoldering remnants of the Cardell Trade Station & Supply Company and whispered urgently over his shoulder, "They've come back! Keep the twins hushed, Mary! They'll get us all killed!" As he spoke, Jamison knew there was something terribly wrong with the side of his head. When he'd touched his hand to his temple earlier all he'd felt had been cold, numb flesh. But attending to his wounds would have to wait. Behind him he heard his young wife reply, yet he could not make out her words very clearly; nor did he notice any letup in the twins' crying. "Pa, are you awake? They've come back on us," he said above the sound of the babies crying and his wife trying to shush them into silence.

Matson Cardell made no reply to his son.

"It's all right, Pa. You get some rest," Jamison said in a thick voice, having trouble focusing on the two riders coming closer. "I'll take care of this, just like you always taught me to." He stood up with a rifle gripped in his bloody hands. The sight of him caused the ranger and Thornis to bring their horses to a halt thirty yards away.

"My God!" Thornis whispered sidelong to Sam. "Look at this poor man's face."

Sam grimaced. "Careful here. He's armed and hurt bad."

"That white lump under his eye . . . is that his broken cheekbone showing?" Thornis whispered, the two putting their horses forward one slow step at a time.

"No," Sam replied grimly, "that *is* his eye."

"Oh, no, you're right!" Thornis repeated. "His face is crushed. What in God's name are we going to do for him?"

"Whatever we can," Sam said.

"Who's there?" Jamison Cardell demanded, raising the rifle to his shoulder, turning his head back and forth like a blind man. "I hear you out there! You're not coming back! You hear me? We've licked you once, we can do it again! My pa and me!" He gave a strong jerk on his rifle lever, shoving a cartridge into the chamber.

"Easy there, young man," Sam called out,

113

speaking quickly but distinctly as he kept Black Pot stepping sideways to keep the young man from drawing a bead on the sound of his voice. "I'm a ranger in pursuit of escaped prisoners. I have an idea they're the ones who did this to you."

"They tried," the young man called out in a thick trancelike voice. "But we gave them whatfor. Right, Pa?" he called over his shoulder. He paused for a moment, listening to his father's voice somewhere behind him. Then he called out to Sam, "Pa says how do we know you ain't them come back on us?"

"I don't see his pa back there anywhere," Thornis whispered, just loud enough for the ranger to hear him.

"Neither do I," said Sam.

"You better answer me!" Jamison Cardell shouted, turning his face back and forth, trying to focus on anything he could find in his fractured vision.

Sam and Thornis gave one another a grim look. "He's hurt awfully bad," Sam whispered. "Try to keep him talking." He stepped down from his saddle and gave Black Pot a gentle shove on his rump, moving him out of danger.

"Believe me, young man," Thornis called out, "we've got nothing to do with that

114

bunch, except that the ranger here is running them down. They came into Olsen and tried to rob our bank. You know where Olsen is, don't you?"

Thornis watched Sam slip quietly around in a wide half-circle and move in closer and closer to the wounded young man.

"I know where Olsen is," said Jamison, "but I don't know you." His face moved back and forth, seeing jumbled broken images that made no sense to him, his left eye dangling bloodily down from its socket onto his cheekbone.

"I'm Ed Thornis, the town blacksmith and part-time constable," Thornis called out, keeping Jamison from noticing any sound of the ranger creeping in on him. "I'm riding with Ranger Burrack, chasing these curs." He paused just long enough to see the ranger about to make a move. "Is your pa hurt? Is the rest of your family all right? We can get all of yas to a doctor. . . ." He let his words trail.

"We're all right," Jamison called out proudly, sounding out of his head. "Me and Pa sent that bunch running for the hills. It's not likely they'll ever want to tangle with the Cardells again —"

His words cut short when he felt the rifle snatched from his hands. Sam tossed the rifle away and jumped quickly to the side as Jamison lunged at him. "Take it easy, son. We only want to help you and your family," Sam said. Jamison turned quickly and lunged again at the broken image before him. This time Sam managed to jump aside and get behind him. He threw his arms around the young man and pinned him in place.

"You dirty, no-good sidewinder!" Jamison screamed in rage. "Shoot him, Pa! Don't mind me — shoot him!"

"Listen to me!" Sam shouted in Jamison's ear. "I'm a lawman. If I was one of the men who did this, you would be dead right now! Can you hear me? Do you understand? We want to help you and your family. Don't fight me."

Jamison struggled a moment longer, but in his condition he soon faltered and sank to his knees. For Jamison's own good, Sam hurriedly snapped a pair of handcuffs on him and said in an attempt to calm him down, "There, you're all right now. Settle down. Let me see about your family."

Jamison nodded his head slowly in submission, breathing hard and shallow from his blood loss. "Okay, you win," he gasped. "You *better* be the law. We need some law out here. Mary, hear that? This is the law.

All of you come out now. This ranger has come to help us. Dory, help Mary bring the twins."

Thornis ran in, knelt beside the young man and draped an arm over his shoulders as Sam stood up and walked over to the remnants of the old Conestoga wagon. "We'll take care of everybody," Thornis reassured him.

Venturing around the wagon, Sam asked, "Is anybody there?" Then he winced and stopped abruptly at the sight of the dead laid out in a neat row, their blank eyes staring skyward. "Oh, no," he murmured to himself.

"Ranger Burrack," Thornis called out, "is everybody all right back there?"

Sam walked back around the wagon and gave the blacksmith a look that told him everything. "I'll go get the horses," Sam said quietly. "We'll have to get that wound covered enough to get him to a doctor."

"How in the world can we do anything with that?" Thornis asked in a hushed tone, giving a pained look at the bloody crushed side of Jamison Cardell's forehead, seeing the eye hanging against his cheek by its long optic nerve.

"Get it covered and keep it clean" is all Sam knew to say, his voice also lowered just between the two of them. "The shape he's in, I don't know how far he's going to make it anyway."

"Give Pa some water first," Jamison said, his voice sounding amazingly stronger than it should, given his condition.

"Don't worry, young man," said the blacksmith, patting Jamison's bowed back as he stood over him. "We'll do all we can." He stayed at Jamison's side while Sam walked away, gathered the horses' reins and returned.

Sam searched through his saddlebags and came up with a roll of gauze. He took down his canteen, walked back over beside Thornis and said quietly, "Once we get him patched up, we'll see if there's some shovels around here. We've got lots of burying to do."

Thornis nodded in agreement, but his attention stayed clearly focused on Sam's task at hand. Looking at the gauze and canteen, he asked, "Are you going to put his eye back in its socket?"

"If I can," Sam replied. "The main thing is to get it as close as possible and get it covered up against the sun and dust." He handed Thornis the canteen. "I'll need you to keep him settled while I do what I can."

Thornis felt his stomach churn a bit.

"Right," he said, stooping down beside the half-conscious young man. "I want you to take it easy, young man," Thornis said to Jamison Cardell. "The ranger here knows what he's doing."

Sam gave the blacksmith a look, took off his gloves and unrolled a long length of gauze. "Here goes," he said to Thornis. "Pour some water over my right hand. Keep it wet so nothing sticks to it."

Thornis swallowed a dry knot in his throat, uncapped the canteen and held it out with a nervous hand. Seeing the pale, sick look on the blacksmith's face, Sam said, as he moved his right hand back and forth under the thin flow of water, "I expect whatever horses might have been here are gone now, don't you?"

Thornis wondered why the ranger would bother asking his opinion on such a matter at a time like this. But he swallowed hard and managed to reply in a raspy tone, "Yes, I suppose," while Sam set about his task, using his wet hand carefully, raising the exposed eye closer to its socket.

"Any guns that they might have found too — don't you suppose?" Sam asked in a calm, level voice as he continued his work.

Averting his eyes from the sight of the ranger gently closing together broken bone and split tissue with his fingertips, Thornis swallowed again, tried to keep his head clear and replied, "Yes, I'm certain of it."

A moment of silence passed, then the ranger asked calmly, "Where are you from, Thornis?"

"Where am I from?" Thornis had felt himself grow light-headed, his left arm draped across Jamison Cardell's shoulders. But the ranger's question caused him to collect himself. "This is a strange time to ask a man where he's from —"

"Where are you from, Thornis?" the ranger asked again in a stronger tone, cutting him off.

"Ohio!" Thornis snapped at him, a level of resentment in his voice. He raised his eyes to Sam and gave him a curious look. Then, as a light of realization came on in his head, he said, "Oh, I see what you're doing. You figure you need to keep me talking, keep me from getting woozy while you do this?"

Sam didn't answer. He continued carefully trying to put Jamison Cardell's face back together enough for the young man to be able to travel. "Do you think you can manage getting him back to Olsen by yourself?" he asked, already back to the matter of Lowry and his men.

"You mean . . . ?" Thornis let his words trail.

"I mean, Lowry and his men have stepped a long way over the line doing something like this. They'll only get worse from here on."

"It's just like you said they would be," Thornis remarked. He watched Sam gently lay Jamison's eye on the outside of the swollen purple flesh covering the empty socket. The blacksmith breathed a little easier watching Sam wrap the gauze gently around the young man's head to hold everything in place. "Yes," Thornis replied finally, as if having given the matter much consideration. "I'll get him back to Olsen." His tone lowered. "God willing he makes it that far."

"Good," Sam replied. "We've pushed hard. I calculate they're no more than eight to ten hours ahead of us. Now that I've got a trail to follow, I don't want to slow down until I have them all in chains."

"I feel the same way, Ranger," said Thornis, forcing himself to observe Sam's medical handiwork.

"You mean about getting on Kaylee and Albright's trail?" Sam asked, just testing the blacksmith's commitment.

"No," said Thornis, "I'm talking about Lowry and his men. I see why it's more important catching them first. Finish up with this man and get back on their trail. I'll handle the burying."

Sam nodded and turned back to Jamison Cardell.

Kaylee Smith and Marvin Albright had not stopped and spent the night under the stars the way she'd promised him they would. Indeed, he thought, watching her from behind as she led the way up the winding hill trail, the farther they'd gotten from Olsen, the more distant she'd become toward him. *Not at all the sort of behavior I expected,* Albright told himself, after him doing everything just the way she'd planned it. Granted, the storm had come upon them at the last moment and caused them to push on even harder in order to stay out of the brunt of it. But storm aside, a noticeable difference had come over her. Albright needed reassuring. He tapped his shoe heels to his horse's sides and rode up beside Kaylee in the long evening light.

"I think this horse may have thrown a shoe a ways back," Albright said, getting her attention.

Kaylee turned a serene gaze to him, then studied his horse's slow, steady gait for a moment and replied, "No, the animal's fine." She turned her face back to the winding hill trail.

"No, I mean it, Kaylee," Albright said, not realizing how childlike he sounded to her. He had to hurry his horse to stay beside her. "I felt something back there, a thrown shoe or something. I need to stop and at least take a look."

"You're just getting tired and restless, being too long in the saddle," Kaylee said, feeling nothing but contempt for Albright's weak, pleading voice. "There could be road agents around here."

"There are no road agents around here," Albright snapped at her, "and being tired and restless has nothing to do with it. I'm stopping! You can go or stay." As he spoke in an emboldened tone, his hand rested down firmly on the canvas bag full of bank money.

Kaylee glanced at his hand, then looked him in the eyes, smiling, and said, "I had hoped we could make it to the top of this trail . . . but if you insist on stopping here, very well." She reined her horse to a quick halt and sat staring at Albright blankly, the serene smile still faintly showing on her face.

"You — you mean it?" Albright asked, amazed that his little gesture with the money bag had been so effective.

"Sure. Why not?" Kaylee said quietly, taking a glance up the winding trail toward the hilltop. "We're in no hurry."

Albright let out a tense little breath. "Yes, what's our hurry?" He beamed with affection for her. "We have the rest of our lives to do as we please, eh?" His eyes went to the money bags, then back to her as he stepped down from his saddle.

"Exactly," said Kaylee. "What's my hurry?" She raised her hat from her head and held it in her lap. She shook out her hair and ran her fingers back through it, closing her eyes, enjoying the feel of a passing breeze.

Watching her, Albright felt his heart quicken. "My God, Kaylee, you are the most beautiful woman on this wide green earth." He saw the impression of her breast on her cotton blouse, the imprint of her nipples pressed against the fabric. "Every day I ask myself what I ever did to deserve someone like you."

Kaylee gave him a flat stare. "It's all that money you had in your reach, you silly boy."

Albright looked stunned by her words for a moment, until he saw a playful smile come upon her face. "Oh, all right," he said, again letting out a tense breath. "You almost had me there for a moment. You looked so serious." He chuckled.

Kaylee also chuckled. But then her smile fell away as she looked up the trail and said to Albright, "Well, well, we have riders coming."

"Oh, dear!" said the banker, getting suddenly anxious, his eyes darting to the money bags. "Perhaps we'd better get out of here! They could be thieves."

"There are no thieves around here," Kaylee said mockingly. "What's our hurry? We have the rest of our lives to do as we please."

"Please, Kaylee, I have a bad feeling about this!" said Albright, hurrying over to his horse and taking the reins in his hand.

"Don't step up in that saddle, Marvin," she warned. "It's a dead giveaway that we have valuables on us."

"Oh, my. Then what shall we do?" Albright asked, trembling.

"We'll just have to play it out, won't we?" said Kaylee, keeping her eyes on the riders, counting six of them as they rounded into sight.

"Hello the trail," a voice called out from the head of the riders, before Albright had the chance to respond to Kaylee.

"Hello, yourselves," Kaylee called out in reply. She sat staring quietly up the trail as the riders drew closer.

Standing beside his horse, Albright whispered in a nervous voice, "If we stay calm perhaps they won't look at the canvas bags. If they do, perhaps they won't conclude that we have any money in them." He rattled on. "Perhaps if we just divert their attention, they will —"

"Good idea!" Kaylee said to Albright, cutting him off. "Why should they even think we have bank money in the bags?"

"Shhhh, speak a little quieter," Albright cautioned her. "Don't mention money!"

But ignoring Albright, Kaylee called out to the riders, "If you're looking for money, we don't have any! If we *did* it wouldn't be in these canvas bank bags." She looked down at Albright and beamed. "That ought to throw them off, don't you think?"

"Oh, good Lord!" Albright murmured, a sick look coming to his face. "Now you've done it! They'll kill us for sure!"

"Not *you*, they won't," said Kaylee, still giving him her wide smile.

"Not me! Why on earth not?" Albright asked, trying to keep his voice lowered.

"Here's why," said Kaylee. She lifted her hat from her lap and fired one shot from the .36-caliber pocket gun in her hand. The bullet struck Marvin Albright above his right eye. He staggered backward a step until he managed to catch his balance and seem to hang on to his last spot on earth for a moment. A look of total surprise came upon his dying face.

"You soft, crawly little pig," Kaylee said, as if hearing his silent question. Her voice turned hard and chilled. "I nearly vomited every time I felt you inside me." She straightened her arm, taking a clearer aim at Albright as he weaved slowly back and forth, his eyes fading away into a distant darkness.

But before Kaylee could squeeze the trigger, Albright sank to his knees, then flopped forward onto his face in the dirt. A dark puddle of blood spread on the ground beneath him. Kaylee smiled to herself.

From the head of the line of riders the same voice called out, "Do you suppose everyone heard that shot for five miles in all four directions?"

Kaylee replied, "I wouldn't be surprised. Want me to shoot him again?" She twirled the smoking pistol on her finger.

The lead rider pushed his horse into a run for the last few yards and snatched her from her saddle and across his lap. "Hell, yes, go ahead, far as I'm concerned." Before his words were finished, Kaylee's lips were on his. The two kissed long and deep while the horse pranced and shuffled in a circle beneath them.

The other five riders stopped a few yards back and sat watching, a bit embarrassed. "Ain't this just the sweetest thing ever?" a man with a severe scar across the bridge of his nose growled under his breath.

"Shut up, Elvey," said a voice beside him. "Doyle is the boss. He can do what he damn well feels like. It ain't your place to pass remarks about it."

"Yeah?" said Elvey Parks in calm defiance. "Let me ask you this, Manfred. Would it be my place to bend this rifle barrel across your hairy neck?"

"You'd be sorely advised to try it," said Manfred Poole.

"Both of yas shut up," said another rider, this one a young Texas gunman named Dallas Spraggs. "I'm tired of hearing the two of yas all the time dirty-jawing one another."

"Yeah," a rider named Tommy Dykes agreed with him. "So's me and Fudd here." He looked at the grizzled old man beside him. "Ain't we, Fudd?"

Denton Fudd only growled under his breath, bared his blackened teeth at him and spit a stream of tobacco juice. "I don't care if they both go rot in hell." He nudged his horse forward. "Let's take a look at all that Morganfield payroll money."

CHAPTER 8

On a blanket a few feet from a crackling fire, Doyle Hollister lay on his back, shirtless and bootless, staring at the stars overhead. Beside him Kaylee Smith relaxed on her stomach, propped up on her elbows, counting bills from a stack in her left hand onto two smaller stacks in front of her. She lay naked, save for Hollister's shirt spread across her rump, her breasts glistening in the soft glow of firelight and bobbing gently with each movement of her hands. Her hair hung in long ringlets, which she took the time to push back each time she reached a hundred in her counting. Across the fire, the rest of the men could not keep themselves from taking guarded glances her way.

"What the hell was it that took you so long getting here?" Hollister asked, now that the two had spent themselves on one another and had time to make conversation. "I was beginning to think you'd run into trouble, got *caught* or something. I thought about riding in."

"Oh," said Kaylee, "so any minute I could have expected you to come charging into Olsen to save me from the gallows?"

"No, but I always enjoy watching a good hanging." Hollister grinned at his little joke, turning his face from the sky and toward her, only to see that her attention remained riveted on the money.

"That's real funny, Doyle," said Kaylee, licking the tip of her thumb and staying steadfast at her counting. "If you've run out of something to do, grab some of this and start counting." She pushed back her hair, gave him a flat sidelong glance and went back to counting.

Doyle relaxed and folded his fingers behind his head, staring back at the stars. "Naw, I'm good with your count."

"Careful you don't get too good with it," Kaylee warned him, giving a quick lick of her thumb. "I'm strictly in business for myself."

"I know," said Doyle, completely relaxed, "but I trust you. I ain't like your banker boyfriend. You're smart enough to know, if I ever caught you shorting me in any way, I'd hang you upside down and slice you open like a tender young elk."

"My, my, Doyle," Kaylee chuckled under her breath without losing her count, "what a lovely thing to say."

Doyle laughed quietly along with her. Near Kaylee's other side lay the ranger's Colt that she had carried shoved down in her waist. "What are you doing with this big shooter?" Hollister asked, picking it up, twirling it.

"Albright gave it to me. It belonged to the ranger."

"Ah, nice," said Hollister. "Mind if I hang on to it?"

"Help yourself," said Kaylee, licking her thumb.

Turning onto his side, Hollister dropped the Colt over on his clothes and idly ran his hand up under the shirt lying across Kaylee's hips. "Maybe I better give you something in return," he whispered with suggestion. He felt the warmth of her and squeezed her gently, liking the feel of her smooth, taut skin.

"In a while," said Kaylee.

"All right," said Hollister. "Then tell me what happened in Olsen."

"It turned into a mess," Kaylee said, still counting, even as she rolled her buttocks up and down slowly beneath his hand. "I spend damn near a year there slinging hash and sleeping with that simpering little turd. Then at the last minute, when everything is in place, here comes four fools on horseback . . . to rob the bank!"

"No," said Doyle, in disbelief. "Who were they? Anybody I know?"

"Oh, you know them all right," said Kaylee. "It was Dick Lowry and his bunch."

"No fooling?" Hollister laughed out loud. "Dick Lowry! They used to call him and his boys the Trouble Creek gang. They had a hideout in an old French garrison along Trouble Creek, across the border in Old Mexico. Ennui Creek," he said with a proud grin. "Ennui is French for 'trouble,' I expect."

"Well, anyway, they were trouble sure enough," said Kaylee, with a dubious look for Hollister's French. "I finally had to break them from jail, give them some money and send them on their way." She paused, then added, "I sent them south, telling them it was the opposite direction me and Albright were headed. I figured once you and I met up, we could turn south ourselves, the way we meant to go. That way if Lowry does double back, all he'll be trailing is our shadows."

"Good thinking," said Hollister, "if Lowry falls for it."

133

"He will," Kaylee said with confidence. "Him and his boys didn't strike me as being real smart."

"That's Lowry all right." Hollister grinned. "Dumb as a stump. But smart ain't all it takes out here. He's stayed ahead of the law for as long as I can remember. He must be doing something right."

"I don't care what he does," said Kaylee, "so long as he stays out of my hair." She paused again for a moment, then went back to the subject, saying, "To make matters worse in Olsen, a territory ranger showed up to foil Lowry's bank robbery. Albright started falling apart on me."

"Whoa, wait a minute," said Doyle, taking on a more serious look. "An Arizona ranger?"

"Yeah," said Kaylee without taking her eyes from the counting. "The one who killed Junior Lake and his gang. The one who rides the big Appaloosa that used to belong to Outrider Sazes or some such shit." She shrugged, licked her thumb again and continued counting. "He scared the hell out of Albright. I thought the poor bastard's heart would stop before it was over."

"Jesus, hold on," said Doyle. He rose on an elbow; his hand stopped enjoying its exploration and lay still on Kaylee's warm behind. "You know who you're talking about, don't you? That's Sam Burrack!"

"Yes, Burrack, I believe that *was* his name," said Kaylee, finishing up the two stacks, blocking them neatly and setting them aside. She turned on her side and looked into Doyle's eyes.

"Christ!" said Doyle, getting a bit excited. "We don't want that son of a bitch on our tails. He's like being tracked by a damn Apache."

Seeing the look on his face, Kaylee smiled and said quietly, "Take it easy. The ranger's dead."

"Dead? How do you know?" said Doyle. "Did you kill him?"

"No, I —"

"Answer me. Did *you* kill him?" Doyle demanded, cutting her off before she even had a chance to respond. "Did *you* see his body?"

"Hey! Slow down, Doyle," Kaylee said. Seeing how excited he'd become, she answered quickly, "I drugged him down with enough black tar opium to kill a horse. So, yes, I killed him. But just to make sure he was dead, I had Albright spike his water with a hard dose of Louisiana swamp poison. The stuff kills twenty-foot bull gators." She paused, then said confidently, "The ranger is dead all right. I'll stake my life on that."

"Careful, Kaylee," said Doyle, raising a finger for emphasis. "If he's *dead,* I want to know it for sure. . . . If he's *not,* I want to know that for sure. This is not a man I want dogging my trail. I've heard too much about him."

"Relax, Doyle," said Kaylee, tossing the shirt from across her middle and pulling Doyle over against her naked body in the soft glow of firelight. "The ranger is dead, and that's that. Marvin Albright said he left him laying dead in the bank. Marvin would not dare lie to me. He knew I'd kill him if he did." She grinned, her hand going between them to Doyle's lower belly. "Now come here. It's been a long time since I had myself a real man."

"What are you talking about?" said Doyle, not wanting to look any more worried about the ranger than he already had. "It's only been a few minutes."

"That's a long time for me," Kaylee teased.

Across the fire, Elvey Parks pulled his hat brim low on his forehead and whispered in a tense voice, "Boys, gawdamn it, I can't watch something like this. There's something a man ought not do in front of one another . . . and this is one of them. I'm moving away and turning in for the night." He stood up, threw a blanket over his shoulder and walked away a few feet, keeping his back turned to the crackling fire.

"Holy Gawd amighty!" Dallas Spraggs said under his breath, watching the two naked bodies through the dancing flames. "Seems like what one gets, the others ought to share in equally."

"Go tell Doyle that," Manfred Poole replied quietly, keeping his eyes lowered but still managing to take a guarded peep now and then. "See how quick he kills you."

"Yeah," Tommy Dykes added in the same lowered tone. "If he don't kill you, that woman will."

Dallas Spraggs said, "There ain't a woman born can kill me. That includes Kaylee Smith."

"Kaylee Smith? *Ha!*" said Denton Fudd. He spit a stream of tobacco juice and ran a weathered hand across his cracked lips. "You don't even know her real gawdamn name, you big-talking Texas cow-humping prick, you."

Spraggs bristled, but managed to keep his temper in check. "All right, *old man,*" he said to Fudd. "You tell me what her real name is."

Fudd roared with mocking laughter. "That's for me to know and you to find out, you big-talking Texas cow-humping prick —"

"Don't call me that again, you dried-out old turd!" said Spraggs. His hand came up cocking the Colt he'd snatched from his tied-down holster. "Don't think I won't blow your scroungy head off!"

"Fire away!" Denton Fudd shouted in defiance. "I've never seen a better gawdamn day to die . . . if you've got the guts to do it!"

"Jesus!" Doyle Hollister said to Kaylee on the other side of the fire. "What's going on over there?" He rose off her.

Kaylee tugged at him to get him to stay. "Forget them," she said, breathless from their passion. "Don't go!"

But Doyle pulled free of her, stood, pulled his trousers up, grabbed his Colt and held the wadded-up shirt in front of himself as he stomped barefoot around the fire. "What the hell is going on here?" he demanded of Fudd and Dallas Spraggs, seeing them as the center of the argument.

As quickly as Spraggs had been to kill, his gun hand lowered upon seeing Doyle step into sight, his own gun in hand. "This old man is calling me names no man should have to tolerate. I figured I'd do the world a favor, shoot a hole through his head." He kept his gaze fixed harshly on Fudd as he spoke to Doyle.

"Holster your gun!" said Doyle. He looked all around at the others and said, "Look at yas. You've got money in your pockets. We pulled this job off slick and clean, thanks to Kaylee. But all you can do is sit around and pick fights with one another? You're acting like a damn bunch of schoolkids!" He stared at Fudd. "Denton, what's stuck in your craw? You've been down everybody's neck since we left Santa Fe."

"Nothing," Fudd muttered under his breath, lowering his head and spitting a stream of tobacco juice.

"Whatever it is, this is the time and place to get it off your chest," said Hollister.

"I said nothing," Fudd repeated. This time he gave Hollister a dark gaze, letting him know the subject was closed.

"All right, then. Let that be the last of it," Hollister said, looking from Fudd to Dallas Spraggs. "Everybody settle the hell down and get some rest. Tomorrow we head south to the border" — he gave each man a look — "with money to burn!"

In spite of Thornis' offer to bury the

Cardells by himself, Sam stayed until the last grave had been filled and the proper words spoken over the dead. Only then did he step into his saddle and get back onto the escaped prisoners' trail. When he'd left the smoldering remains of the Cardell Trade, he looked back once from atop a rise of loose rock and sandy soil and watched Thornis ride away slowly toward the trail to Olsen. Beside Thornis, Jamison Cardell sat slumped atop a bareback mule that had been left wandering on its own when Lowry and his men had finished sacking and burning the place. Sam shook his head slightly and murmured to the Appaloosa beneath him.

"He just might make it, Black Pot," he said, as if answering any doubts the stallion might have about Jamison Cardell's condition. He rubbed the big stallion's withers with his gloved hand. "But that's all you and I could do for him. We've got to stop this bunch from doing more of the same."

He touched his heels lightly to the stallion's sides and felt the animal snap forward along the crest of the rise. Following the prints left by Lowry and his men on fresh horses, Sam put the stallion down at an easy gait on the other side of the rise, feeling a warm breeze on his face. Ahead of him, Sam looked down onto a lower level of flatlands and saw the tracks circle back and head north. "You've got yourselves some guns and fresh horses, Lowry," he said idly to himself, the stallion's hooves at work beneath him, taking in the trail. "What's so important to you north of here?"

He rode on until the long evening shadows surrendered themselves to the closing darkness. But when he stepped down from the saddle because he could no longer see the tracks in the dark, wild grass, instead of making camp for the night, he continued on foot, leading the stallion by its reins. At midnight the ranger topped a sloping plane and stood at the edge of a long stretch of barren sand flats. In the light of a waxing three-quarter moon, his eyes followed the tracks clearly out across the silvery-gray terrain.

"All right, Black Pot, back to work," he said quietly to the stallion. He stepped up into the saddle and nudged the big Appaloosa forward, keeping a close watch on the long, meandering hoofprints.

Thirty miles ahead on the other side of the sand flats, Dick Lowry stood up from a thin blanket and wiped sleep from his eyes with both hands. "Damn! Soon as we take that money away from the banker and his woman, I'm going to sleep for a week straight. I'll kill any sonsabitch who tries to wake me."

Next to him, Black Cat Thompson and Pony Phil rose grudgingly to their feet, having had no more than an hour of sleep. Clarence Hawk continued to lie on the ground, his blanket pulled around him like the wrapper on a cheap cigar. "Come on, Hawk, time to go," said Black Cat, giving him a prod with the toe of his boot.

Hawk cursed under his breath and rolled onto his other side. "I'm hurting too bad to get up. Leave me the hell alone," he growled.

Lowry and Pony Phil looked at one another, then reached down without warning, grabbed Hawk's blanket by its edge and yanked it up, spinning the wounded gunman into the dirt with a painful scream. "Gawdamn it!" Hawk cried out, clutching the side of his blood-crusted shirt. "Can't you see I'm in no shape to ride?"

"You best *get* in shape," Lowry warned him. "If you think the law is on our trail for jailbreak and bank robbery, wait until somebody sees what we did back at that trading post. Now get into the saddle. Let's ride!" He booted Hawk in the rump, causing him to let out another painful yelp.

Pony Phil and Black Cat mounted their

horses and circled impatiently. "Come on, Hawk, act like a damn man!" Pony Phil coaxed him.

"Yeah," Black Cat joined in. "Think of all the pretty senoritas we'll have waiting on us once we get that money and skin across the border."

"Sonsabitches," Hawk grumbled, struggling to his feet and taking his horse's reins from Black Cat's outstretched hand.

"Catch up, Hawk!" Lowry commanded. He jerked his horse around and batted his boots to its sides, sending it bolting away in a rise of dust. Black Cat and Pony Phil followed.

Fanning the dust with his hand, Hawk crawled up into his saddle with much effort and jerked his horse around toward the thin trail. But when he batted his heels to the horse, a sharp pain caused him to pull back soundly on the reins instead of allowing the animal to spring forward. In its confusion the horse let out a long whinny and reared straight up, causing Hawk to spill backward from his saddle as the animal spun and charged away across the desert floor. Hawk hit the ground with a painful outcry for help.

"Jesus!" said Lowry, the three having turned in their saddles at the sound of Hawk's voice. "The sonsabitch can't even sit his saddle!" He trotted his horse back to where Hawk struggled to his feet and staggered in place, his hand pressed firmly to his wounded side.

"Somebody go catch the ornery bastard for me," said Hawk, gesturing toward the fleeing horse, not liking the look that had come over Lowry's face. "My damn money is in the saddlebags!"

"I've got it," said Pony Phil, who had hurried his horse alongside Lowry.

"Stay put," Lowry demanded, reaching sidelong and grabbing Phil by his shirtsleeve before Phil could turn and give chase to the animal. "It's Hawk's horse. Let him attend to it himself."

"Aw, hell, Dick, his money's in the saddlebags," said Pony Phil. "It's dark out there. I'll go fetch his horse. It don't make me no difference —"

"Are you simpleminded?" Lowry asked Phil harshly, giving him a dark stare. "I *said,* let Hawk attend to it."

"Sure, let Hawk fetch it," Pony Phil replied, starting to understand Lowry's intentions.

"How the hell can I catch it on foot?" said Hawk, bowed slightly with the pain in his side. "I'm doing well to stand on my own! What's wrong with you three? Can't you get it through your heads, I'm hurt *bad!*"

"Yeah," said Lowry, "I'm starting to understand." He stared at Hawk for a moment in silence, then said coolly, "Either go catch your horse and catch up to us, or find yourself a spot where you can sit and lick your wound for a few days."

"What?" Hawk gave him a look of disbelief. "You're cutting out on me? Just like that?"

"Yep, just like that," said Lowry. "You've harped too much about that damn wound. I'm sick of hearing it. You know the direction we're headed in. Either get your horse and catch up to us, or find yourself a place to lay down and mend."

"Lay down and *die,* is what you really mean!" Hawk bristled, but kept himself in check, knowing that Lowry would think nothing of putting a bullet in him now that things had gone this far.

Lowry shrugged. "Take it however it suits you," he said. Nodding toward the distance, he said, "There used to be some Mexican goat herders out that away, soon as the flats turn green. "Maybe it would suit you better to head that way once you catch the horse." His gaze bored into Hawk. "Anything else we need to talk about?"

Hawk knew better than to push his luck

with Lowry. "Naw, hell, no," he said, shaking his head. "I'll be all right. Go on. I'll get that damn horse and catch up before you know it."

"That's the spirit," said Lowry, backing his horse a few steps before turning it and riding away.

A few yards behind him Pony Phil turned to Black Cat, who rode along beside him, and cast a look back over his shoulder in the darkness at Clarence Hawk. "I reckon that ought to open a man's eyes, show him where he stands in *this life*," Phil whispered.

Turning his eyes away from Hawk as if dismissing him, Black Cat stared straight ahead and said in a rigid tone, "If a man didn't know that much coming into this life, he was dead before he started."

Behind them on the hard, flat belly of the desert, Hawk stood for a moment, his head bowed as if in prayer, his hand still pressed to his aching side. He shook his head slowly, took a deep breath and walked away, following his horse's hoofprints into the moonlight.

CHAPTER 9

At daylight the ranger stepped down from his saddle on the spot where Hawk had taken a spill from his horse in the night. He stooped and held his fingertips to the sand, as if to do so would somehow reveal to him all that had gone on there a few hours before. But as he sat, stooped, with his rifle across his lap, studying the ground and the boot prints walking out across the sand, he realized that for whatever reason one of Lowry's men had now gone off on his own. He looked at the other three sets of hoofprints headed off along the north trail and knew he didn't have a moment to spare if he wanted the whole gang.

In sore need of sleep and a hot cup of coffee, Sam stood up, stepped back into his saddle and said to the big stallion as he reined him around, "We'll have to rest later, Black Pot. It looks like one of these killers has just about run out of road." He nudged

147

the animal forward and rode on.

Fifteen miles out across the sand flats where pale green clumps of wild grass began to hold their own against the encroaching desert, Clarence Hawk sat on a flat rock, his left arm cradling his aching stomach. The horse stood beside him, head down, picking at the sparse blades of grass. "Gawdamn it," Hawk said aloud to the horse. "I finally catch your flea-bitten ass, now I'm too sore to climb up your side."

He sat with his head bowed until a breeze drew his attention toward two riders headed his way from a short line of rooftops farther along the trail. "With my luck this will be the devil himself and his right-hand demon, come to drag me to hell on the points of a pitchfork."

But as the riders drew closer and Hawk saw the wide brims of their battered straw sombreros and their billowing white peasant shirts, he drew the big pistol from his waist, cocked it and held it across his knee. He eyed the saddlebags on the horse and said to the animal, "If you try to run off this time, I swear to God I'll kill you."

Moments later when the two Mexicans rode up to him and stopped a few feet away, Hawk looked them up and down and said gruffly, *"Hola, buenos días* and all like that.

What brings you two *jinetes* so far out this way? Don't tell me I smell *that bad.*" He sniffed close to his arm, as if checking himself.

"Hola," said one of the serious-looking young men, ignoring Hawk's remark. "And good morning to you as well," he added in stiff English. They both carried muzzleloader rifles across their laps. Long machetes stood in the sashes around their waists. "Why do you sit out here all alone?"

"I enjoy the quiet," Hawk replied with a shrug and a trace of sarcasm. He looked both men over a good while before he spoke, noting their lack of up-to-date shooting gear and their shoeless horses.

"What did he say?" the other one asked, keeping his eyes on Hawk.

"He makes the little joke," the other replied.

"Ah, *sí*, a little joke." The Mexican stepped his horse forward beside his friend's and stopped. He gave a look at the saddlebags and said to Hawk, "Your belly is bloody. I think you have a bullet in you."

"Hey, that's good," said Hawk. "Go on."

"I think you are a bandito," the Mexican continued, "a man who is on the run. I think if I look in those bags I will find money that does not belong to you."

The big gun came up from Hawk's lap, pointed and ready. Both Mexicans stiffened in their saddles. "You did good till you got to that 'Look in the bags' part. That's the sort of thing will get a man killed quick where I live, *José.*"

"José?" said the second man. "Why does he call you José —"

"Do not shoot, mister!" the first Mexican said quickly, cutting his friend off. "We mean you no harm!" His left hand rose in a show of peace, but his right hand remained clasped around the small of his rifle stock, his finger inside the trigger guard. "We are desperadoes ourselves, Hector and me!" He patted himself firmly on his chest. "I am Paco. That is the same as the name Frank in your language." He made a tight fist and added with a smile, "You know, like Frank James, *sí?*"

"Yeah?" said Hawk, eyeing them closely. "Okay, *Frank James,*" he said with a sarcastic twist in his voice. "If we're going to be engaging in sociable conversation, maybe you two best drop them rifles to the ground."

Paco's smile left his face, replaced by a serious expression. "I don't think so, mister," he said. "We do not drop our rifles. You must think we are fools."

"Whatever you *are,* they can carve it on your grave marker if either one of yas start to raise your rifles from your lap," Hawk warned, seeing the two weren't about to give up their guns.

"We understand," said Paco, nodding in agreement. "What about your stomach? How bad are you shot?"

"Not that bad," said Hawk. "But the doctor left the bullet inside me. It's turned sore as hell and starting to knot up on me. I need to get it cut out, I reckon."

"Then get on your horse and come with us," said Paco. "We will give you some whiskey and cut it out for you."

Hawk chuckled and shook his head with a wise look in his eyes. "Huh-uh," he said with resolve. "Now who's thinking *who* is a fool?" He stood up, the pain showing on his face. "Anyway, I thought all that was over that way is a bunch of goat herders. What are two bold desperadoes like you doing out there — making cheese?"

"Do we look like goat herders to you?" Hector asked in a frosty tone.

"Nothing against goat herders," said Hawk, his pistol still up, cocked and ready. "I'm just asking for the sake of curiosity."

Before Hector could speak again, Paco cut in, saying, "It is true our fathers and uncles used to tend goats in this country. But we are not them. We are the generation who refuses to tend goats. We see what we want and we take it." He looked proudly at Hector, then back to Hawk. "When I tell you we are desperadoes, you can believe my words are true."

"All the more reason for me to leave the whiskey alone and keep my money close at hand," said Hawk.

"If you can stay awake while we cut open your belly and dig out the bullet, you have big balls. We would not steal money from a man of such courage and honor."

Hawk lowered the pistol an inch and gazed back toward the trail where Lowry and the others had left him. "Yeah, right," said Hawk, not believing a word of it. "I'll tell you what I'll do, *Frank James.* Take me to your camp, get me mended up some, and I'll give you some of this money. . . . Hell, I'll even take you somewhere we can make a robbery or two, if you'll play straight with me."

"We will play straight with you, mister," said Paco. "You have our word on that."

"All right then, *Frank James,*" said Hawk, keeping the gun cocked. "You step down and help me up into the saddle. All the while I'll have a bead drawn on your *amigo,* ole *Jesse* here. If I feel a gun to my back or a knife to my throat, or so much as a sharp finger near my ass, for that matter, I'll kill him deader than he ever thought he could be, *comprende?*"

"*Sí,* we understand, mister," said Paco, swinging down from his aged California-style saddle. He walked over to Hawk, with his rifle hanging loosely in his hand, seeing Hawk's battered old pistol pointed at his friend Hector. With a shove upward on Hawk's rump, he stood back and watched the wounded man seat himself painfully into the saddle, his left hand still gripping his side. Noting the condition of Hawk's pistol, Paco commented, "Maybe things have not gone so well for you lately, *sí?*"

"The hell does that mean?" Hawk asked haughtily. But then he saw Paco looking at the battered pistol that he'd taken from the Cardells and said, "Oh, this? Hell, that's a long story. I'll tell you about it when we've got the bullet out and made friends of one another." With his pistol barrel he gestured Paco back toward his horse.

As Paco stepped up into his weathered California saddle, he noticed Hawk looking back across the sand flats and asked, "Is there someone following you, *mi amigo?* If so you must tell us."

"Ha!" said Hawk. "There's been some-body *following* me for some reason or an-other ever since I was fourteen years old." He squinted skeptically at Paco. "Why? What's it to you?"

"Because if someone is following you, Hector and me will warn that person to turn his trail and leave you alone."

"Oh, you would *warn* that person," said Hawk. "And if that person don't heed your warning?"

Paco shrugged. "Then we will kill him for you, of course."

"Now that's the kind of talk I like to hear," Hawk said with a pained grin. "And you boys will do all of this for me out of our newfound friendship? Because we're all just good ole desperadoes?"

"*Sí*, that is why," Paco replied.

Hawk looked along the trail, then back to Paco and Hector. "Man," he said, "you can't beat that kind of friendship with a stick."

"And because you will give us a taste of the money you carry," Hector cut in, pinch-ing his finger and thumb together. "*Un poco*, eh?"

Hawk let out a breath and said, "*Sí*, maybe just a little . . . for watching my back."

154

■ ■ ■ ■

Sam stopped the big stallion but stayed in his saddle, looking down at the spot where the two shoeless horses had stood earlier. He saw a pair of thin-soled moccasin prints lead over to the rock where they joined a pair of boot prints in the sand. As if watching the scene play itself out in his mind, Sam saw the moccasins stand beside a third horse, then walk back to the two shoeless horses, then vanish as they stepped up and rode away, the third horse being held a bit to one side. Contemplating what had gone on, Sam whispered, "A bit standoffish with your new friends?"

Sam's eyes followed the three sets of prints out across the sparse grasslands. Before going any farther he drew his Winchester rifle, checked it and laid it across his lap. He slipped his Colt upward an inch, loosening it, then eased it back down in its holster. "Well, Black Pot, here we go," he whispered to the stallion, nudging it forward with only a twitch of his knees.

He rode steadily but with caution, watching the jagged rooflines grow closer, the clumps of grass grow thicker, and the feel of eyes upon him grow more intense with each rise and fall of the stallion's hooves. At a distance equal to the range of a good rifle shot, Sam swung Black Pot in a quarter-circle and rode out of his way for almost a half mile, until he put the glaring sunlight behind his back. When he turned back toward the rooftops, beneath him the stallion seemed to take on an understanding of the situation. He slung his big head back and forth and rode on with a wariness that made Sam reach down with a gloved hand and pat his withers. "Good boy," Sam whispered.

Behind a crumbling adobe wall, Hector's older brother, Phillipi, squinted against the sunlight, rubbed his right eye and said, "He is one clever gringo, this son-of-a-whore lawman." He spat in disgust and turned to Hector, Paco and Hawk. The three stood examining the wound in Hawk's side. "He knows we wait for him, I think," Phillipi added. "He rides in with the sun shielding him."

"He don't know shit," said Hawk, figuring right away that it was the ranger on his trail. Standing shirtless, a wet rag in his left hand, his right still clutching the big battered pistol, Hawk continued, "Any lawman *still breathing air* knows better than to ride straight into a place, if he's got any choice in the matter."

Phillipi shook his head. "No, this one is smarter than most, I think. I can tell by the way he sits his saddle."

"By the way he *sits?*" Hawk looked bemused. To Hector he said, "Far be it for me to undercut your brother's wide knowledge of lawmen, *Jesse.* But I have outrun more badges than a bear has flies. The one coming here is a bad hombre, I'll admit. But if you desperadoes want some of *my* money, you and *Frank James* will earn it by blowing his gawdamned brains all over the sand."

"Who is this lawman?" Paco asked.

"Hell, some half-assed sheriff or some such thing," Hawk lied. "He got lucky, caught me when I was dog drunk. . . . He had a full posse backing him up. I was unarmed."

"Oh," said Paco, "you were drunk, unarmed. He had a posse on his side. No wonder he was able to take you, this sheriff or *some such thing.*"

"Yeah, that was sort of how things went," said Hawk, giving Paco a look. "Does that suit you?"

"Maybe, maybe not," said Paco. A young woman had walked up to them, carrying soft, clean rags and a pot of hot water from a nearby chiminea. But Paco stepped over between her and Hawk and said, "We have

157

not yet *seen* any of this money you speak of. I think it is time you show us what we get for shooting this lawman."

Hawk looked at the woman and said, "Sit that stuff down and go fetch my saddlebags, pronto!"

The young woman looked first to Paco for a nod of permission. Getting it, she set down the water and rags and hurried over to Hawk's horse. She returned with the saddlebags slung over her shoulder. When Paco reached out to take the saddlebags, Hawk stepped in, saying, "Not so fast, *Frank James.*" He backed away a step, swung the saddlebags to the ground and opened them.

Paco, Hector and his brother Phillipi stared as if in awe at the banded stack of money Hawk pulled from inside the saddlebags and shook back and forth in front of them, grinning as he did so. "There's three more just like it in here. Get me taken care of, who knows, maybe we can all go arm ourselves to the teeth, get some fine riding horses and go in business headfirst. Anybody with me on that?"

Slowly the three men began to smile, first at one another, then at Hawk. Paco said to Phillipi, "You heard our *amigo.* Go shoot holes in this lawman."

Phillipi turned quickly, throwing his rifle

butt to his shoulder and squinting out through the glittering sunlight. He scanned back and forth, slowly at first, then more rapidly, until finally he lowered the gun from his shoulder, rubbed his right eye and said, "The lawman is gone."

"What do you mean he is gone? Look out!" Hector demanded, jerking the rifle from his brother's hand and throwing it up to his shoulder. He scanned back and forth, then lowered the rifle and looked at it as if something didn't work properly.

"What are you doing?" Paco shouted. "Somebody shoot the lawman and be done with it!"

"But he's gone, Paco!" Hector replied.

"Well, hell, that figures," said Hawk, dropping the stack of money back into the saddlebags in disgust. "The three of yas can't shoot one gawdamn ranger!"

"He has disappeared!" Hector said, stunned.

Paco jerked his head around, facing Hawk. "What did you say? One *ranger?* You said it was a sheriff, or *some such thing.*"

"Sheriff, ranger — what the hell's the difference?" Hawk growled. "You don't seem to be able to shoot him, whatever he is!"

"Because he is gone," Hector shouted, his eyes still searching frantically for the lone rider who had been there only moments earlier.

Doing some quick thinking, Paco turned to Hawk, shrugged and said with a half-confident smile, "This is good. We have scared him away! He saw we were here, and he knew better than to ride in. This has been happening more and more lately, now that people are learning of us and knowing we will —"

"Nice try, *Frank James,*" Hawk said wryly. "But if that ranger was there a while ago, you can bet your sister's wedding night that he's *still* here some-damn-wheres." As he spoke, Hawk looked all around suspiciously, as if at any moment the ranger would appear. In a lowered but sarcastic tone, he added, "You *James boys* have let him slip past you some way. Now all three of yas spread out and start looking."

Chapter 10

In the cover of rubble and crumbling adobe walls, Sam stepped down from his saddle. He led the big stallion quietly into a narrow alleyway, where an old basket weaver and his wife sat beneath a dirt roof. They stared at him blankly, the material of their trade lying coiled in a pile beside them. With his Colt in hand, Sam whispered to the old man in Spanish, "Go on about your work. I'm here to take an outlaw back to jail."

The old woman bowed her head back to the half-finished basket in her lap. But the old man replied, saying in a whisper himself, "You can speak English to me."

Sam nodded, then said in English, "Did you see the man who rode in here with two of your people?"

"We saw him ride in with them," the old man replied, his English having grown stiff from lack of use but coming back to him. "He is wounded. Yet he refused to allow

Hector or Paco to carry his saddlebags for him." The old man had a knowing look. "He is a thief, yes?"

"Yes," said Sam, "he is a thief." Making sure the old man saw the badge on his chest, he said, "I had him locked in a jail, but he and his friends escaped. Where is he wounded?"

"He favors his side," the old man said.

"Gracias," said Sam, realizing it had to be Clarence Hawk. He paused for a moment, then asked in a tone that let the man understand his intentions, "Are Hector and Paco your family?"

The old man shook his head slowly, gesturing toward the old woman. "I have no family except my *esposa.* Hector and Phillipi are young men whose family were goatherders here for many years. Now they have all died or gone back to Mexico. The other young man is Paco. We know little about him." He gave Sam a warning look and added, "He has a woman with him."

"Obliged," Sam said, grateful for the information. "Are these good boys?" he asked, looking the old man in his eyes.

The old man shrugged a bony shoulder. "They are foolish young men. But they are not bad men . . . not yet."

"Gracias," Sam said again, this time in a

162

whisper as he laid Black Pot's reins over a knee-high earthen wall, drew his rifle from the saddle boot and stepped away through strewn rock and rubble. The old basket weavers continued their work as if the ranger had never been there.

On a wider street that had once been paved with tiles of stone and accommodated the legends of some Spanish conquistador, Sam walked with caution through clumps of sage brush and broken hewn timbers. At the end of the ancient thoroughfare he spotted a long adobe building where four horses stood at a weathered timber hitch rail. He stopped when a solitary figure stepped into view in the dark, opened the doorway and called out along the street to him.

"Hey, lawman!" said Paco loudly, wanting the other two to hear him and hurry back from their search. "What do you want here?"

"You know what I want here," the ranger called out. The young man's tone of voice tipped him off to the presence of other gunmen. Sam looked around warily as he spoke. "You watched me ride in from your rear door there. You've had plenty of time to talk it over. What's it going to be? Will you give him up, or will I come take him?" Sam stepped forward slowly, his Colt half raised and cocked in his right hand, his rifle cocked in his left.

"If you try to take him you will die, lawman!" Paco shouted, putting a warning growl in his voice that Sam recognized as fear, whether the young man knew it or not.

"He's a killer and a thief," Sam said as he continued walking slowly forward, scanning the street peripherally. "Why are you and your friends protecting him? I have heard that you are not bad hombres. Don't make me kill you over a man like Hawk."

"Ha!" said Paco. "Then you have heard wrong, lawman. We are bad hombres. We ride the outlaw trail for our fortune, and we all stick together! Hawk is one of us, and if you try to take him you will die!"

"How much is he paying you?" Sam called out, not buying the young man's words for a minute.

"What he pays us is none of your business," Paco replied, sounding almost childlike to the ranger in spite of the growl in his voice. After a second of hesitation, Paco added, "Why do you ask me this?"

Sam caught a glimpse of movement on his left, a figure in a white shirt and straw sombrero sprinting from cover to cover along the rear of crumbling adobe structures. But he didn't turn his eyes toward the figure; instead he made mental note of the man's position as he walked on. "I'm asking because I've got a feeling that whatever he's paying you, it's not *real* money."

"Not real money!" Paco shouted. "Of course, it is real money. We are not fools, lawman!"

"You haven't looked at the money yet, have you?" Sam asked, each step putting him closer to the young man.

Instead of an answer, Sam felt a tense silence set in. He stopped less than fifteen yards from the open doorway, knowing he'd planted enough doubt to make the young man start using his head. Along his right side, another figure wearing a sombrero ran from cover to cover back toward the building where Paco waited with Clarence Hawk.

Inside the adobe, Paco turned to Clarence Hawk as Hector and his brother, Phillipi, came rushing in through the open rear wall, stumbling over broken stone and chunks of fallen earthworks. "What is he talking about?" Paco asked, giving Hawk a cold stare.

"Yes," said Hector, "what does he mean the money is *not real?*"

"Damned if I know!" said Hawk sincerely, looking worried. "It's some lawdog trick, is what I'm guessing!"

"Lupe!" Paco ordered the woman who sat

huddled to the wall. "Take the money out of his saddlebags again!"

"I'll be damned if she's going to!" bellowed Hawk, grabbing the saddlebags in his left hand, clutching them to his chest. He pointed his revolver at Paco.

"We're going to take another look at it!" Paco demanded, shaking his rifle at Hawk. The woman moved forward with a frightened look, then stopped when Hawk swung his pistol toward her.

"Like hell!" said Hawk. "We're in the midst of a gunfight here! Kill that lawdog sonsabitch before he kills us! Then we'll all sit around and take turns looking at the damn money!"

"Give them over to her!" Paco demanded. To the woman he said, "Lupe! Do as I tell you. Take out the money!"

Hector and Phillipi closed in menacingly around Hawk. Hector's rifle was cocked and pointed. Phillipi clutched a big French dueling pistol and a long, glinting machete.

"All right, gawdamn it!" said Hawk, tossing the bags to Lupe. "Take it out and look at it, you mongrel sonsabitches! You bean suckers wouldn't know a gawdamn real American dollar bill if it dropped out of your ass!"

Lupe opened the saddlebags, took out a

stack of bills and pitched it to Paco, who raised it close and studied it intently. Hector and Phillipi closed in to do the same, still keeping watch on Hawk.

Out in the wide thoroughfare, Sam had listened to the cursing and threatening, knowing that at any minute all hell would bust loose. When the voices fell silent, he stepped sideways out of the front of the open doorway and stood tense and ready.

"Wait! I didn't know! Son of a —" Hawk shouted, his words clipped by the sudden sound of rifle fire.

Sam waited, hearing Hawk's big pistol explode within the sound of two more rifle shots and the loud, flat sound of the French dueling pistol. He heard the woman scream. He heard the solid *thunk* of the machete blade chopping against the side of the door frame as it barely missed Hawk's back. The wounded outlaw limped frantically out into the street, screaming, looking back and firing over his shoulder. Blood spewed from a fresh wound high up in his left thigh. A rifle shot kicked up dirt at his feet. He swung back and forth wildly and shouted, "All right, Ranger, you lousy lawdog bastard! Come and get me!"

"Over here, Hawk," said Sam, his Colt out at arm's length, cocked and ready. "Drop the gun and surrender. You're under arrest!"

"Ayyiiiieee!" Hawk cried out, like some enraged mountain cat with its paw caught in a trap. Swinging toward the ranger, he pulled one wild shot after another, until Sam's big Colt bucked once in his hand and sent the outlaw flying backward onto the broken stone-paved street. A cloud of dust rose up around Hawk as Sam turned back to the adobe and called out, "All right, I've got him. It's over. Throw out the money and I'll be on my way." He stepped sidelong over to where Clarence Hawk lay gasping for air, and kicked the pistol out of his reach. "Lay still, Hawk," he said, seeing the gaping chest wound. "I'll get you patched up in a minute."

"No . . . patching is going to . . . help," Hawk wheezed, squeezing his hands to the wound, unable to slow the flowing blood.

"Where's Lowry and the others headed?" Sam asked.

But before answering, Hawk asked, "How the . . . hell did I get stuck . . . with bad money?"

"That story would take longer than you've got time to listen," said Sam, looking closer, seeing the severity of the chest wound and realizing Hawk wouldn't be alive much longer. "Where's Lowry headed?"

"Trouble Creek," Hawk managed to say. Then he gasped and coughed and said, "Just tell me this. . . . The woman had something to do with it . . . didn't she?"

"Yep, a whole lot," Sam said. "It looked like you and your friends came to rob the right bank at the wrong time. She set you boys up to take the blame. All you got was play money."

"I knew she . . . was no good," Hawk murmured. "Well, hell. I reckon I . . . had one last good screwing coming. At least . . . she was pretty. . . ."

Turning from Hawk and facing the adobe building, Sam watched the woman run away from an open side doorway and disappear deeper into the shelter of rubble and earthen walls. *A bad sign,* he told himself, stepping farther away from Clarence Hawk, both rifle and pistol ready. "If you're thinking about keeping the money, it's a bad idea," he called out to the three men inside.

"Oh?" said Paco. "If the money is not real, why do you want it?"

"I'll turn it in," said Sam. "Counterfeit money gets turned in and burned. You can't keep it."

"I think maybe we do keep it," said Paco. "We will take it to Mexico and you will never have to worry about seeing us again."

"I can't do it," said Sam firmly, his feet spread shoulder length apart. "Throw out the money. Don't turn this into a fight."

"What is the harm, señor?" Hector called out in an almost pleading tone. "Nobody will know it in Mexico. It is a good thing for your country, no? American money that we spend in Mexico? Explain the harm in that!"

"My job is not to explain things to you," said Sam. "Throw out the money, or I'm coming after it."

"Come in after it and you will die like the outlaw laying out there," Paco replied to him.

Here goes . . . Sam said to himself.

Standing to the side of the open doorway, Paco said to the other two, "All right, when I count three, we charge him. We shoot him down, take the money and go to Mexico! Ready — *uno!*"

"Wait, Paco!" said Hector. He gestured with his rifle toward the open rear wall looking out toward the sand flats. "We don't have to fight this lawman! We can take the money and make a run for it! What is there to stop us?"

Paco looked out longingly through the open back wall and stifled a sigh. "If only it was so, Hector," he said. "But our horses are out front. Do you think this man will just let us go?"

"Then maybe we should give him this money," said Phillipi with a worried tone to his voice. "If it is not real, why do we risk our lives for it?" He gestured toward the dusty stone street. "We see that this man doesn't mind killing to enforce his law."

"Are you loco?" Paco asked, his rifle growing sweaty in his anxious hands. "Whether the money is real or not doesn't matter! We have it. We can spend it. We must not give it up! How long will it be before any of us sees this much money again in our lives? Never — that is how long!"

Seeing his words had no effect on Paco, Hector turned to his brother with his hands spread, pleading for his help.

"Hector is right, Paco!" said Phillipi. "The money is not worth anything. We will only get in trouble spending it!"

"What does it matter that we will get in trouble spending counterfeit money?" Paco asked. "Is that any more trouble than spending *real* money that we have stolen somewhere?"

The two brothers looked at one another.

"Who can say what money is real and what money is not real?" Paco asked, taking quick, nervous glances toward the street to make sure the ranger had not begun sneaking up on them. "A government prints on paper — here, this is our money. It is *real!* Why? Because we declare that it is real! And if you say otherwise or try to take our money from us, we have an army that will come shoot holes in you and burn down your haciendas!"

"But, Paco, listen to yourself!" said Hector. "We are not the government. We do not even live here! This is not even our country!"

"Oh?" said Paco indignantly. "It used to be our country. I never said anybody could have it. Did you?"

"Paco, please, *por favor!*" said Phillipi, getting more and more concerned, seeing Paco slip further and further away from reality.

"You must hear from a *government* what is real and what is not?" said Paco. He patted himself soundly on the chest. "All right, then. I am my own government. I say this money is real! I declare that this is our money, and that no one can take it from us." He raised his battered old rifle and jiggled it in his hands. "If we need an army to defend our money, I *am* that army!"

Hector shook his head and nervously checked his rifle. "This is not good," he said in a shaky voice.

"No, it is not," said Phillipi, agreeing with

his brother, but at the same time readying himself to follow Paco into the street to wage battle.

"All right, then," said Paco, satisfied that he'd won them over. *"Dos!"* He gave them a cavalier grin and leaned nearer to the open doorway.

Hector crossed himself. Phillipi swallowed a dry knot in his throat.

"Tres!" said Paco, lunging forward out the doorway and into the street.

The ranger's first shot sent Paco staggering sideways, turning his running charge into a broken, stumbling descent into the billowing dust. A shot exploded wildly from the rifle in his hands. Sam had no time to see if his bullet left the young man dead or alive. As quickly as he could turn and fire, he saw the flame of powder explode from the dueling pistol in Phillipi's hand. The round lead ball zipped past the ranger's ear just as his next shot dropped Phillipi face-down, sliding him to a halt on the street stones, leaving a smear of blood behind him.

Swinging his Colt away from Phillipi, Sam heard Hector let out a long, gut-wrenching scream at the sight of his brother's blood. In a frenzy, Hector let the rifle fly from his hands and raced to where Phillipi lay dead in the dirt. Sam held his fire and waited, hoping Hector would give up the fight. But Hector wasn't about to stop. A thirst for vengeance suddenly overcame him. He picked up the machete that had fallen from Phillipi's hand and charged at Sam, swinging it back and forth like a madman.

"Halt, or I'll shoot!" Sam shouted. But neither his warning nor the sight of the Colt in his hand had the slightest effect on Hector. With no further delay and without batting an eye, the ranger squeezed off another shot. He felt the big Colt buck once in his hand, silencing the screaming young man and stopping the machete from slicing the air.

Sam stood in the street and looked back and forth as he cradled his rifle in his left arm, opened his Colt and let the spent round fall to the dirt at his feet. Holding the Colt in his left hand, he scanned in each direction as he stuck fresh cartridges into the cylinder and clicked it shut.

"Nooooo!" a voice cried out, followed by the sound of moccasins running across the street stones.

Sam turned toward the sound, cocking his Colt, but eased down as he saw the woman running past him, unarmed, with tears in her eyes, to the body of Paco lying ten yards away. He watched her make the sign of the cross. Then he began walking toward her slowly when he saw her eyes go to the rifle on the ground. "Ma'am, leave it lay," he warned her.

But before the words were out of his mouth he saw her grab the rifle and cock it. He raced forward, pointing, taking aim, hoping to reach her in time to knock the rifle away before she could fire it. Yet, to his surprise, she did not point the rifle at him. Instead she cocked the rifle, turned the barrel to a spot beneath her chin, reached down with her bare foot and hooked her toe into the trigger guard. "No!" Sam shouted, diving headlong toward her the last few yards.

He saw a tight grimace come upon her face as the rifle exploded, lifting a long gout of blood from the top of her head, before he landed against her in time to shove the rifle barrel away from her face.

He lay on the ground for a moment as if to collect himself. When he finally rose to his feet and brushed dust from his shirt, instead of turning his eyes to the dead woman's face, he looked away, out across the horizon, as if searching for something of extreme importance. In the silence that followed, the old basket weaver walked up beside him, looked down at Paco, the woman, and the other two dead men lying on the stone street. Then his eyes turned down to Clarence Hawk's dead, blank face and he said to it, "All this because of you and your money."

"Play money," Sam said quietly, slipping his Colt into its holster.

"*Play* money?" said the basket weaver. His weathered hand made a slow, sweeping gesture, taking in the carnage the counterfeit bills had caused. "All money is *play* money."

■ ■ ■ ■

PART 2

■ ■ ■ ■

CHAPTER 11

Dick Lowry had no way of knowing that he and his men had taken the right trail until they spotted the circling buzzards and allowed the birds to lead them to the body of Marvin Albright lying a few feet down off the rocky ledge. When the three outlaws rode up to the spot where Kaylee had rolled Albright across the dust and gave it a final shove, the sound of squawking buzzards and their powerful batting wings caused Lowry to give a knowing smile.

"Well, well. Sounds like somebody is eating good this evening," he said, nudging his horse closer to the edge and stepping down from the saddle. Catlan Thompson and Pony Phil joined him. Catlan carried a canteen he'd taken from his saddle horn. He uncapped it as he gazed skyward and watched the circling buzzards. From a distance more of the big birds sailed in and swooped and circled lower overhead. "Easy, boys, it's all yours," Lowry chuckled, looking upward, hearing the birds squawk in protest.

"Jesus!" said Pony Phil. The three of them looked down at a dozen of the big scavengers perched on or around Albright's half-eaten remains. "I always hate seeing something like this."

One of the birds shook its head vigorously inside Albright's open chest cavity and backed away, pulling a long string of viscera. Black Cat spat out a mouthful of tepid water he'd sipped from the canteen in his hand and said, "Hell, it's all just meat once it hits the ground."

Looking at the big black man, Pony Phil started to comment; but then he thought better of it and swallowed a bitter taste in his throat. He reached out a hand for the canteen. Catlan passed it to him without taking his eyes off the feeding buzzards.

Nodding down at Albright's body, Lowry said, "That's what a lying, low-down bitch like her will do to a man."

"Every time," said Black Cat.

"Let's get out of here," said Pony Phil, looking up at the buzzards, then back down at Albright's body.

"What's your hurry?" Lowry said, teasing him. But even as he spoke, a large splatter of bird excrement plopped into the dust at his feet, causing him to step backward toward his horse.

"It won't be hard catching up to her from here," Pony Phil said, handing the canteen back to Thompson. "A woman like her, traveling all alone across this desert." He grinned and swung up onto his horse's back without using his stirrup. "Hell, she might be *glad* to see us ole boys coming."

"Hmmpff," Black Cat grunted, sounding doubtful. "I don't know about that," he said, capping the canteen, stepping up into his saddle. "But I don't see her as the kind of woman who'll be traveling alone for long."

Atop his horse, Dick Lowry nodded at the extra sets of hoofprints less than ten feet away, then looked upward along the winding trail. "She ain't the *kind of woman* who ever has to travel alone. She was already with somebody else before the birds set into the banker's belly."

"She sure enough was," Black Cat marveled, shaking his head. "That banker was set up from the start!"

"We should have seen that all along," said Lowry. "A woman like that, with a man like him?" He shook his head. "It didn't look right to begin with."

"Looks like there's a whole gang involved here," said Thompson, gazing at the hoof-prints.

"Damn right, it does!" said Pony Phil. He glanced back along the lower trail and added, "I wish Hawk would hurry up. From the looks of all this, we're going to need every gun we've got."

Thompson and Lowry exchanged a knowing look. "I wouldn't count on Hawk showing up, Pony," said Thompson. "He's wounded pretty bad."

"Then what are we going to do, Dick?" Pony asked, turning to Lowry for guidance. "We're short on men. . . . All we've got for guns are these bunch of scrapes." His hand patted the older Remington pistol in his waist.

"We're going to do what makes sense," said Lowry. "We're going to stay on these people's trail and check them out. Soon as the time is right, we're taking that money from them and hightailing it to Mexico."

The three hurried their horses to the top of the hill trail and rode on in silence for the next few miles along the edge of the hills, until Lowry stopped and pointed down at the hoofprints as they circled wide and turned south on the flatlands below. "Look at this," said Lowry. "They've circled back and headed south." He grinned. "Hell, boys, we won't have to hightail it to Mexico. . . . These folks are going to lead us there!"

"We can save ourselves some time catching up to them," said Thompson, nodding out across the flatlands toward a set of hills south of them. "We could cut right down to the trail from here and straight across the flatlands."

"Yes," said Lowry, "and that's exactly what we're going to do." He jerked his horse toward a thin, steep trail leading almost straight down the flatlands. "We'll be close enough to buy that woman and her friends breakfast come morning," he said with a dark grin.

No sooner than the last of the Cardells' bodies were in the ground and he'd spoken a hurried prayer over their graves then Ed Thornis seated Jamison Cardell atop a mule he'd found wandering aimlessly around the yard of the trading post, and headed along the trail back to Olsen. Throughout the entire trip, Thornis kept expecting to look around beside him and find that Jamison Cardell had fallen dead from his saddle. The truth be known, he reminded himself, dying might be the best thing . . .

But something kept the young man alive

all the way to Olsen, and by the time Thornis led his mule onto the dirt street at the edge of town, Jamison's good eye swam back and forth for a moment and he said in a detached voice, "Where am I?"

Surprised, Thornis brought both animals almost to a stop and replied, "This is Olsen, young fella. We've got a good doctor here. He's going to get you fixed right up." As he spoke Thornis saw three townsmen come down off the boardwalks and hurry toward him. Jamison tried to focus on the townsmen, but the difficulty in doing so caused him to swoon a bit, and he began to lean dangerously to one side.

"Hold on, now," said Thornis, grabbing him by his shoulder, pulling him back and bracing him until the townsmen arrived at the young man's side and eased him down from the saddle.

"Ed, what's happened to him?" asked Albert Hubert.

"Who is he?" asked Dexter Swan.

"He's one of the Cardells, from the trading post," Thornis replied, stepping down from his saddle to help them with Jamison. "Be careful with his head. It's busted something awful."

"What's this bandage?" Swan asked, almost touching the lump of bandage on

Jamison's cheek.

"Don't touch that!" Thornis cried out. "It's got his eye covered!"

"His eye?" Swan gave him a peculiar look. "Hell, his eye's up here." He pointed, again almost touching the bandage until Thornis stepped around and pulled his hand away.

"I told you *don't touch nothing!*" said Thornis. "His eye is laying out on his cheek. It's been knocked out of the socket!" He winced just talking about it. "For God's sake, let's get him to the doctor — let him handle this."

"Oh, Jesus!" said Swan. "I've never seen nothing like that!"

"Nor have I," said Thornis, all of them hurrying along the center of the street, carrying Jamison between them. "Where is Nebberly?"

"Nebberly's busy with some of Morganfield's men," said Swan, using one hand to help with Jamison, his other to hold his bowler hat down on his head. The townsmen hurried along toward the doctor's office.

"Morganfield's men?" Thornis looked stunned. "When did they get here?"

"The day after you left," said Swan, already puffing, getting out of breath. "I never seen nothing like it! They came charging in here like the bank was being robbed right then!"

"How did they get here so fast?" Thornis asked.

"Beats me," said Swan. "Nebberly telegraphed Morganfield's Chicago office right away, of course. Seemed like within hours these men came riding in. I figure they were on a railcar somewhere nearby, took the message aboard the train and came running. Their leader is a detective named Bo Maydeen. From the way he's acting, Morganfield must be madder than a wet hornet."

"I've heard of Maydeen," said Thornis. "He made a reputation for himself killing rustlers for a big English cattle association."

"So?" said Swan. "I have no problem with cattle thieves getting what's coming to them. Do you?"

"None at all," said Thornis, "except some of these alleged cattle rustlers happened to own land that the English growers wanted. Do you understand what I'm saying, Councilman Swan?" he asked pointedly.

"Yeah, I do, now that you put it that way," said Swan. His eyes made a quick, guarded sweep of the other townsmen carrying Jamison Cardell. "I swear it's getting to where you can't find one honest man in a thousand. I don't know who to befriend anymore."

"Befriend the one who's apt to kill you if you don't," an old townsman named Rusty Hienz added to the conversation. He gave Swan and Thornis a piercing stare as they stepped up onto the boardwalk outside the doctor's office and Thornis opened the door with his free hand. "I learned a long time ago that when a man like Morganfield goes to all the trouble of hiring a killer like Maydeen, it's a sure sign some poor sonsabitch is about to die. Best thing I know to do is make sure that poor sonsabitch ain't me."

"Your sage advice is well considered, sir," said Swan. "I assure you I have nothing bad to say about Laslow Morganfield or any of his associates."

"Nor do I," said Thornis. Rushing into the office with Jamison Cardell in his arms, Thornis turned to the elderly doctor when he stepped in from the other room, already rolling up his sleeves.

After recounting what had happened to Jamison Cardell to Dr. Fisher, Thornis and Dexter Swan sent the other men away and waited in an adjoining parlor while the doctor worked on the wounded man in private. At the end of a tense half hour, the two men stood up as if coming to attention when the door opened and Dr. Fisher stepped in, taking his thick spectacles from the bridge of his crooked nose. "Doctor, how is he?" Thornis asked anxiously. "Is he going to live?"

"He's young and strong," said the doctor. "So, yes, I believe he might live. But he has taken an awfully severe blow to his head."

"Do you think he'll get over it all right?" Thornis asked. "Will you be able to save his eye?"

"Save his eye?" The doctor shook his head slowly. "I doubt it. Will he be *all right?* I doubt that too, but it's too soon to tell. I came out here to tell you both to go on about your business. I know how to reach you if anything changes."

"I'm obliged, Doctor," said Thornis. "I don't know the young man, but I'd like to know how he's doing."

"And so you will," said the doctor, sweeping a hand toward the front door. "Now, if you'll excuse me, I need to stay by his side."

Leaving the doctor's office, Thornis and Swan walked along the boardwalk toward the Nebberly Land & Mineral Development Company. "Doc Fisher doesn't sound very optimistic to me," Swan said, still out of breath. "If I were you I wouldn't have my hopes up in that young man surviving."

"Jamison Cardell has an awfully strong will to live," said Thornis. "I believe he'll make it now. When we found him I wouldn't have given two cents for him living through the day. Then I expected him to die any minute all the way here. But he's fooled me at every turn." He paused for a moment, then said, "I ain't ordinarily a religious man, Swan. But damn, it looks like *something* or *somebody* wants this boy alive."

"I understand you've been through a lot," said Swan. "I just don't want to see you too badly disappointed if he dies."

"Disappointed?" said Thornis. "I shouldn't say this, but the shape he's in, I've thought death would be a blessing for him."

Swan looked confused. "But you just said you believed he'd make it."

"I said I *believed he would make it,*" said Thornis. "I never said that I saw any good reason why he should."

"Oh." Swan looked no less confused as they continued along the dirt-crusted boardwalk.

When the two stepped inside the door of Stewart Nebberly's office, Thornis let out a breath, seeing Stewart Nebberly stand up from his desk and look at him as if in awe. Beside Nebberly's desk sat two men in wooden chairs. They turned and looked Thornis up and down without standing. "Ed Thornis!" said Nebberly. "I can't tell you how good it is to see that you are alive and well."

"Thank you, Councilman," said Thornis. "I'm sorry I've failed to bring back either the money or the thieves who stole it."

"We all know you've done the very best you can, Ed," said Nebberly.

"Which thieves are you talking about?" one of the men asked impatiently. "Do you mean that little snake Marvin Albright? Or do you mean Dick Lowry and his band of range trash?" He idly brushed a fleck of cigar ash from his lapel as he spoke. "It must be difficult having so many guilty parties to choose from." He ended his words with a sour smile.

Noting the accusation in his voice, Thornis stood at a loss for a moment, not sure of how he should answer the man. But Nebberly cut in quickly, taking him off the spot by saying to the two men, "Excuse me, gentlemen. I want you to meet Ed Thornis, the man I told you about who went off searching for Miss Smith and Mr. Albright."

The men nodded, but neither offered any gesture of manners. "Oh, the blacksmith," said the larger of the two, who gave Thornis an appraising stare and let his thick hand rest on a bone-handled Colt standing in a belly holster across his broad stomach.

"Ed," Nebberly continued, "these gentlemen are Mr. Bo Maydeen" — his hand swept toward the large man — "and his associate, Mr. Cobb."

"Mr. Nebberly tells us you were a close friend of the young lady in question, Thornis," said Maydeen, almost before Nebberly finished the introduction.

Thornis gave Nebberly a sharp glance, then said to Maydeen, "I thought we had become friends, but as it turns out, I must have been wrong. I had no idea she might be up to something like —"

"What business does the town *blacksmith* have trailing bank robbers?" Cobb asked, cutting Thornis off. His words sounded like an implication.

"Gentlemen," said Nebberly, cutting in on Thornis' behalf, "Ed here is civic-minded enough to serve as a sort of constable, if you will, in times like these."

"A sort of constable, huh?" said Cobb, eyeing Thornis closer now, but no more cordially than Maydeen. "What the hell is a *sort of constable?*"

Maydeen silenced Cobb with a wave of his thick hand. "Give the blacksmith a chance to speak, Mr. Cobb." He offered his same flat sour smile to Thornis. "What went on out there? Did you do any good at all? Did you find Albright's trail?"

"No," said Thornis. "I'm afraid I did not find Albright's trail." He turned his answer away from Maydeen and Cobb and directed his words to Stewart Nebberly, answering to him in his capacity as councilman. "I joined the ranger on the tail end of the storm. We followed a line of smoke that led us to Cardell's Trading Post. Lowry and his men killed the Cardells, except for Matson's son, Jamison. I brought the young man here for medical treatment. The side of his head is crushed. . . . His eye was knocked out of its socket."

"My goodness," Nebberly said quietly.

Cobb stifled a short chuckle. "Ouch! That must've hurt."

Thornis ignored Cobb and said to Nebberly, "Doc Fisher says he thinks Jamison might make it. He'll lose the eye, though."

"I take it you know this young man?" Maydeen asked.

"I do now," Thornis replied. Turning his attention back to Nebberly, he said, "Ranger Burrack stuck tight on the Lowry gang's trail. We both decided it would be best if he kept tracking the gang. I have faith in him catching them."

"Did you say Burrack?" Branard Cobb asked, his eyes narrowing. He winced, and before Thornis could respond, said to Maydeen, "We don't need Burrack out there sticking his nose into company business."

"I could care less what Burrack and the Lowry gang does to one another," said Maydeen. He swung his sharp eyes back to Thornis. "What has any of *this* got to do with Albright and Mr. Morganfield's money?"

Thornis stared at the two detectives for a moment, sizing them up, seeing nothing about them that inspired confidence. These men were paid thugs and nothing more, it occurred to him. He could picture either of them crushing Jamison Cardell's skull with a rifle butt as easily as he could picture one of the Lowry gang doing it.

"Well, *blacksmith?*" Cobb asked in a sarcastic tone. "Are you going to tell us what this has to do with Morganfield's money?"

"Not a damn thing," Thornis surprised himself by saying. He returned Maydeen's and Cobb's stare, determined not to say another word to either of these men. Instead he turned to Nebberly and said, "When Dr. Fisher sends word about Jamison Cardell, please tell him much obliged for me."

"Of course, Ed," said Nebberly, seeing that Thornis had stepped back and appeared ready to turn and leave. "I suppose you must intend to go somewhere and get some rest."

"Yes," said Thornis, but he knew he had just lied. He wasn't about to let Morganfield's men know his business. He saw that as long as the money from Olsen-Morganfield Bank & Land Trust remained missing he would always be subject to someone's accusations and suspicions.

Leaving the councilman's office, he walked straight to the livery barn, picked out what he knew to be the strongest, best-shod rental horse in the corral and prepared it for the trail. He wasn't coming back to Olsen without the bank money in hand.

CHAPTER 12

With the counterfeit money in his saddle-bags, Sam followed both the hoofprints and the circling buzzards until he found the body of Marvin Albright lying half devoured in the baking desert sun. In addition to the buzzards, coyotes had slinked out during the previous night and yapped, chewed and stripped Albright's clothes from his body. Sam looked at the banker's strewn-out remains and saw where some larger predator had prowled forward on the cusp of dawn and twisted and gnawed the banker's head off. The remnants of the face lay turned toward the ranger. Stepping down closer, Sam shooed flies away with his sombrero and identified Albright's mangled purple features as best he could.

Raising his bandanna up over the bridge of his nose to help block out the smell and the swarming flies, Sam dragged Albright's remains over against a short breastwork of rock and piled small stones over it until at length the banker disappeared into the belly of the desert. With no words to say over the pile of rocks, Sam walked back to Black Pot, stepped up into his saddle and rode on, following a gathering of hoofprints upward along the trail until he reached the spot on the hillside where Lowry himself had looked down onto the flatlands and sighted the wide circle of tracks swinging out across the desert floor.

Looking to the left he also saw where the three sets of hoofprints he'd been following reached straight across the sand and disappeared over a distant rise. "Whoever she's with now, she's got Lowry on her trail, Black Pot," Sam murmured to the stallion beneath him. He gave a slight tap of his heels to the animal's sides and rode down onto the flatlands.

Without pushing the stallion, he spent the rest of the day crossing the wide, empty land and did not stop until the sunlight lay long across the rocky soil. Then, not wanting to suddenly come upon so large a body of riders as he now knew lay ahead of him, Sam made a dark camp for the night and hobbled Black Pot in a nearby stand of wild grass. He slept guardedly, fully dressed, and awakened instinctively two hours before daylight began to form a glowing wreath on the eastern edge of the earth.

For breakfast Sam stirred a palm full of pemmican powder into a tin cup filled with tepid canteen water. With his hands wrapped around the cup out of habit, he sat hunkered down beside his saddle and sipped the gritty substance, his blanket thrown across his shoulders, against the desert chill. When he'd finished, he stood up, took off the blanket, picked up the saddle and walked over to Black Pot.

"Time to go," he said, pitching the saddle up on the stallion's back. As if the big animal understood his words, Sam said, "We're going to ride extra easy till daylight. I don't want anybody to see us coming." He gazed out across gray, starlit darkness and prepared Black Pot for the trail.

Once back upon the trail he stopped now and then, leaned from the saddle long enough to make sure he still had kept the many hoofprints beneath him, and rode on. By sunup the stallion had taken him onto a long upward slope headed off the flatlands and into a stretch of blunt low hills. When morning light gave him a better view of the rugged, desolate terrain, he tracked the riders off the main trail and onto a thin path leading through tangles of dry brush, deadfall and sharp ravines.

Black Pot followed the winding paths, stopping only long enough to take a draw of cool water where a stream meandered down out of the boulders and braided its way along its bracken-lined bed of white sand and black-red gravel. In the early afternoon, Sam rested himself and the stallion by such a stream, risking a low, smokeless fire just long enough to boil a pot of coffee. As soon as the coffee had boiled dark and strong, he put out the fire with his bootheel and sat down beside the stream and sipped his coffee. In the quiet of a warm breeze through the dry brush, he took in the land in a long, sweeping gaze, but kept his eyes coming back every so often to the hoofprints, as if they might otherwise disappear.

His coffee finished, he stood up and dusted his trousers. He put away the pot and the cup, tightened Black Pot's cinch, mounted and rode on. He put the stallion into a faster pace once they rode out off the brushy hills and onto a level trail. In the late afternoon he met a stagecoach rolling toward him in front of a billowing cloud of dust, as if rising up from some smoky netherworld. Seeing the shotgun rider's ten-gauge come up from his lap at the man's sight of him, Sam slowed Black Pot to a walk and eased him off of the narrow trail. But as he held the stallion to allow the stage to pass, Sam made it a point to open his duster wide enough to reveal the badge on his chest.

"Whoa . . ." came the voice of the stage driver, sitting back firmly in his wooden seat, laying his weight back on the rein traces and brake handle at the same time.

Sam turned Black Pot beneath him, both of them watching the stage slide past until it came to halt. Through the swirl of dust, a bearded face leaned out from the driver's seat and stared back at him. "Hello the trail?" the driver called out, making it more of a question than a greeting.

"Hello the stage," the ranger replied. He swung the stallion out a few feet to avoid the worst of the dust, and circled to the front of the big Concord coach until both driver and shotgun rider could see him clearly.

"Did you flag us down, Ranger?" the driver asked, having identified the badge on Sam's chest.

"No," said Sam. "I sidled off to clear the trail for you." He'd glanced inside the empty passenger area as he rode around to the front.

"It don't matter none," the driver said.

"I'm Piearcy, from Kansas." He touched his dusty Stetson brim. "Ethel and me most always stop when we meet a lawman out here, especially if it's a ranger like yourself."

Touching the brim of his sombrero in response, Sam said, "Howdy, Piearcy, I'm Ranger Sam Burrack." Then, leaning a bit in his saddle for a better look at the shotgun rider, he asked, "Is that Ethel *Moody* you're talking about?"

The shotgun rider leaned out around the driver, her hair bushing out beneath her hat brim on one side, and said with a broken-toothed grin, "What other *Ethel* have you ever seen out here, Ranger?" A thin, willowy mustache mantled her upper lip. "I bet you're tracking the hell out of somebody, ain't ya?"

"Howdy, Ethel," said Sam, touching the brim of his sombrero. "I'm trailing jailbreakers, all the way from Olsen."

"See? I told you," said Ethel, nudging the driver with her elbow. "He's always dogging some outlaw or other." She turned her grin back to the ranger and asked, "I can't believe we run into you out here. But then, it has been a strange trip all the way around."

"Have you seen any riders?" Sam asked.

"No, I can't say that we have," said Ethel,

seeming to ponder the question as she replied.

"We got put off our usual route," said the driver. "It's got us both out of sorts."

Ethel jerked her head toward a set of low hills to the southeast. "Storm washed out our hill trail. We swung down here. . . . Had to duck mud puddles the first twenty miles."

"I don't like it down here," the driver said, shaking his head. "It's too close to the border to suit me. We get all the saddle trash from both sides."

"We even lost our only two passengers," Ethel said. "Two gun toters in suits and bowlers. No sooner than we hit the flatlands, two other men in suits, leading spare horses, flagged us down." She made a sliding gesture with her hand. "Those two got off and *ziiiip,* they was gone!"

"Oh?" Sam's interest was piqued. He immediately thought of Laslow Morganfield. "Did they look like detectives?"

"If *they didn't,* I do," said Ethel, sweeping a hand down the front of her ragged buckskin shirt and trousers, her battered hat and knee-high boots.

Sam smiled. "Headed for the border, were they?"

"At a *run,* the last we saw of them," said the driver.

Sam started to back Black Pot and bid them good day, but before he could, Ethel Moody said, "Say, Ranger, did you ever marry that pretty young woman, Ella something-or-other?"

"Ella Lang," Sam said, feeling a twinge of pain upon having her name brought up. "No, it never happened," he said, not wanting to start a conversation.

"Well, hell," said Ethel, "I thought you would have by now."

"Gawdamn it, Ethel, can't you see he ain't wanting to talk about it?" the driver admonished her.

"Sorry, Ranger," said Ethel. She grinned as Sam backed the stallion and touched his gloved fingers to the brim of his sombrero. "If you don't want her I'll take her."

The driver's eyes widened. "Don't talk like that! That ain't decent!"

"Hell, he knows I'm only joshing!" said Ethel, giving the driver a solid punch on his arm. "Take care, now, Ranger!" she called out, seeing that Sam had already turned and started riding away.

It would be midafternoon before he stopped again. By then the Mexican border had slipped unnoticed beneath the big stallion's hooves. At a fork in the trail he turned and followed many sets of hoofprints southwest toward a farming village, where no more than a year earlier he'd taken a wanted killer by the name of Earl Hackly off the villagers' hands. He'd ridden away with Hackly's body lying limp across his saddle, his arms dangling, his blue tongue a-loll like that of a wild dog.

"Here's where it might get a little tricky, Black Pot," he said to the stallion.

Knowing the riders had gone into the village, Sam cut off the trail and rode wide around an old stone wall that had in centuries past protected an ancient race of warriors from their many enemies. Now the wall served only to protect lush green stalks of corn from wild pigs and stray cattle. Halfway around the wall, he rode into a small vine-covered courtyard and stopped when he saw an old man rise up from a wooden swing and step forward with a curious look of recognition on his weathered face.

"Hola, Guardabosques, mi amigo!" the old man called out. He swept a wide, faded black sombrero from his head and hurried forward.

Sam eased the stallion forward and stepped down from the saddle. *"Hola, Don Ramón, mi amigo y confidente,"* he said quietly, looking around, a bit concerned that the man had so boldly called him *Guarda-bosques* (Ranger) at a time when Sam needed to keep his presence a secret.

In Spanish, the old man asked, "What brings you here?" Then, seeing the way Sam had lowered his tone and looked all around, he asked with a raised brow, "Is there trouble once again in my little village?"

"There have been riders come here today, yes?" Sam asked in his blunt but respectful border Spanish.

"*Si*, many riders," said Don Ramón. "All of a sudden my little village has become most popular!" He spread his hands and swayed slightly as he said, "They come in business suits and in range clothes. Some come the day before yesterday and leave the next morning. Others have come and gone since then. And others yet rode in early today and are still here. They spend two hours eating beans and goat meat. . . . Then the rest of the day they drink at the cantina."

"The last ones? Are there three of them?" Sam asked.

"Yes, three of them," Ramón answered, holding up three long, thin fingers. "One of them black and two of them white. They smoke *mucho* marijuana and feed themselves *loco droga*."

"Drunk and doped, huh?" said Sam, pondering the situation.

"Sí," the old man said. "They look like they have already had trouble with someone." Recalling one man having a battered forehead and another with a wounded shoulder, he grinned and asked, "You did this to them, no?"

Sam nodded and slipped his big Colt from his holster. He checked it as he spoke, saying in English now, "How about trading sombreros with me for a while?"

"Ah, I see how it is," Don Ramón grinned, dusting his palm across the brim of his black sombrero before handing it to him. "Do you want to trade shirts as well?" He plucked at the front of his loose white shirt.

"No," said Sam, "but if you have a poncho handy, I'm much obliged."

"I have no poncho," said Ramón, "but I have a blanket and a knife. I will make one for you."

"Gracias," said the ranger, handing the old man his silver-gray sombrero and putting the faded black one on in its place.

Wearing the newly made poncho draped down over his shoulders to hide his gun belt, and the broad black sombrero low on his forehead, Sam left Black Pot in the old

Mexican's courtyard and walked in the dimming evening sunlight to the cantina at the far end of the village. But as he walked along past the town well in the center of the wide, dusty thoroughfare, Dick Lowry had just stepped away from relieving himself against a stone wall, his saddlebags draped over his shoulder. He stood watching curiously, recognizing something familiar in the walk, the slow swing of the ranger's arms.

"Gawdamn it!" Lowry growled to himself, hurrying with the buttons on his fly as he backed farther away from the edge of the adobe cantina. His first impulse was to run back inside through the side door, his Colt coming out of his belt, cocked and ready. But then he stopped short, hearing Pony Phil snickering loudly and drunkenly from the small plank bar.

Hold on . . . Lowry told himself. Looking in through the darkening gloom, he saw Black Cat Thompson twirling a young barefoot village girl around on the dirt floor. A long, twisted marijuana *cigarro* stuck out from between his teeth. Black Cat grinned wildly from within a blue haze of looming smoke. At the bar, Pony Phil stood in a thin puddle of urine, snickering, laughing and crying, out of control, his arms holding his sides as if he'd been kicked in the gut.

Huh-uh . . . Lowry thought. He wasn't going back in there. On the bar lay a half-dozen empty mescal bottles and a mound of pale brownish powder that matched the powder caked in Phil's mustache stubble. A pistol lay only inches away.

"Sorry, boys," Lowry whispered under his breath. "You both died happy." Slipping back away from the cantina, he raced along the narrow alleyway to where their horses stood hitched out back. He hastily jerked his saddle up off of a public rack where it lay between Phil's and Black Cat's, slung it up onto his horse's back and tightened the cinch quickly. Grabbing the reins to the other two horses, he climbed into his saddle, nailed his spurs to his horse, and jerked the other two along roughly, saying, "Come on, gawdamn it! They won't be joining us this evening!"

Out front, Sam stepped inside the cantina and quietly walked along the wall. While Black Cat and the young woman stopped dancing and stood clinging to one another in the midst of the dirt floor, Sam eased across the floor and stopped at the far end of the plank bar, ten feet from Pony Phil. Against the wall two ragged men stopped playing a wooden flute and guitar when they saw him. They rose quickly and silently with their instruments and disappeared like wisps of smoke through the rear door.

"Hey, what the hell?" Black Cat called out in a blurry tone, looking up from across the young woman's bare shoulder when he realized the music had stopped. Holding the woman against him with one arm, he walked toward the rear door as if to see where the musicians had gone. "You don't stop playing till I say you stop playing!" he called out the open doorway. "These lazy beaners," he growled, turning back toward the dirt dance floor. "We don't need them, honey," he said sidelong to the woman, nuzzling his face into the side of her throat. "We'll make our own music."

The woman stopped abruptly with a gasp as she saw the dark figure standing less than two feet from them, a corner of the blanket thrown up over his shoulder, a big Colt hanging in his hand. "The party's over, Thompson," he said as Black Cat raised his dreamy, smiling face from the woman's throat.

"Huh?" Black Cat replied.

At the bar Pony Phil turned at the sound of gunmetal against skull. The woman let out a short scream, seeing Black Cat stagger backward, flip over a tall stool and land with a solid thud on the hard dirt floor.

"Jesus, Cat! Watch where you're going!" Phil said through an outbreak of uncontrollable snickering and tearful, wheezing laughter, his arms still wrapped across his belly.

Seeing that Black Cat wouldn't be causing any trouble for a while, Sam turned to Pony Phil and walked forward. The outlaw's gun lay on the bar. He wanted to keep down any shooting for the woman's sake; but if Phil made a wild grab for the pistol, Sam knew he'd have to kill him on the spot. "Step away from the bar, Pony," Sam demanded.

But Phil only continued with his delirious tears and laughter, bowed at the waist as if cramping from it. "I — I can't!" he managed to wheeze, the urine puddle at his feet growing wider. "Oh, God! Stay back!" He did get a hand raised as if to ward the ranger back from him. "Don't come any —" But he couldn't finish his words. Instead he went into a deeper fit of laughter. "I . . . can't stop!" He sank to his knees, paralyzed, and fell forward onto his face.

"Get out of here," Sam said to the woman. He stepped past the convulsing Pony Phil Watson and picked up the pistol from the bar. All the while he kept watch for Dick Lowry.

"I won't get out," the woman said defiantly in stiff English. She pointed a drunken finger toward Black Cat. "He promises me money! I do not leave without it!"

"Ma'am, get out," Sam said firmly. "Any money he has will only get you into trouble. His money's not real."

"Not real? What does this mean, *not real?*" She shoved a hand down inside the low bosom of her dress and pulled out wadded-up bills she'd already siphoned off Black Cat during his drinking-and-smoking spree. Looking at the wadded bills without straightening them out, she said, "This money is as real as any I ever seen!"

"You'll have to give it to me," Sam said, realizing that he had no way of making her comply if she didn't want to. "The money is counterfeit, and I have to take it back with me."

"Not my money," she said, clutching the bills to her breasts, backing toward the open door. "I am not giving it up! Shoot me, but I still will not turn it loose!"

On the floor, Phil wheezed and panted, and at the sound of the woman's voice, he fell into a renewed fit of sobbing laughter.

"Suit yourself, then," Sam said to himself, seeing the woman back out the door and run away. Still looking all around for any sign of Lowry, he shoved Phil's pistol into his belt and reached down, grabbing Phil by his shoulder. "Pony Phil, you're under arrest again. This time for murder. Now I expect you'll hang."

"Murder? Hang?" Phil rose painfully to his feet, still convulsing. "Please!" he wheezed, still crippled by laughter.

Sam leaned the delirious, urine-soaked outlaw against the bar, pulled his arms behind his back and cuffed him. Phil buckled over the bar, gagging in his laughter. Sam stepped over to where Black Cat lay moaning, slowly regaining consciousness. "Who — who are you?" the blurry-eyed gunman asked.

"It's me, Sam Burrack," said the ranger.

"Ranger?" Black Cat said in disbelief.

"Yes, and you're under arrest — again." As Sam spoke, he took out another pair of cuffs and snapped them on the big man's wrists. "Where's Dick Lowry?" he asked.

Black Cat shook his throbbing head a bit as if to clear it. He tried to steady his swimming eyes, looking all around the darkening cantina. "That's what the hell I'd like to know," he moaned.

CHAPTER 13

With two spare horses in tow, Dick Lowry knew he could get a long head start on the ranger. The problem would be to keep the lawman off his trail long enough for him to disappear deep into the rough, hilly terrain along Ennui Creek. There were places in there where Lowry knew he could hold off an army if he had to. "Trouble Creek," he said aloud to himself. *Yeah!* That's where he was headed. The thought of it caused him to slap his reins harder to his horse's sides. *Tough break for Black Cat and Pony Phil,* he told himself. But damn, wouldn't either of them have done the same had they been in his boots?

He looked back over his shoulder in the growing darkness, wondering why he hadn't heard any shots. "Give him hell, boys!" he called out. Then he faced forward, pushing the horse with determination along the cactus-lined trail.

He continued riding hard, paying no mind to the darkness and the rough, rocky trail. He only stopped long enough to change horses when the one beneath him began to lose its pace in spite of the slapping reins and his constant spurring. Past midnight he stopped to change horses again. This time, in the quiet of night, he heard voices speaking in English not far off the trail to his right. Tensing into a crouch, his hand instinctively drawing the Colt from his belt, he searched the brush and sparse woods until he caught the glimmer of a small campfire.

"Easy, boys," he whispered to the three horses, in the same manner as he might have done with Phil and Black Cat had they been alongside him. "Let's go see who we have here."

He led the horses a few yards farther, found a short stub of juniper, hitched them to it and crept forward on foot, the voices growing clearer as he went. At a thin circle of mesquite brush he stooped down and belly-crawled beneath the brush until he saw three men in bowler hats and business suits seated around the campfire, sipping coffee from steaming tin cups. He lay quiet and listened for a moment, deciding whether or not these men had anything to do with Kaylee Smith.

"I'm just grateful that you and Peak came and got us off that stagecoach," a thin, hard-edged man named Ben Winton said. "Four-wheel traveling doesn't agree with me."

"I knew you'd want to join us as soon as possible," said a rough-looking man named George Hope. His prizefighter nose and cauliflower ear stood out almost in mockery of his brown wool suit and crisp brown bowler hat. "Once Maydeen and Cobb got the wiretapper's message, you can bet they got under way. They're on their way here right now, but probably coming from the other direction." He nodded off toward the distance ahead of them.

"Yeah, I agree with George," said Ben Winton. "A damn handy invention, those wiretappers, eh?" He grinned and tipped his cup as if in a toast to the other two.

"I've never seen them," said young Dar-man Peak, a tough, sullen gunman from the Boston slums. "But they're everywhere, I hear."

"All they are is two long poles with metal hooks on the ends," said Winton. "Hook them over a telegraph line and you can send and hear telegraphs just like you can from a telegraph station somewhere."

"Damn," said George Hope. "What are

they going to come up with next? It's enough to spook a man, all this science."

"Ain't that the truth?" said Ben Winton. "It's all too damn fast for me to keep up with." He sipped his coffee, then went on, saying, "Anyway, Maydeen and Cobb got the message. They're coming. You can bet on it. And I want to be there when Maydeen drags that woman away, kicking and screaming."

"You can have all that," said Hope, his big knuckles standing out hard and thick around his cup. "I just want to bash Hollister's head in and watch him die."

"You just want to see him die?" Peak asked, looking a little confused by such an attitude. "You don't want the reward Morganfield's paying?"

"Hell, yes, I want the reward," said Hope, sounding disgusted that the younger man would have thought otherwise. "But I like killing a slick outlaw like him." He spread a wide grin. "He's been running around, doing as he damn well pleases — thinks he's gotten by with something all his life. I like that look that comes to that kind of man's eyes when he's figured out he's dying . . . and that he's looking into the eyes of the man who did the job on him. I like that better than sleeping with naked women."

"Christ, Hope . . ." Peak murmured, staring at the big ex-pugilist.

A tense silence passed, broken at length by Hope and Winton no longer able to stifle their laughter.

Peak still stared, a bit puzzled.

"I'm joshing you," Hope said finally. Winton let loose with his laugh now that the joke was over.

Peak smiled weakly, a little embarrassed. Letting out a breath he said, "Damn, I'm glad to hear that. I started wondering if it was safe to sleep around the same fire with you of a night."

"He's joshing, Peak," said Winton, "but not entirely. I've seen him choke a man to death instead of shooting him, just so he can see that look he's talking about."

Hope shrugged a big shoulder. "There's some truth to that, I suppose."

Listening, Lowry had already realized these were Laslow Morganfield's private gunmen. That was all he needed to hear. But before Lowry crawled backward and away, it dawned on him that across the fire and to the right of the three men stood *four* horses. *Oh, hell!* He should have taken note of that right away. He started to back out of there in a hurry now, but it was too late. The cold tip of a rifle barrel at the base of his skull stopped him.

"Who the hell are you?" said a sinister-sounding voice. Before Lowry could swing around with his pistol, a boot came down and clamped his gun hand to the ground. "Huh-uh, you don't want to do nothing stupid," said the voice. "I'm apt to kill you anyways, for sneaking past me."

"What's going on out there, Clifford?" Winton asked. All three men rose to their feet, drawing pistols from behind their suit coats.

"I've found us a snake crawling around out here," said Clifford Devoe, holding the cocked rifle aimed down on Lowry. In his other hand, he held the reins to Lowry's main horse, the one with the counterfeit money in the saddlebags. "It's a two-legged snake," he added. "One of Doyle Hollister's, is my guess."

"Drag it on in here, Clifford," said Winton. "Let's all take a look at it before we mash its head."

"You heard him, flunky," Clifford said to Lowry, poking the back of his head with the hard rifle barrel. "Turn loose of the gun and start crawling."

Lowry took his hand off of the gun and crawled forward, leaving it in the dirt for

Clifford to pick up and carry in his free hand.

The other three men stared down at the parting brush near their feet as Lowry came crawling into sight. "Damn, I guess it really is a snake," said Winton, poking Lowry's shoulder with the toe of his boot. Lowry turned his eyes upward and saw three pistols cocked and aimed at his face.

"I swear to God, I don't know no Doyle Hollister," said Lowry.

"How would you like us to start chopping you up into tiny pieces, Apache style, starting at the tips of your toes?" Winton asked casually.

"Mister, I ain't lying," said Lowry.

"Jerk his boots off, George," Winton said to Hope. He reached behind his back beneath his suit coat and pulled a dagger from its sheath. "Help hold his feet down for us, Clifford."

"Wait! My God, mister!" Lowry shouted, kicking his feet wildly. "I'm just an innocent traveler here! I swear to God I don't know the man you're talking about!"

Standing behind him, Clifford Devoe clamped a boot down on the small of Lowry's back, pinning him to the ground. Lowry let out a hard grunt as the air rushed out of his lungs. "An *innocent traveler*." Winton chuckled. "Now that would certainly be a novelty here in Old *Mejico.* That lie alone should cost you both big toes." He flashed the blade down near Lowry's face. "If you're not with Doyle Hollister, you most certainly must be riding with the rapscallions his girlfriend duped into taking the counterfeit money."

"Huh?" Lowry stared up at him dumbfounded, clearly knowing nothing about the phony money and, as Winton quickly deduced, probably nothing else about Hollister, his gang or the woman. "What the hell are you talking about, mister?" Lowry asked, straining his neck to look at Winton in the darkness. "What counterfeit money? I don't have any money at all! If I did, I wouldn't be out here traipsing through the —"

"This money," Clifford Devoe said, dropping a pack of bound bills on the ground in front of him.

Winton said, "Get him on his feet! Maybe we'll just jerk his tongue out."

In spite of the threat, Lowry felt better now. He stood up with help from Clifford Devoe. "I'll tell you everything, mister," he said. He began brushing dirt from the belly of his shirt. "What do you men know about that money being no good? How'd you fellows find out about all this? Through those *wiretappers* I heard you talking about?"

"Hey, shut up!" Ben Winton snapped at him, poking him in the chest with the tip of his pistol barrel. "Keep your hands raised. I'll ask all the questions here."

Lowry raised his hands. "My mistake, mister. Ask what you will. I figure if you're looking for that woman and her friends, you and me are on the same side anyway."

"Oh, you think so?" Winton asked, wondering what, if anything, this man might know about Hollister's gang. "Then tell us where they're headed — maybe you'll keep toes, tongue and all."

Without one forward thought on the matter, Lowry blurted out confidently, "Trouble Creek." He looked back and forth from one pair of eyes to the next, judging whether or not they believed him.

"Where is this Trouble Creek, Clifford?" Winton asked without taking his eyes off of Lowry.

"Two days southwest of here," said Devoe. "That's where the French kept a full command of soldiers, to protect folks from the Apache. Ennui Creek, they called it." His face twisted slowly into a cruel grin. "They say on a quiet night you can hear the soldiers' screams."

"Meaning their protection plan didn't work?" Darman Peak asked.

"Ha!" Lowry chuckled aloud.

"Did I say something funny, snake?" Peak asked, pushing his cocked pistol a little closer to Lowry's belly.

"No, sir," Lowry said, his expression turning serious again.

"The Apache killed them all," said Devoe, "some of them in ways I don't like to even mention."

"Oh," said Peak, taking a step back, lowering his gun barrel an inch.

"Ever been there, Clifford?" asked Winton, still studying Lowry's eyes.

"No, but I think I can fi—"

"I know the place like the back of my hand," Lowry cut in. He returned Winton's stare without a flicker of an eye.

"Oh, and how come?" Winton asked, knowing this man would say most anything to save his own life.

Now Lowry hesitated for a moment, but purely for effect. Letting out a breath as if in resignation he said, "All right, here it is. I'm Dick Lowry." He gave Winton an even firmer stare. "*The* Dick Lowry. Leader of the Trouble Creek gang. You've got me fair and square." He shook his head slowly and bowed it in resolve. "I just hope to God you ain't bounty hunters. That's all I can say."

"Who the fuck is *the* Dick Lowry? Who the fuck are the Trouble Creek gang?" Winton asked with a bemused expression.

"I heard of them a few years back," Devoe offered with a shrug. "They were a bunch of third-rate bank robbers. Lowry *was* the man's name."

"Not *was,* gawdamn it, still *is!*" Lowry said, having suffered all the insults he could take, guns or no guns. "And you think I'm third-rate, you best stop and remind yourself who rode into Olsen and robbed that bank in the first place." He thumbed himself on the chest. "Me, that's who! Me and the Trouble Creek gang!"

"Oh, I see," said Winton, slowly fanning back and forth the stack of bound bills he'd picked up from the ground. "So if I ever wanted to steal a lot of worthless money, you'd be the man for the job?"

The men laughed; Lowry seethed. "I'm saying the gawdamn money is real," he declared boldly. "And I'm saying if you want the woman and this Hollister fellow, that's where they're heading, right now, while you stand here poking fun at my hard-earned reputation."

"If it's true that you're not a part of Hollister's gang, how do you know this?" Winton asked sharply.

"I heard the woman say so, before she let me and my boys out of jail in Olsen," said Lowry, lying straight-faced, seeing that so far he'd done pretty well for himself. "Boy, oh, boy, what I wouldn't give to get my hands around that woman's throat. That's who I'm trailing, to tell you the truth. I'd like to cut her lying heart out!"

"Watch your language now," Winton said, passing a thin smile and a knowing look to the others, then back to Lowry.

"What'd I say?" Lowry shrugged.

Winton didn't answer. He seemed to consider things for a moment. "Where are your men, Lowry?" he asked.

Lowry felt better hearing the man call him by name. "The ranger just killed them back there in the village. I had gone outside to the jakes ditch. I heard all the shooting. There was nothing I could do. . . . It made me sick. By the time I got back there the ranger was gone." He looked down as if in mourning. "I never want to see nothing like that again, my pards — damn good boys, both of them — laying there dead, shot full of holes, bloody as hell." He winced at the thought of it.

"He's got two more horses back there,"

Devoe interjected. "This one is almost ready to fall."

"Oh, I see," said Winton.

"Of course I've got their horses," said Lowry. "Think I was going to leave them behind? Let those villagers have my dead pards' riding stock? Hell, no."

"He must be one fast son of a bitch, this ranger," Winton said with a twist of skepticism, "to get in there, kill your pards, then get away that quick."

"Yes, you're damn right. He is fast. There's no doubt about it," said Lowry. "He's fast and full of tricks. He's a back shooter, a coward and a rotten sonsabitch. That's another one I vow to kill, first chance I get."

"I take it we're talking about Sam Burrack, the same Arizona ranger Bo Maydeen warned us about — the one who killed Junior Lake and his whole gang."

"See?" said Lowry. "Ain't it strange how you remember Junior Lake and his idiots like they was some special turds rolled in sugar. But you never heard of me and the Trouble Creek gang."

"I don't know if I can ride with you as far as Trouble Creek without putting a bullet between your eyes," said Winton.

Lowry breathed a little easier now. "You can if you really want to get there and find this Hollister and his bunch," he said, lowering his hands a bit just to test where he stood with these men.

"All right, let's kill the fire and get riding," Winton said to the others. "Before some more riffraff crawls in on us."

"All right, snake," said Clifford Devoe, nudging Lowry with his rifle barrel. "Get your saddle off this horse. Let's go get a fresh horse under you. I hope you try something funny. I'd enjoy busting all your ribs with a rifle butt."

Lowry turned to his tired horse, loosened the cinch and flipped the saddle and saddlebags up onto his shoulder, letting one wooden stirrup hang down over his forearm in front of him. "We're riding together now," he said. "I see no need in any more rooster talking one another, do you?" He walked away through the brush as he spoke back over his loaded shoulder to Devoe.

"Just so you understand," said Devoe. "We don't ride together, you and us. I'll put a bullet in you at the drop of a hat."

"Oh, I understand that, all right," said Lowry, gauging his steps, hearing the other men head across the campfire to their horses. "You don't owe me anything. . . . I don't owe you anything."

"That's right, snake," said Devoe. "Keep

that in mind and you and I will get along fine."

"Wait! What was that?" Lowry asked, coming to a sudden halt.

"What was what?" Devoe asked, tensing, his eyes going out into the darkness with Lowry's.

"That!" said Lowry, dropping into a half-crouch and spinning around quickly. Using the heavy wooden stirrup like some ancient gladiator might use a mace and chain, he swung it in a hard circle, right at jaw level. The unsuspecting gunman let out a loud grunt and flew sideways into sharp, dry brush, knocked cold, his jaw hanging slack toward the starry sky.

"Clifford?" Winton called out from the line of horses on the other side of the camp, where the other two men stood scraping the fire out with their boots.

"Yeah?" said Lowry, lowering his voice to imitate that of the big, deep-spoken gunman.

Hurriedly Lowry dropped his saddle — keeping the saddlebags — and grabbed Devoe's rifle. He slung his saddlebags up onto one of the fresh horses, unhitched the animal and jumped up into the saddle.

"Hey! That wasn't Clifford," said Winton, jerking his Colt from inside his suit coat.

"Damn right, it wasn't!" said Peak. The three hurried toward the spot where Clifford had led Lowry into the brush. George Hope snatched a rifle from his saddle boot and hurried along behind them.

"Yeeehiiii!!!" Lowry bellowed, ripping through their midst on horseback, causing Peak and Winton to leap to one side to keep from being run over by a thundering flurry of hooves.

Collecting themselves quickly, Winton and Peak ran through the thin moonlight to where George Hope stood taking aim along his raised rifle barrel. "No, don't fire that shot, George!" Winton called out, stopping the big gunman. "It's too dark to hit anything," he said, seeing Hope turn to him with a questioning look on his face. He stood staring after the sound of fading hoofbeats. "For all we know, Hollister and his gang could be close enough to hear it. We don't want to tip him off."

"But he's killed Clifford!" said Peak.

"I doubt that," said Winton. "Go check on him, though." He stood staring out into the darkness. "Come daylight, we'll start following everybody's hoofprints again. If this fool takes us to Hollister, that's good. If not, we're still on the right track. Trouble Creek, eh?" He considered it for a moment.

"He might just have been telling the truth about that. We'll have to see where tomorrow leads us."

CHAPTER 14

On an unfamiliar trail that had grown worse with each passing mile, rather than risk harming Black Pot or the two gangly donkeys he'd purchased from the village stock trader, Sam and his prisoners made a camp off the side of the trail in the deep shelter of tangled juniper and scrub piñon. They built a small fire long enough to boil a pot of coffee. As soon as the coffee smelled ready to pour, Sam instructed the two cuffed men to put out the fire.

"What? Are you serious?" Pony Phil asked, as if he found the ranger's request hard to believe.

"I'm serious, Pony," Sam said. "Both of you put out the fire. Right now."

"Surely you don't mean with cuffs on." Pony Phil said, raising his cuffed wrists for the ranger to see. His voice still sounded a bit thick from the drugs, the drinking, and from the ranger having to knock him cold as a last resort back in the cantina when nothing else could stop his laughing delirium.

"Do as you're told," Sam said, staring hard-eyed at him. "You're lucky I didn't kill you both and leave you laying for the buzzards after what you did to the poor trading post family."

Realizing that any response on the matter of the Cardells would touch on a raw nerve, Pony shook his bowed head. "Come on, Black Cat, let's put it out before he shoots us down like dogs."

Black Cat rose to his feet with a painful groan, the knot on his forehead having grown to the size of a ripe purple plum, with its skin split across its middle. "The way I feel now, I'd as soon you would go ahead and shoot me. If I'm going to hang anyways, what's the point in doing all this labor?"

"Yeah, that's what I say," Phil Watson cut in, a slight chuckle coming back into his voice. He caught himself, got rid of the chuckle before it got out of control and said in a more somber tone, "What if we was to tell you it was Dick Lowry and nobody else who killed that family? Would that help us any?"

Sam didn't answer. He sipped his coffee until the two had stamped out the fire and started to sit back down to their coffee, having to share the only other battered tin cup the ranger had in his saddlebags.

"Don't get comfortable yet," Sam said. "We're going to rest the animals here for a couple of hours."

"Oh, man, Ranger," Black Cat moaned. "Are you getting ready to do what I *think* you're getting ready to do?"

"If you think I'm getting ready to cuff you two together, yes," said Sam, setting his coffee down and standing up. "Turn facing one another," he said, taking out the key to the handcuffs from his vest pocket. "Don't either one of you make any sudden moves against me."

"This is inhumane treatment of a prisoner," Pony Phil complained, he and Black Cat holding their cuffed hands out.

"There's laws against this in some places," said Pony Phil, siding with his partner.

"But not out here," said Sam. He loosened one set of cuffs at a time and recuffed the two men, wrist to wrist, to one another. "Out here I'm the law. So keep that in mind, both of you."

"I feel like we're getting ready to dance," said Phil. He stared at his left wrist and Black Cat's right wrist cuffed together and shook his head. "I'm glad my sainted ma didn't live to see this."

"How are we supposed to drink our coffee cuffed together like this?" Black Cat asked, shaking a wrist in frustration.

"Hey, take it easy, Black Cat!" said Phil. "That's my damn hand you're slinging around too."

"On the ground now," said Sam, giving them a nudge to get them started. "I'll hand you the cup and you can take turns with it."

"It's inhumane, I'm telling you," Phil repeated.

"It's better than you deserve," Sam responded. He picked up the coffee cup and jammed it into Phil's hand as soon as the two men plopped down onto the ground, facing one another. "Now keep quiet and drink your coffee."

Sitting a few feet away with his rifle across his lap, the ranger kept an eye on the two men, watching them finish their coffee and adjust themselves in a way that finally allowed them to sleep flat on their backs, each with a cuffed wrist lying across their chests. For the next two and a half hours Sam rested without sleeping. Then he stood up, stepped over to the prisoners and nudged them with the toe of his boot. "The horses are rested," he said, "let's go."

They mounted and rode on, following the long, running hoofprints of Lowry and the two horses he led behind him. At a turn in the trail where the hillside lay thick with brush, they came upon Lowry and Black Cat's horses standing at rest in the thin moonlight, foraging with their muzzles through lowstanding brush and pale blades of wild grass. "It's about time something good came our way," Pony Phil said, looking to the ranger for permission to drop from the donkeys and get their horses.

Sam gave them a nod and followed them over without leaving his saddle. "Check them good," he said, "and don't turn the donkeys loose. We're leading them with us until we know the horses are all right for the trail."

"I don't care how far we lead them," said Black Cat, "so long as I don't have to ride them. Riding a donkey is bad luck, I always heard."

Phil checked the horse Lowry had last ridden and said, "This one's been rode hard. But he's cooled out now."

"Then hurry it up," said Sam. "We're going to ride all night to make up for all the time we lost with you two riding donkeys."

The two groaned but went about checking and readying the horses. In moments they stepped up into their saddles and turned toward the trail in front of the ranger. "Stay close," said Sam. "Both of you keep in mind that I will kill you if you take a notion and try to bolt on me."

"Why do you keep on bringing it up about us not trying to get away, Ranger?" asked Black Cat.

"Yeah, we got the message the first time," said Pony Phil.

"I'm saying it because you're both hard-headed and likely to forget any minute and make a run for it."

"Oh, I see," said Pony Phil. He looked around and asked, "How are we going to know how *close* we're staying, riding in front of you?"

"You best just keep looking back at me and paying attention," Sam said. "Now get moving." He reached out with the end of his reins and slapped Pony Phil's horse on its rump.

They rode on.

At dawn the morning sunlight lifted above the horizon and brought the wide, purple-shadowed land into clear sight. The three stopped for a moment at a point where their trail opened out onto a long stretch of flat-lands strewn with impenetrable thickets of yellow-flowered cactus, broken gullies and mammoth black boulders. Sam's eyes followed the many fresh hoofprints beneath them to a shimmering flat surface of backwater fewer than fifty yards ahead of them. "Rest the animals. Water them and yourselves. We're leaving here as quick as we can. We make too good a target around that water hole."

"Man, Ranger," Pony Phil said, "me and Black Cat are worn down to a crawl. When do we get to rest?"

"As soon as you get to prison," Sam said flatly.

The two shook their tired heads and nudged the horses forward.

Arriving at the water's edge, Sam stepped down with his rifle in hand and walked a few feet away from the prisoners, in order to keep an eye on them without being close enough for them to suddenly make a move against him. He loosened Black Pot's cinch and let the stallion draw water while he himself stooped down, cupped his hand and raised a short drink to his mouth. Fifteen feet away, Black Cat and Pony Phil plunged forward onto their chests into the cool water and drank with their faces submerged.

Sam scanned the far horizon warily as he sipped.

Coming up from the water and slinging

his wet hair back, Pony Phil looked at Sam and said, chuckling, "Ranger, it won't hurt for you to let down long enough to take a damn drink of water."

"Attend to yourself, and don't worry about me," said Sam, his eyes still searching intently along the rough, broken land. "You two spread out a little from one another. You make too tight of a target that close."

"Come on, Ranger!" said Phil, chuckling more. "If Lowry's out there, the only person needs to be concerned is *you.* Maybe you need to spread yourself out some."

"There's others out there to worry about besides Dick Lowry," the ranger reminded him, still searching the distance.

Beside Pony Phil, Black Cat rose up from the water and spat a long stream. Having heard the words between them, he said, "It would take a coldhearted sonsabitch to shoot a man down whilst he's slaking his thirst." He stood up, wiping his face with a wet hand, and said, facing the empty distance, "Ain't nobody going to show themselves to you anyway, Ranger. What do you expect to see out there?"

No sooner did Black Cat finish his words than the ranger saw a glint of sunlight on metal among a line of rocks at the base of a small hill. "A rifle! Get down, Cat!" he shouted.

But before the big man could heed the ranger's warning, he buckled forward as if stricken by a deep, sudden stomach cramp. A long string of blood erupted from his back, followed by the faraway explosion of a single rifle shot.

"Jesus, Cat!" Pony Phil bellowed. He rose halfway to his feet and lunged forward toward Black Cat as the big man left his feet and landed backward with a splash. Their horses spooked and ran back from the commotion.

"Get away from him, Pony!" Sam demanded, rising quickly, giving Black Pot a hard slap on his rear, making the stallion bolt away from the water's edge.

Pony caught on to the ranger's words and turned to run. But as soon as he turned, his back stiffened into a hard arch. His eyes and mouth flew open wide and a similar gout of blood exploded forward from a gaping hole in the center of his rib cage. A second powerful shot exploded from within the distant rocks as Pony Phil pitched dead on his face in the glittering water.

The ranger quickly dived forward into the shallow sparkling water, stirring it as much as possible, knowing what effect this kind of glare had on the eyes of the shooter. Scurrying, crawling, rolling toward three broken rocks standing twenty feet away on the other side of the water, Sam took cover, his wet rifle in hand, and turned immediately to make sure Black Pot had run away and disappeared safely over a slight rise of sandy earth. A third shot kicked up a tall spur of water and spun upward on the spot he'd just left.

"Black Cat? Pony? Are either of you alive?" the ranger called out to the two bodies bobbing in the thin six-inch-deep water. A wide reddish circle had already begun to spread around the two men. They made no reply. . . .

Across the flatlands in the long stretch of rocks, Ben Winton lowered the leather-covered binoculars from his eyes. "Damn, fellows, it looks like Mr. Peak here has gained a rightful spot in our ranks. He is quite the shootist, as it turns out." He turned to George Hope and Clifford Devoe, grinning, and said, "Well, gentlemen. You owe Peak twenty dollars each. Pay up."

"He didn't get the third one," Clifford said, his nose and jaw swollen and dark purple from where Lowry had swiped him a knockout blow with the stirrup.

"Don't be a stiff, Clifford," said Winton.

"You both bet him he couldn't take down two men with two shots from here. He did, you lose, pay up," Winton said sharply, holding out his hand and rubbing his thumb and fingertip together.

Beside him, crouched against a rock, Darman Peak rubbed his right eye to get rid of the sun's glare glittering strongly on the stirred-up surface of the water. A big Austrian sporting rifle lay across his lap, a curl of smoke still drifting upward from its hand-engraved barrel. A long, shiny brass scope stood attached along its barrel. "I was just showing off, shooting at the third man. Best I can tell I just might have nailed him too." He turned his eyes to Winton for support.

"That is true," said Winton. He shrugged slightly. "Least-wise, I saw nothing left standing."

In a gruff tone, George Hope stepped forward and shoved a twenty-dollar gold piece out to Peak. "What the hell . . . good shooting."

Devoe grumbled and touched a careful hand to the swollen side of his head. "All right, damn it." He reached down inside his pocket and pulled up a respectable-size roll of bills, held together by a gold money clip. Pulling off a twenty, he stuck it out to Peak. "You better be that good when a fight comes in close. It's one thing hitting a man this far away . . . a whole other thing when you do your killing looking square into his eyes."

Peak took the bill and just stared at him with a half-smile. "I'll try my very best to remember that," he said, folding the bill neatly and putting it away inside his shirt.

"Pay no attention to Clifford, Peak," said Winton. "He's still smarting over a fool like Lowry catching him unaware with a saddle stirrup." He laughed and slapped Devoe on his back.

"That son of a bitch," Devoe growled. If I ever get my hands on him again —"

"Ah, but you had your hands on him, Clifford," Winton said, teasing him in a cutting tone. "Perhaps you're lucky he didn't kill you, famed outlaw that he is."

"If Lowry told the truth and that was the ranger trailing us, I sure put his lights out for him, eh, Ben?" Peak patted the Austrian rifle proudly, then handed it up to Winton.

Winton's smile half faded. "Don't start feeling too cocky, Peak," he said, taking the rifle. "But to be sure, Mr. Morganfield will be hearing about your marksmanship as soon as we meet up with Maydeen." He looked forward along the trail, as if Bo Maydeen might appear at any moment. "Which should be real soon, I'm thinking."

"Yeah," said George Hope. "Getting that lawman out of our way might be worth a good little bonus to you."

Peak grinned. "I like the idea of a *good* bonus. I'm not sure I like the idea of a *little* one."

Winton and Hope laughed along with him. Clifford Devoe nurtured his swollen jaw and made a grimacing face.

Doyle Hollister heard his name through a veil of sleep and felt the toe of a boot nudge him into consciousness. He rolled over onto his side and felt a cool breeze against his bare behind. "Hunh?" he said in a thick, sleepy voice, reaching back and covering himself with the corner of the blanket. "What's going on?"

Tommy Dykes had looked away from the sight of Hollister's naked rear end. "What's going on is it's past daylight and we're still bedded down here."

Hollister opened his eyes and immediately felt them stabbed by the harsh glare of the sun. "Jesus, leave me alone," he whispered, throwing a forearm over his face.

"She said get you up, Doyle, so I did," said Dykes, wanting no bad repercussions for awakening him.

"She's already up?" Hollister asked, seeming to awaken a bit quicker.

"Yeah, she's been up, bright-eyed, right along with the rest of us," said Dykes. He turned and walked away, feeling no need to say any more.

Even in his sleepy state Hollister caught the implication. He half rose onto his elbow, yawned and pushed his fingers back through his hair. "Jesus," he whispered again. The woman had him worn out. He forced himself up from the blanket, stepped into his trousers, slung his gun belt over his shoulder and plodded along barefoot to where Kaylee Smith stood atop a rock, looking back along the trail across the flatlands below. *"Buenas días,"* he said, a bit embarrassed, seeing the rest of the men hanging around their extinguished campfire, their horses saddled and ready to ride.

But Kaylee didn't respond to his greeting. Instead she turned to him with a cold look and thrust the used army telescope toward his naked belly. "Here, maybe you can see something. You're rested," she added.

What the hell is all this . . . ? Hollister stared at her for a moment. Then he took the telescope and pulled it open in his hands. "What am I looking for?"

"We heard rifle shots," said Kaylee. "Fudd

and the others said it sounded like *big* rifle shots." She gave him a dark, knowing gaze.

"Yeah?" That got his attention. "How many?"

"Three," she said.

"How long ago?" he asked as he raised the lens to his eye and scanned the wide flatlands.

"Ten minutes, twenty at the most," she replied.

"Twenty minutes! Gawdamn it!" he said tightly. "Why the hell didn't somebody wake me?"

"We did," she said coolly.

"I mean *sooner!*" he said, his voice getting tighter, his temper ready to flare.

"I tried to wake you sooner," she said, lowering her voice. "You wouldn't wake up. So I told them I wanted to let you sleep." She waited, then said, "Should I have told them you wouldn't wake up? Because next time I will if that's what you want."

"Gawdamn it," he murmured under his breath, lowering the lens and looking away from her. "A big rifle, huh?" He collapsed the telescope and handed it back to her.

"That's what Fudd said," she replied quietly. As she spoke she stooped down and picked up a tin cup half filled with coffee. "Here, I saved this for you." Her tone softened. She reached out with the end of the telescope and ran it lightly down his hard, flat stomach.

"There won't *be* no *next time*," he said, looking down at the cup of coffee. He took the coffee, drew a long sip of it and pitched the rest of it out of the cup. Kaylee smiled to herself, watching him turn and stomp back toward the rest of his clothes lying on the ground.

Before Hollister had finished pulling on his boots and tucking in his shirttail, Dallas Spraggs called out from where the men stood waiting by their horses, "Looks like we've got a rider coming this way."

"Son of a bitch!" Hollister growled, trying to hurry, feeling like everything had started moving too fast for him. He finished poking his shirttail into his trousers and swung his gun belt around his waist. "Coming on which trail?" he called out, sounding irritated at Spraggs for telling him.

Dallas Spraggs looked at Denton Fudd and didn't answer.

"The high trail," Fudd called out. "Get your pecker put away and let's go see who it is!"

Hollister stomped over to the horses, giving Fudd a hard stare. When he got close Fudd pitched him the reins to his already-saddled horse. Hollister grabbed them, stepped into his saddle and growled sidelong to the old man, "Fudd, if you ever say something like that to me again, I'll kill you."

Denton Fudd didn't respond.

Kaylee sidled her horse close to Hollister's and turned with him and the others as they kicked their horses out along the narrow trail they'd ridden up from the flatlands.

CHAPTER 15

Dick Lowry didn't know what had hit him. One minute he'd been riding along at a good, fast clip; the next minute he'd felt the horse shoot out from under him and leave him hanging in midair, as if suspended for a second. He'd heard a hard twanging sound, like the plucking of some large, powerful guitar string as the tightened rope caught him across his chest, lifted him from his saddle and caused his breath to explode from his chest. Then he'd hit the ground hard, flat on his back in a rise of dust.

"Whooo*iee*," said Manfred Poole, sitting amid the rest of the riders alongside the narrow trail. "Six inches higher, that would've snapped his head off!"

"Go get his horse, Poole," said Hollister, he and Kaylee stepping their horses forward ahead of the others. At the center of the trail the riders formed a circle around Dick Lowry, who lay rolled in a ball, gagging, stunned, trying to collect himself and figure out what to do next. "I don't believe it," Kaylee said with a short laugh. "It's that fool Lowry! One of the ones I let out of the jail!" She turned a genuine smile of surprise to Hollister.

Poole circled back with Lowry's horse in tow. Hollister reached over and rummaged through Lowry's saddlebags. He recognized the counterfiet bills and dropped them. "No kidding!" he replied to Kaylee, glad to hear her laughter after a rocky start to the morning. "You mean this idiot has managed to find your trail? Follow you all this way?" Even as he said it laughingly, it dawned on him that this was not really a joking matter. If Lowry trailed her, who else might have? But he let it pass for now, grateful for a lighter mood.

"Evidently so," said Kaylee, still grinning, chuckling a little. "Somebody get him on his feet," she said, issuing an order to the men just like Hollister would. Hollister noted it but said nothing, even when he saw Dallas Spraggs and Elvey Parks. Both stepped down quickly and hurried to where Lowry had rolled onto his knees, still in a ball and making a strange squeaking sound.

"Boy!" Dallas Spraggs said to Parks as they hurried out to Lowry. "Did she fuck him up, or what?"

"It was her idea, but it's *my* rope, don't forget," said Parks.

The two pulled Lowry to his feet, the outlaw coming unrolled slowly. But when they tried to turn him loose, he collapsed to his knees, the strange squeaking sound returning to his chest.

"Hold him up!" said Hollister, getting the order in before Kaylee had a chance to say the same thing.

Spraggs and Parks pulled Lowry up again. This time Lowry put more effort into standing. His eyes were red and watery, his grimacing face the same color, with a bit of a bluish tone to it. "Go-*d!*" he wheezed, clutching the width of his chest. Spraggs caught him and steadied him as he staggered backward a step.

"Lowry, what the hell is it going to take to get rid of you?" Kaylee asked. As she spoke she raised the small pistol from inside her riding blouse and held it pointed loosely in his direction.

Lowry raised a weak hand toward her and struggled with his breathing. "Wait," he managed to squeeze out in a failing tone. "I'm . . . on *yo-ur* side!"

Hollister grinned, staring at Lowry. "What did he say?"

"He's on *our* side," Kaylee said, smiling.

"Oh," said Hollister with a nod, still smiling amiably. Then he said to Spraggs and Parks, "Shoot him."

Spraggs drew his Colt quickly, cocked it and put it to Lowry's head.

"Wait!" cried Lowry, his voice raspy but suddenly coming back to him. "Hear me out! Please! It's important!"

"I don't think so," said Kaylee, giving Spraggs a go-ahead nod to kill the conniving outlaw.

Not liking the way Kaylee had promoted herself to giving orders, Hollister said to Spraggs, "Hold on. . . . I want to hear what he's got to say."

"Thank you, mister," said Lowry, still clutching his chest, his face starting to regain its original color. "It's true I was trailing her! I admit it. She took bank money that rightfully belonged to me and my men. She stuck me with a bunch of counterfeit money! Can you blame me?" He tried to shrug but it hurt too bad.

"Go on," said Hollister, crossing his wrists on his saddle horn as if preparing for a long-winded spiel.

Kaylee looked at Hollister. "Are we going to waste time with him, after hearing rifle shots on our trail?"

"I had nothing to do with those shots, ma'am," said Lowry. "But I'll tell you this. It most likely came from a bunch of Laslow Morganfield's men. They're on your trail, you know. Whether you know it or not, that was *his* money in the bank!" He paused to see what expression that information brought to their faces. Seeing no noticeable change, he went on, saying, "They caught me last night, you see. Oh yes! And they meant to kill me, but I saw a chance and got away. That's when I figured instead of coming to you as an enemy, bent on vengeance and getting my money back . . . maybe it would be best if we partnered up. At least for a while, just till we kill those gunmen. You know what they say about a bundle of sticks being strongest and all." He paused again, waiting for a response.

"Shoot him," Kaylee said, this time to Elvey Parks.

Elvey drew his gun, but then looked to Hollister for authorization.

"No, let's listen. This is good," said Hollister. He said to Lowry, "Where's your men now? Did Morganfield's men get them?"

"No," said Lowry. He shook his head. "I almost can't talk about those poor, brave men without choking up. They were both killed in a blazing gun battle not two days ago in that shit hole of a village." He shook his bowed head. "They made the mistake of riding on ahead of me while I stopped and checked my horse for a stone bruise. Before I knew it they rode right into a trap. They was dead by the time I got to them. Nothing I could do by then."

"But it wasn't Morganfield's men?" Hollister asked, his wrists still crossed.

"No, this wasn't Morganfield's men," said Lowry.

"How do you know, if they were dead when you got there?" Kaylee asked.

Lowry took on a trapped expression, but only for a second. "Did I say they was dead? Hell, all of this has got me not thinking straight. My poor pards weren't *dead* when I got to them, but they was damn near." Turning loose of his chest for a moment, he made a cradling gesture and said, "They died in my arms, you might say."

"Who killed them, if not Morganfield's men?" Hollister asked bluntly, appearing to grow bored with Lowry's story.

"Some lowlife, cowardly, back-shooting lawdog, that's who," said Lowry in a bitter tone, starting to wonder if he could pull this off, get on their side and lead them to Trouble Creek. The proposition looked shaky, he had to admit.

"Oh?" Hollister's interest returned. He gave Kaylee a quizzical look, then asked Lowry, "Who is this lawdog? What's his stake in this?"

Kaylee shifted uneasily in her saddle. "I'm sick of listening to this fool, Doyle. Tell somebody to shoot him."

"Go on, Lowry," said Hollister, ignoring Kaylee all of a sudden.

All right! Lowry wasn't sure what he'd said that did it, but he'd seen a sudden change, a shift in his favor. He breathed easier, realizing that once again he'd managed to save his life by some quick thinking and slick talking. "His name is Sam Burrack. The lady saw him." He nodded toward Kaylee. "She'll tell you that he had me and my men jailed and ready for prison." He stopped talking long enough to turn his attention to Kaylee. He had this man Hollister won over; now he wanted to win the woman over as well. "Ma'am, in all the commotion there in Olsen, I hope I did stop and tell you much obliged for setting me and my poor pards loose. Did I?"

Kaylee just stared at him. "He's lying. The ranger is dead," she said flatly.

"Yes, I remember you telling me that," Hollister said coolly, feeling himself coming back into control. He offered Lowry a half-smile. "Any chance you could be mistaken? You know these rangers. . . . If you've seen one, you've seen them all."

"That's true. You've got a point," said Lowry, feeling better by the minute. "But this one is Burrack, all right. And if I know him, he's back there dogging my trail right now, along with Morganfield's men and God knows who else. That's why I'm saying we need to *partner up.*" He made a sweeping gesture with his arms, the pain in his chest subsiding a bit. "There's a place called Trouble Creek up ahead. I can lead you in there! Once we're in there an army can't drag us out!" He grinned. Yep, he had Hollister. Not the woman, at least not yet, but Hollister, oh yeah. *Everything is going to be all right,* he said to himself. "I can take us there in less than two days. There's even a railhead forty miles on the other side. So when you're ready to leave, after things cool off, you can ride out in style." His grin widened.

Hollister returned his grin with a flat but friendly smile and called out over his shoulder, "Fudd, what about this Trouble Creek? Ever heard of it?"

"Sure have," said Denton Fudd, pushing his horse a step forward, staring hard at Lowry. "He ain't lying. It's a damn good place to lay the rocks and pick a fellow's eye out."

"And you already know the way there, right?"

"Yeah, it's not hard to find," said Fudd.

Hollister shrugged at Lowry. "Sorry, we already have a guide."

"Not like me you don't!" Lowry said quickly, feeling his gains slipping away. "It's easy getting lost going in there! If you don't know the place like the back of your hand, you can go in and never be seen again!"

"Is that right, Fudd?" asked Hollister.

"It can get tricky," Fudd conceded.

"So maybe you know the place, but not as well as Lowry does?" Hollister asked.

"I can't say, since I don't know *how well* he knows it," said Fudd, still staring hard at Lowry.

"Like the back of your hand, eh, Lowry?" Hollister asked.

All right, you're still in. . . . Lowry took a deep, calming breath and reminded himself that as soon as the time was right, he'd make it a point to put a bullet in this old man Fudd's head. "That's the truth," said Lowry. "I know the place up, down, back and sideways!" He found the grin again and spread it wide. "Hell, there's some who'll tell you that I *am* Trouble Creek!"

"So we're taking this two-bit punk along?" Fudd asked, again with the hard stare at Lowry.

Two-bit punk? No doubt about it, Lowry told himself. First chance he got, this evil-eyed old bastard was dead.

"No," Hollister said bluntly, "shoot him."

Shoot him? What the — Lowry couldn't believe his ears. "No! Wait!" He threw a hand up toward Parks and Spraggs. "There's more!" He wasn't sure what else he could say, but as long as he remained alive, something would come to him.

"No, there's not," said Kaylee.

Lowry's eyes turned toward her in time to see the pistol buck in her hand. The shot hit him square in his chest and sent him flying backward in a spray of blood.

"Not a bad shot," said Hollister, cocking his head slightly to one side. He took a scrutinizing look at Lowry's shattered chest, the outlaw lying less than eighteen feet away. "Interesting what he said about the ranger. . . . You know, about him being alive and all." As he spoke, Hollister idly reached back into Lowry's saddlebags, lifted the stack of counterfeit bills and stuck them inside his shirt.

"I told you he was lying," said Kaylee firmly. She drew a fresh cartridge from the pocket of her riding skirt, quickly replaced the one she'd just used and clicked the chamber shut.

"Yeah, he was quite a liar, all right," said Hollister.

But Kaylee didn't like the tone of voice. "You can believe him or me," she said boldly, "I really don't give a damn."

"I believe *you,*" said Hollister. "I saw that he was lying, making things up to suit him as he went along."

"Good," said Kaylee, still in a firm voice, "because I don't want this fool's lies standing between us."

"Don't talk crazy, Kaylee." Hollister smiled. "You know I wasn't taking him seriously. What say we forget he ever rode up on us? He's nothing worth thinking about."

"That suits me," said Kaylee, studying him closely to see if there would be a catch to what he said.

Hollister casually reached his hand out toward her, saying, "Hey, let me take a look at that pistol of yours. It must be a real dandy."

"You've seen it before," said Kaylee, not handing the gun over to him. Instead she laid her thumb over the hammer as if ready to cock it.

The men sat watching intently, their

expressions giving nothing away. "Forget it, then," said Hollister. "I'm starting to think you don't trust me."

"I trust you, Doyle," said Kaylee. "But I can see you're taking what he said about the ranger as the truth. . . . And it's not, it's a *damn lie*."

Hollister turned his horse a step, then stopped and asked matter-of-factly, "You're sure the ranger's dead?"

"I'm sure," said Kaylee, feeling the men's eyes on her.

"Then that's the end of it," he said, dismissing the matter. He looked over at Lowry's body; blood ran down from the hole in his chest a thick, widening puddle in the dirt. "What about this Trouble Creek he talked about, Fudd? Wasn't we pretty much headed that direction anyhow?"

Fudd shrugged. "Yeah, pretty much. Trouble Creek is where this man and his gang used to be known to hide out. They used to call themselves the Trouble Creek gang. It's a good place sure enough."

"Hell, let's go there, then," said Lowry. "Lay low for a while and get all these folks off our backs." He looked at Lowry's body and touched his gloved fingers to the brim of his Stetson. "*Gracias* for the tip, ole pard." He raised his reins and started to collect his horse and nudge it forward. But then he halted again and said sidelong to Kaylee, with emphasis, "The ranger *is* dead?"

"Yes," said Kaylee, getting more and more irritated.

"Not wounded, not sick . . . but *dead?*" Hollister asked, even more pointedly, staring deep into her eyes.

"Gawdamn it, Doyle!" Kaylee said. She jerked her horse back a step, the pistol in her hand, the barrel still warm from taking a man's life.

"Hey, that's all I wanted to know," said Hollister, raising a hand toward her as if ending the conversation. "Is that he's dead, *right?*" he asked. He had to know how badly this got on her nerves.

"Go to hell!" she shouted, jerking her horse away and kicking it out ahead of the others on the trail.

"He better be!" Hollister called out after her.

Behind him, Fudd leaned closer to Elvey Parks, having held his horse for him while Parks and Spraggs dealt with Lowry. "I think they've reached that point all men and women in love reach sooner or later. . . . Where they both know one is bound to kill the other, but they're both waiting for just the right thing to set it off."

Elvey Parks nodded in agreement and leaned closer to Fudd. "So far my money's on the woman."

■ ■ ■ ■

PART 3

■ ■ ■ ■

CHAPTER 16

Beneath a battered, sun-faded sign that read ESTACIÓN DE LA ROCA ROJA, Bo Maydeen and Branard Cobb stood in fine red dust an inch deep, watching the engine slow its three-car train to a halt. Behind the engine came the ornate Pullman car, followed by a stock car and a brightly painted and highly decorated Mexican caboose. The train passed them by fifty yards and stopped beneath a tall wooden water tank. The two men looked at one another, having just come eye to eye with Laslow Morganfield, only to have him drift past them, standing on the rear Pullman platform, his fingers holding a cigar clasped between them, scissor style. "Follow me, men," Morganfield had said in passing.

"Well, hell," said Cobb, "he's already leading us around where he wants us."

"That what a rich man does," Maydeen replied flatly, "leads people around." They turned and started walking, rifles in hand, breathing the fine, choking red dust.

At the stopped Pullman car platform, Bo Maydeen stood at the bottom iron step and said to Morganfield over the chain hooked across the gateway, "Welcome to Red Rock Station, Mexico, Mr. M."

"Look at these two, Stokes," Morganfield said to the black man standing beside him in a white waistcoat. "They're covered with red dust." He spoke without humor and inflection. His words sounded like nothing more than a commentary to himself.

"Yes, sir, they are, Mr. Morganfield," said Stokes.

"Quickly, let them in then," Morganfield said, wearing a thin, flat smile, leering a bit at Bo Maydeen.

Stokes stepped over curtly, unhooked the chain from across the iron gateway and stood back, holding it as if at attention while the two stepped onto the rear platform. Bo Maydeen walked up the steps and straight to Morganfield's outstretched hand, shaking it firmly. Cobb turned a distasteful glance to Stokes and said under his breath, "How's the chickens?" Stokes stared straight ahead as if he didn't hear him.

"What news have you for me, Maydeen?" Morganfield asked bluntly.

"Good news, I think, Mr. M.," said Maydeen, accepting a cigar from a gold-trimmed cigar box that Stokes appeared with, magically and held open for him. "I heard from Winton. He and some of our men have trailed Hollister's gang into the Mexican hill country not far from here."

"And I take it *she's* still with them?" Morganfield asked.

"Yes, it's our belief that she's still with Hollister and his men. We're headed out to meet up with Winton and the others directly. With any luck we'll have Hollister's gang trapped and killed . . . and your money from Olsen back in hand, of course."

"Let's not leave this to *luck,* Maydeen," said Morganfield. "If I wanted to risk the outcome to *luck,* I'd have had some of Stokes' relatives come take care of things. Show me some *skill,* fellows," he said, making a fist for emphasis. "Show me some guts and ingenuity!"

"You got it, Mr. M.," said Cobb. He stepped forward for a cigar, but the box snapped shut in Stokes' hand, as if Cobb weren't there.

"I brought along Cage Thomas and the Freely brothers to help us out. And I'll be joining you myself, to take this matter personally in hand," Morganfield said, staring at Maydeen to see how he would take the news. "I have some experimental military *treats,* compliments of the United States Army. These might come in handy."

But Maydeen saw it and kept a poker face. "We'll be honored to have you riding with us, Mr. M., military treats or not." He wasn't about to ask what sort of experimental weapons Morganfield might have some money invested in. He only hoped it wasn't something that might get him killed.

Morganfield puffed his cigar and let out a long stream of smoke. "This is the sort of thing a man must do for himself. I feel it my duty to bring Hollister and the rest of his trash to their knees." He studied Maydeen's eyes closely. "But you do understand that a man in my position must keep this sort of thing low in profile. I wouldn't want any of this reaching the newspapers. Nor would the high brass in the army want it known what I have in my possession."

"I understand, Mr. M.," said Maydeen. "And that's why you have me here. Your trouble is *my* trouble. I understand that you want to go along and handle this yourself, but I'd consider it an honor to take care of this bunch of riffraff for you." He pressed a hand on his chest and patted himself. "I would do it just to show you my appreciation."

"Me too," said Cobb, cutting in on Maydeen's conversation. "I know you haven't known me as long, but gawdamn, Mr. M., I'll be right in there, fighting for you like a pit bulldog!"

"I'm *coming*," Morganfield said with finality on the matter.

"Of course, Mr. M.," said Maydeen.

"Whatever you say, sir!" said Cobb. "That's how we want to do it."

Laslow Morganfield looked him up and down and said with a bland expression, "Cobb, isn't it?"

"Well, yes, Mr. M.," Cobb said, trying not to let his embarrassment show. "I'm Branard Cobb. Me and Bo here have been looking out for your mining interests up in the badlands for going on —"

"Stokes," said Morganfield, ignoring Cobb, "bring Maydeen a brandy." As if in afterthought, he said, "Oh, and bring this Cobb fellow one too, I suppose."

Maydeen sniffed his cigar and managed to give Cobb a devilish grin without Morganfield seeing it. When Morganfield turned back to him, Maydeen said, "I take it we'll want all of Hollister's gang to never be seen or heard from again?" His voice lowered just between them.

"That's right — we'll kill them all," Morganfield said boldly. "Every last gawdamn one of them!"

Maydeen gave a look all around the area, making sure their conversation wasn't being overheard.

"What's the matter, Maydeen?" Morganfield asked. "You're not getting shy on me, are you?"

"No, Mr. M.," said Maydeen, "it's just that you never know who might be hanging around, listening."

"I don't give a damn who's listening!" Morganfield roared. "If I want a son of a bitch killed, or a whole army of son of a bitches killed, for that matter, where's the harm in that? I'm a rich man. My money clothes and feeds thousands of people all across this land, every damn day of the year! If I want *a few* of them killed now and then — for damn good reason, I might add — why shouldn't I be able to *have* them killed?"

Maydeen smiled, studying Morganfield's eyes, trying to know how to take all this. He was unsure if this was all just his strange sense of humor or if the rich man truly felt this way. Finally Maydeen cleared his throat and said, "Hearing it put that way, I'm with you one hundred percent. We'll kill them all for you, right Cobb?"

Cobb looked stunned, but said, "Hell, yes, they're all dead already. They just don't know it yet." He grinned.

"Yes, yes, we will kill all of them, to be sure," said Morganfield, seeming preoccupied, running things back and forth through his mind. But then he stopped and raised a finger, saying, "All of them except the woman, of course . . . it goes without saying I want her brought to me unharmed."

"Of course, Mr. M.," said Maydeen, "it goes without saying."

Suddenly Morganfield shouted loudly above the pulse of the big engine, "Garrity! Get up here! Right now!"

A door squeaked open on the stock car and a wiry man in rawhides jumped to the ground and came strutting back toward them. "Aye, sir," he said, "at your service." As he spoke to Morganfield he looked Maydeen and Cobb up and down, as if appraising them for the first time, although he'd had occasion to meet them more than he cared to over the past two years.

"You remember Bo Maydeen and . . . this *other* fellow, don't you?" Morganfield asked, stalling on Cobb's name for a second, pointing the men out with his cigar.

"Yeah, sure," said Garrity, a bit of contempt in his voice, "I remember them."

"Saddle us up five fresh horses and let's be off right away," said Morganfield. "Have your helper take their horses on board and see to them until we return."

"Saddle *five* horses, sir?" Garrity asked.

"Yes, saddle five," said Morganfield. "And bring spares for each of us. You and Stokes are riding along. Fetch both of those oversize army saddlebags I have in the stock car. Be especially careful with them, mind you."

Garrity knew better than to inquire about the two large army saddlebags. But that didn't stop him from asking, "Five spare horses, sir?" He gave Stokes a look, knowing the manservant hated riding with Morganfield as much as he himself did. But Stokes showed no sign of his displeasure. "Might I ask how far it is we'll be going, that we'll need the five extra animals?"

Morganfield referred the question to Maydeen with a glance.

"Fifty, sixty miles," said Maydeen.

"Hard terrain, is it?" Garrity asked.

"It's damn hard terrain!" Morganfield cut in abruptly. "Now get the horses and the army bags, and stop fooling around!"

"Aye, sir," said Garrity. But as he turned to leave, Morganfield stopped him.

"We'll need food too, Garrity," said Morganfield. "We'll need food, coffee, blankets, whiskey, brandy, grain for the animals" — he spun a finger in the air and dismissed the matter to Garrity by saying — "and anything else you can think of."

Garrity, Stokes, Maydeen and Cobb all exchanged glances.

"We're going to do this right, from start to finish," Morganfield said, clamping the cigar between his teeth.

The ranger waited a long time before he ventured out and hurried across the shimmering water. He found Black Pot and the two prisoners' horses chewing on coarse wild grass in the long shade of a large barrel cactus. He stripped the two horses' saddles from their backs and led them along with Black Pot, managing to keep himself between the two animals for cover. In that manner, he walked out and dragged the two bodies back away from the water, where he covered them with rocks too large for coyotes and buzzards to overturn.

"I can't say you didn't both deserve it," Sam said when he'd finished covering the men and took off the faded black sombrero he still wore, along with the homemade poncho Ramón had fashioned for him. "But

God's your judge now, not me." He put the sombrero back on, stepped up into his saddle with the two spare horses' reins in his hand, and rode away, wanting to get off the flatland as quickly as possible and into the better cover of the hill country. He'd lost valuable time here. He counted on having two spare horses to help him make up for it.

Staying on the hoofprints, he crossed the flatlands and rode almost straight to the spot where the rifle shots had been fired. He picked up one of the brass shells and squeezed it in his gloved hand, as if to do so would reveal the shooter to him. He looked out toward the water across the flatlands, getting an idea of how good this shooter must be in order to orchestrate two killing shots back-to-back from such a distance. Then he looked all around at the hoofprints and saw them lead onto the trail, where they intermingled with the set of tracks he'd been following. In a moment he'd mounted, turned the stallion and put him back onto the trail, leading the spare horses right beside him.

The next time he stopped it was to see the hoofprints end in the middle of the thin trail leading up off the flatlands. As he looked all around and nudged the stallion forward, he saw the face of Dick Lowry staring at him from beside the trail where he'd fallen and been left for dead. But Lowry wasn't dead. Seeing the ranger, he managed to call out faintly, "Ranger . . ."

Sam stepped down, grabbing his canteen from his saddle horn. He threw the horses' reins around a scrub juniper, hurried over to the mortally wounded outlaw, and stooped down beside him. "Look — look at what she . . . done to me, Ranger," he wheezed. "I'm done for. . . ."

Sam pressed the canteen to Lowry's lips and wet them, seeing the man was in no condition to swallow water. "Somebody finally dropped you, eh?" Sam said quietly.

Lowry managed a thin, faint smile. "You don't . . . look surprised," he whispered.

"I can't say that I am," Sam said quietly. "I'm only surprised you made it this far." He pressed the canteen to Lowry's lips, this time letting him decide whether or not he could drink and hold it down. Lowry ventured a long sip. "You've carried lots of trouble with you, Lowry," Sam said. "I keep running into more of it at every turn in the trail."

"Yeah?" Lowry looked proud of himself. A little of the water came back up, having turned pinkish with blood. But he held most of it down. "Think if you lifted me onto a horse, I could . . . give you a run . . . for it?"

"We're not going to find out, Lowry," Sam said quietly. "Which one shot you?" he asked matter-of-factly.

"Why? Are you going . . . after her?" Lowry asked.

"The woman shot you?"

"Yeah, what the hell?" said Lowry, trying to shrug. "I tried talking my way in with Hollister and her. . . . It didn't work." He coughed, then sounded stronger, saying, "She tricked me, took my money . . . gave me phony money. Finally she shot me. I never got so screwed . . . by one woman. Never even took my pants off."

"She's got all the bank money?" Sam asked.

"Yeah . . . far as I know, unless Morganfield's men caught up to her on the . . . way to Trouble Creek," Lowry said, sounding weaker again.

Sam wanted to ask him more but he saw the glazed look come to Lowry's eyes, and decided to let him die in peace. "For what it's worth," he said quietly, "I don't like having my prisoners killed this way. It's not the way the law intends it."

Lowry nodded slowly and seemed to understand. Then he stared straight up at the sky, the kind of stare the ranger knew too well. Sam sighed, capped the canteen and stood up. He walked back to the stallion and his spare horses and stood still for a moment, glad the hunt had ended. He'd started to take the harnesses from the spare horses and turn them loose. Yet, before he'd made a move to free the animals, he raised his eyes toward the distant sound of a single rifle shot coming from a stretch of flatlands beneath another row of green-brown hills. The shot gave him pause. He listened intently, knowing the sound came from the same shooter he and his prisoners had encountered earlier.

"Looks like you two are with me a while longer," he said to the spare horses, unwrapping their reins from Black Pot's saddle horn and stepping up into his saddle. Leading the horses, he turned the stallion back onto the trail and said under his breath, "Come on, Black Pot, we'll turn back at Trouble Creek. Since we're here we might as well get back the money for all the folks in Olsen."

Less than five miles ahead of the ranger, Doyle Hollister ran limping away from his downed horse. The animal lay, neighing pitifully, a bullet hole in its side pumping blood with each beat of its heart. "Damn it!"

Doyle shouted, grabbing Kaylee's out-stretched arm and swinging up behind her. "Get us out of here!"

Kaylee batted her boots to her horse's sides and sent it bolting along the trail behind Dallas Spraggs and the others. "Are you hit?" Kaylee called out over her shoulder.

"No, but my leg feels cracked from taking the fall!" Hollister said. He looked back toward the clearing they had passed through along the high trail. He expected to hear another rifle shot, but none came. "Whoever it is, he's good!" Hollister said. "He doesn't waste a damned shot!"

Only ten yards up the thin trail, the gang had pulled off into the shelter of high-reaching piñon and thick juniper. "Hell," said Fudd to the others as Kaylee and Hollister rode in, "we know it's Morganfield's men. They just managed to catch up to us on that flatland trail. They spotted us riding along up here and took a shot. If the shooter had known we would be coming and been set up and waiting for us, we'd be counting our dead right now."

Seeing Kaylee and Hollister ride in, Dallas Spraggs, Parks, Poole and Tommy Dykes turned their attention to him. "Fudd's right," said Hollister, hearing most of what the old gunman had said. "This shooter didn't aim for my horse. He just didn't have time to get ready. Next time he will be."

"Are you all right, Doyle?" Fudd asked.

"I'm all right. I think my leg's hurt. I won't know how bad till I step down. And I'm not stepping down till we top this hill and find cover. Now that this shooter is on to us, there'll be little letup."

"How much farther to that creek we're headed to?" Dallas Spraggs asked Fudd.

"It comes up from the ground on the other side of this hill," said Fudd, "not more than two miles. We'll have plenty of cover once we get there."

"Then let's quit talking about it and get to it," said Hollister. He managed a grin in spite of the pain stabbing deep into his leg. "We can't take much more of this sharp-shooting."

On the flatlands, behind a row of chest-high rocks, Ben Winton laughed and said to Clifford Devoe, "You can't win if you don't bet, Clifford. Didn't anybody ever tell you that?"

"It figures," Clifford said tightly. "I bet him, he hits his mark. I don't bet him, he misses. Makes me wonder if this is a fixed game."

"You can wonder all you like, friend," said

Peak, "just don't go accusing me, not out loud anyway." He grinned and handed the rifle back up to Winton.

Winton turned the rifle down, saying, "Naw, you hang onto it awhile, Peak. You're the best with it anyway. Once we get past this hill we're going to be dogging this bunch hard." He looked up along the high trail. "Wouldn't it be just dandy if Maydeen and Cobb got here and we already had this bunch slung over their saddles?"

George Hope laughed and said in his deep voice, "Cobb would shit his boots full, is my guess."

Looking back along the flatlands through his binoculars, Winton's smiling expression turned serious. "Well, it's not going to happen," he said, lowering the binoculars. "Here they come now. You won't believe who's with them."

"Jefferson *by-God* Davis?" Clifford Devoe asked, not wanting to take a guess.

Devoe's sarcasm drew a cold stare from Winton. "No, guess again," Winton said sharply.

"Hell, who is it?" Hope asked, stretching his thick neck upward and straining his eyes across the flatlands in the sun's glare.

"It's none other than our own Laslow Morganfield." Winton grinned and added,

"Or *Mr. M.,* as Maydeen might say."

"Are you kidding me?" Hope asked, straining even harder, making a visor of his hand above his eyes, just below the rolled brim of his bowler hat.

"I would not kid about such a matter as this," Winton said, his binoculars up to his eyes again, bemused by the sight of men, horses and supplies coming toward them over a slight roll on the belly of the flatlands. "Jesus, he's even brought his stable man, Garrity, and his manservant, Stokes!"

"Stokes on horseback?" said Devoe. "Give me the binoculars. I've got to see this. How does he ride?"

Winton lowered the binoculars from his eyes but did not put them into Devoe's expectant hand. "Far better than you, it appears," he replied, turning and walking to his horse. "Let's ride out and meet them."

"Yeah," said Devoe. "You know Morganfield didn't ride out here without some good sipping whiskey."

"Of course not. He'll have plenty of whiskey," said Winton. "He'll have it, but you will play hell getting it." He smiled. "Not if Maydeen has any say-so on it."

"Well, that's *one hell* of an attitude," said Devoe. "The shape my face is in, I could use a belt or two of whiskey for the pain."

"Good luck, then," said Winton, "but don't look to me for any support when you ask for it. Morganfield might just fire you."

"Damn it!" said Devoe, stepping up onto his horse. "Why the hell would he bring whiskey if he's not going to allow anybody to drink it?"

"I didn't say he brought whiskey for you and me," Winton chuckled. "Man, do you have a high opinion of yourself." He shook his head and nudged his horse forward toward the distant riders.

CHAPTER 17

On the flatlands, Bo Maydeen raised a hand and brought the men and animals to a halt upon seeing the riders appear, moving toward them across the flatlands. When he recognized Winton at the head, he said to Cobb, "Keep everybody back here. Give me a chance to find out what's going on."

"You mean about the rifle shot a while ago?" Cobb asked.

Maydeen gave him a look. "Yes, that, among other things. Just see to it that everybody stays back here. If Morganfield asks, tell him I rode to make sure this is Winton and our men. We've got to work together to keep Mr. M. happy — do you understand?"

"Yeah, I understand," said Cobb, returning the look Winton gave him.

No sooner did Maydeen turn his horse and head out to meet Winton and the others than Morganfield called out, "Who is that coming up ahead?"

"We think it's our men, sir," Cobb replied. "But it always pays to check and make sure. That's what I always tell Maydeen."

From his horse, Morganfield turned in his saddle and waved Stokes and Garrity forward. "Both of you get up here beside me. Hurry up! I want those saddlebags close at hand!"

"Damn it!" Garrity said under his breath, looking back at the heavy, bulging saddlebags behind his and Stokes' saddles. "I shudder to think of what he's got us toting around with him."

Stokes also cast a wary eye back on the saddlebags, but he only shook his head without commenting and rode forward. He and Garrity flanked Morganfield with their horses and sat watching the riders draw closer.

Bo Maydeen rode ahead and met Ben Winton and the other three men on the sandy flatlands. Darman Peak, George Hope and Clifford Devoe halted their horses a few yards back and awaited a signal from Winton or Maydeen. "I see you had to bring a new man along," Maydeen said as the two touched their hat brims in greeting.

"New, but *one hell* of a shot," said Winton.

"That's good," said Maydeen. "I take it that was his rifle shot we heard?"

"It was," said Winton. He nodded upward toward the hills and said, "We saw Hollister and his gang riding past a clearing along the trail. Bang. He knocked one's horse out from under him."

Maydeen looked up along the hill trail, appreciating the difficulty of the shot. "I'm glad he's on *our* side," he commented.

"Me too," Winton grinned. "Now listen to this. That ranger everybody wants dead? The one who's always such a pain in the ass?"

"Burrack?" said Maydeen.

"Yep," said Winton. "Peak killed him and two prisoners he had with him, at a distance I wouldn't want to have to *walk* on a hot day."

"That's great." Maydeen looked past Winton at Peak and gave the young gunman a nod of acknowledgment. Then he looked at Clifford Devoe's battered face and asked, "What happened to Clifford? He looks like he ran into a low-hanging branch."

Winton chuckled. "The poor son of a bitch has had a hard time of it this trip. I'll tell you about it later. How long do you think all this is going to take?"

Maydeen considered it for a moment.

"Not long," he said. "You've got the ranger taken care of, so he won't be jumping down everybody's shirt. From what I remember about this country, they'll soon be running out of room up there. We'll take them down pretty easy once they do. All we have to do now is press them hard. Once they try to hole up somewhere, we'll move in quick and finish them off."

"Trouble Creek," said Winton.

"What?" Maydeen asked.

"That's where they're headed," said Winton.

"I've heard of that place," said Maydeen. "How'd you hear that's where they're headed?"

"One of the ranger's escaped prisoners told me that," said Winton. "A shifty low-life prick named Dick Lowry. Ever heard of him?"

"Can't say that I have offhand," Maydeen replied. "But I might recognize him if I saw him."

"If you saw him now, you'd see a bullet hole in his chest," said Winton. "He's the one who put the hurting on ole Clifford. Got the drop on Clifford with a saddle stirrup and got away from him. I'm speculating that he tried joining up with Hollister's gang. But somebody plugged him dead —

pow! Straight in his chest." He held a long index finger to his breast as if it were a gun, and dropped his thumb for the hammer. "He's laying back along one of the hill trails, birds eating his belly."

"Damn, it sounds like there's been a hell of a lot going on here in the Old Mexico badlands," Maydeen said, appearing impressed.

"Yep," said Winton, nudging his horse slightly, awaiting a sign from Maydeen to ride back to where Morganfield sat waiting. "To be such a big, empty land, there's sure been lots of dead folks along the way."

"Morganfield says he wants every one of them killed," said Maydeen, turning his horse beside Winton.

Winton gave a slight hand signal to the other three, getting them to come ahead as he turned his horse beside Maydeen's. "*All* of them?" Winton asked pointedly.

"Except for the woman," said Maydeen. "You *know* how he feels regarding that woman."

"Yeah, I know," Winton said, shaking his head as if remembering.

Hollister and Kaylee stopped at the edge of a cliff and looked down at the long, winding creek and the small assortment of adobe and wooden-frame structures lining both rocky banks. "That fool Lowry was right," said Kaylee, assessing the old French settlement, seeing remnants of an old earth-covered timber fort wall that had at one time encircled most of the clearing below.

"Yeah," said old man Fudd, his eye going to a high, sheer rock wall standing on the other side of the deep clearing. "One man with a rifle and enough ammunition could perch over there and keep this whole trail shut down for as long as he felt like it."

Hollister slipped down carefully from behind Kaylee's saddle and limped over to a rock. He leaned down and examined his leg just below his knee. "I hope to hell they've got lots of tequila and mescal," he said. "Somebody's gonna have to get me drunk and set this leg for me."

"I'll set it for you, Doyle," Fudd volunteered with a cruel grin. "Just to get to hear you yelp about it."

"I hate to disappoint you, Fudd," said Hollister, "but I ain't much of a yelper." He straightened up from leaning against the rock and had started to step back over to Kaylee's horse when five mounted young Mexicans appeared silently on the trail behind them.

"All of you, freeze!" shouted the lead

rider, holding a pair of battered Walker Colts aimed at Hollister. "Raise your hands in the air!" Bandoleers of ammunition crossed his thin chest. Flanking him, the other four riders held cocked rifles and pistols older than themselves.

"Like hell," Manfred Poole shouted, seeing nothing to fear from these young men and their ancient weaponry. His gun streaked up from his holster. But as his shot exploded, so did one of the Mexicans' rifles. Poole's shot grazed the rifleman's shoulder, but the rifle shot lifted Poole from his saddle and sent him backward off the edge of the cliff. He rushed down through breaking limbs and brush and bounced off of the rocky hillside. He came to rest limply on the edge of another cliff.

"Hold your fire!" the lead Mexican shouted at his men in Spanish. Four men were close around him; two more sat their horses a few yards back along the trail, as if making sure no one else came up behind them.

Dykes, Parks, Spraggs and old man Fudd brought their guns up quickly. But Hollister, hearing the young man's order and seeing the tight spot he and his gang were in, pressed as they were to the edge of the cliff, shouted loudly at his own men, "No, *don't shoot!*"

Both sides remained tense, but neither disobeyed their leader.

"He killed Poole," Denton Fudd said, staring at the young rifleman, ready to fire at the slightest flicker of an eye.

"I know, gawdamn it!" shouted Hollister, he himself holding his Colt cocked and ready to fire. "Nobody fires unless I say otherwise!" He ventured a quick glance at the edge of the ground behind him. Two steps away stood nothing but open air and a two-hundred-foot drop for him and his party. Looking back at the lead rider, he said, "Who the hell are you?"

If fear or doubt registered in the young man's mind, his dark eyes revealed neither. "I am the hombre who patrols this road! Who the hell are *you?*"

"Travelers," Hollister said flatly. "What do you want?"

"We came to collect a simple fee for using the road," the man said. "But now that one of yours has wounded Javier, there will be a larger fee for you to pay."

"They're half-assed mountain banditos!" Fudd cut in. "Say the word, Doyle! We'll turn them into sausage!"

"Easy, Fudd!" said Hollister. He noted

that even Kaylee had drawn her pistol and had it at the ready. "I didn't bring us this far to die in some French shit hole!"

"Shit hole?" said the young Mexican leader. "You call our Ennui Creek a shit hole?"

"I call it Trouble Creek," said Hollister, "and you're getting ready to see why if you don't back those horses, turn and let us off this ledge."

"If you look at the rocks below," said the young man, "you will see the bones of all those who chose to fly instead of paying us our road fees."

"I'm not going to look," said Hollister. "I've seen goat bones before. Are you going to back away or die right here with us?"

"Goat bones, eh?" said the young man, giving his companions a look, as if admitting that what Hollister had said about goat bones might be true. "You are one clever-thinking gringo, you are." With his free hand he reached up slowly and tapped a finger to the side of his head. "But it makes no difference what bones lie on the hillside. Tomorrow it will be your bones if you do not pay up."

"Let's get to killing, Doyle," Fudd growled.

"No, I don't think so, Fudd," said Hollister, keeping his eyes on the young Mexican. "I think we'll just pay this fee he's asking us for." He slowly spread a friendly yet cautious grin. His free hand went inside his shirt. With his gloved hand he busted open the paper binder around the counterfeit money, took out a small portion of bills and spread them in front of the bandits. "Will this be enough to cover our road fees?" he asked, knowing that these mountain bandits had never seen this much money in their lives, real or otherwise.

The young Mexican leader's eyes lit up. "I think for this much money you can use our road for . . . *hmm.*" He stopped as if considering an appropriate amount of time, then said, "Two months, señor!" He held up two thin fingers.

"Gracias," said Hollister. He stepped closer, still holding his Colt ready to fire at the slightest mood change, and handed the money up to the leader. "I didn't catch your name, mister," he said, as the money left his hand.

"My name is Manuel River—"

Hollister cut him off. "Let's keep one another on a first-name basis, Manuel," said Hollister. He took a step back and said, "I believe you and me are both wolves working the sheep. I just happen to have drawn the larger herd. My name's Joe," he lied, "and if you like the feel of this kind of money, there's a way you can make yourself plenty of it."

"Wolves . . . *lobos,* eh? I like that." Manuel sat grinning, holding the bills in his hand, knowing that if these men had more money, this would be the best time to take it. Turning to his men he said, "He says we are *lobos,* me and him, eh? *Dos lobos!* Two *bold* wolves, I call us!" But Manuel also knew that some of *his* men would die, perhaps even himself, in the ensuing gun battle. He nodded agreeably, fanning the bills in his hand. "You know what, *Joe,*" he said, "I think *I* like how *you* think." He pointed first at himself, then at Hollister.

"I knew we could come to some sort of agreement." Hollister smiled. "The way reasonable men always do." He reached inside his shirt again and pulled out more money. Without counting it, he said, "Here is half of what I will pay you to keep everybody off this road until we leave Trouble Creek."

"Ah, there are people following you, *mi amigo?*" said Manuel. "People who do not like wolves like us?"

"Exactly," said Hollister. "These are the kind of people who would kill wolves like us if they got the chance." He stepped closer, with the money held out for the Mexican leader. "I'm betting this much money, plus this much *more,* that you and your *amigos* here will kill them before they get the chance."

"*Sí,*" Manuel said, taking the money eagerly. "We will kill anybody who comes along this trail, and we will bring their bodies to you, to show you the work we do, eh?"

"That will work out fine, Manuel," said Hollister. "Now back your men away, *por favor,* so we can get down to Trouble Creek and get some food and drink. It's been a long trail for us."

"Javier, Paolo, Dejero, Juan!" Manuel called out to the four men around him, "Give our *amigos* room to pass. Show some manners, all of you." Behind him on the trail the other two men stepped their horses aside.

As one, the Mexicans lowered their weapons and backed their animals around on the trail until the way was no longer blocked. "*Gracias,*" said Hollister, swinging up behind Kaylee, his Colt still in hand. Kaylee held her horse back until the others had filed past one at a time. As Fudd passed, his Colt across his lap, his thumb still over the hammer, he growled under his breath to Hollister, "What about Poole?"

"Sure," said Hollister, "I didn't forget." Quickly he swung his Colt upward, out at arm's length and shot the unsuspecting Javier through the head. Then, before the other Mexicans could even get collected, Hollister swung the cocked Colt toward Manuel, who sat stunned in his saddle, less than four feet from him. "I lost a man. . . . You lost a man. Now we're even! Agreed?" Hollister asked, leaving no doubt in his voice as to what would happen if Manuel disagreed. It dawned on him that in the turn of a few seconds, he had given up the best of the two positions and allowed the American gunman to take it.

"Hold your fire," Manuel said to his tensed gunmen. He raised a hand in a show of peace. "It is only fair, in this world of ours." Down the trail the other two Mexicans raised their hands away from the big flintlock pistols on their laps.

"Yeah," Hollister said to Manuel, feeling Kaylee nudge the horse forward, "look at it this way. All of you just got a bonus to split up."

Manuel nodded. "We will not think about this and let it cause trouble between us. We will still protect this trail as we said we will do . . . for the money, of course."

"Of course," said Hollister, looking back at the Mexicans as Kaylee stepped up the horse's pace and fell in behind Denton Fudd and the others.

Moments later, headed down the steep, winding trail, the riders reined their horses off onto a narrow flat spot and looked all around the valley below before continuing down into it. As he looked back up along the trail, Fudd said to Hollister, "You did right shooting that quick-triggered son of a bitch."

"It made a point," said Hollister, his broken leg aching with each movement of the horse beneath him.

"How much do you suppose we can count on those banditos?" Dallas Spraggs asked, also looking back up the steep trail.

"I count on them as long as this play money holds up," Hollister said, forcing a pained smile. He looked across the creek to the high, sheer wall of rock above the valley more than a hundred yards away. "I figure with them holding that trail, we won't have to keep anybody perched up there unless we hear shooting."

"So either they protect us and kill Morganfield's men, or they get themselves killed and we hear it as a warning," said Dykes.

"That ain't half bad, Doyle."

"Not at all," said Fudd, letting out a dark laugh, "especially when it only cost us a handful of scrap paper."

The others laughed too, except for Kaylee, who nudged her horse forward. "Let's get down there and get his leg fixed," she said. "We've got plenty to keep us busy for a while."

"Yeah," said Hollister in a pained voice, feeling he should be the one giving the last word on the matter. "Get ourselves ready for Morganfield's men, if Manuel doesn't manage to kill them."

CHAPTER 18

The ranger heard the gunfire to his right, behind him, up in the hills above Trouble Creek. This had been a rifle shot — but not a powerful rifle — followed by a pistol shot, and another pistol shot moments later. He wasn't going to speculate on what had just transpired up there along the steep hill trail, but he felt certain it had nothing to do with the long-distance shooter or any of Morganfield's men. Having the two spare horses with him had afforded him the opportunity to get a strong lead on the long-distance shooter and his pals. He'd swung wide of the hill trail, giving up the hoofprints for awhile, knowing that whoever went up one side of the hills would have to come down the other. He planned on getting there beforehand and staking out the best position.

Along the shimmering water of Trouble Creek, he stopped on the outskirts of the small, almost abandoned town and swapped his saddle from one of the spare horses back to Black Pot, who had taken a good, long bareback rest for the past thirty miles. He let the three animals drink their fill from the cool, clear water while he looked back and forth and all around the hillside and half-circle of sheer rock wall surrounding the valley.

"Are you looking for the best spot, señor?" a small boy asked him in Spanish. Sam looked toward him, seeing a bamboo fishing pole over his shoulder as the child plodded barefoot into view from around a turn in the creek bank.

Sam gave him a smile. "Well, yes, young man, as a matter of fact, I am," Sam returned to him in his broken border Spanish. He'd just looked up along the rock wall and saw narrow ledges there that faced straight across the valley, covering the trails leading down to Trouble Creek. "But I think I've already found it."

"Then I wish you luck, señor," the boy said, "so long as you will not be on my spot." He looked the horses up and down and started to continue on his way.

But Sam stopped him by saying, "May I buy your spot from you?"

The boy stopped and looked at him with

dark, questioning eyes. "Buy my fishing spot? For how long? For how much?"

"For this much," Sam said. He fished a ten-dollar gold piece from beneath his poncho and flipped it to the boy for inspection.

The boy looked the coin over closely, keeping his composure in spite of the excitement the gold brought him. Finally he nodded and cocked his head slightly as if expecting a catch to this transaction. "And for how long?" he asked.

"Until you see me leave town," Sam said. "One day, maybe two days. I'll want you to stay away from the creek until you know I have left town."

Even with the poncho draped over the ranger's shoulders, the bottom two inches of the tied-down holster showed clearly. The boy nodded to the guns and asked, "Are you here to take away Manuel and the banditos?"

"No," Sam said, "I don't know the men you're speaking of." He saw a slight look of disappointment in the boy's eyes. "But I heard shooting in the hills a while ago. Could that have been from them?"

"Always there is shooting coming from the hills," the boy said, nodding. "And always it is from them." He looked expect-antly. "My mother prays to the Blessed Mother that someone will come and take Manuel and his men away. She says they choke the life out of our town."

"I am sorry, young man," said Sam. It pained him to say, "But I am not here to do that. I am here for other reasons. Do we have a deal?"

"One day, maybe two," said the boy. He held the coin up in his closed fist. "When I see you leave town, I will come back. . . . And I will give this to my mother, so if the Blessed Virgin Mother does not send someone for the banditos, we can use this money until we can pay someone to do it."

Sam nodded and watched the boy hurry back around the turn in the creek bank. Again Sam looked all around, but he had already chosen his spot. A thin, jutting platform of rock lay high up the wall, with a broken path leading down to it. The path went in and out of sight from where he stood on the valley floor. "Finish up, boys," he murmured to the horses. "We only rented this place for a couple of days."

When the horses had drunk their fill, Sam picked up the canteen he sank at the water's edge, capped it and hung its strap back around his saddle horn. "Let's get on up there," he murmured, drawing the cinch on

Black Pot's belly. Gathering the reins to all three horses, he walked slowly along the deserted dirt street of the once-vital and busy army garrison.

From the window of their modest adobe that had at one time been a high-ranking French officer's quarters, the woman and her son watched the stranger in the poncho and black faded sombrero walk along the dusty street, leading the three horses behind him. The woman noted the tip of the gun barrel in the tied-down holster her son had told her about, and she crossed herself with the same hand that held the shiny gold coin her son had brought to her. "You must be an honorable man and hold up your end of the agreement, Simon," she said in a somber tone to her son.

"I will, Mother," Simon said, standing beside her. He watched the stranger and his horses walk out of sight toward the narrow trail leading across the valley floor. "He is a gunman, *sí?*"

"*Sí*, from the looks of him, I must believe that he is," said the woman. She looked away from the disappearing stranger and all along the hill in the direction the shots had come from earlier, her dark eyes searching warily, for what she did not know. "Until we know he has left Trouble Creek, I think you must stay inside and help me with the weaving," she said.

Up on the hillside trail, at the same spot where the Mexican bandits had slipped in behind Hollister and his gang, Laslow Morganfield sat atop his horse, staring down onto Trouble Creek. Beside him, Stokes said both quietly and cautiously, "Not too close, sir. These rocks can give way."

Morganfield turned a sharp glance to his manservant. *"Hmmphf,"* he said gruffly. "Do I look to you like I can't sit a horse?"

"No, sir," Stokes said crisply, and he sat in silence.

On the other side of Morganfield sat Garrity, staring down through his own set of binoculars at the figure in the poncho and sombrero, leading three horses across the narrow valley floor. "Now this strikes me a wee bit peculiar," Garrity said idly to no one in particular.

"Get back here, man!" said Morganfield, looking first at the oversize army saddlebags, then grabbing Garrity's reins and jerking his horse back a step. "Your job is to stay close beside me. That's important cargo you have behind your saddle! I can't risk you stumbling off the end of a cliff!"

Garrity and Stokes gave one another a guarded look. No, sir. . . . I mean, *yes, sir,*" said Garrity. "That is, you're right, sir. . . . I'll be more careful." He offered his employer the binoculars. "Take a look at this Mexican, Mr. Morganfield, sir. Something doesn't look right about him."

Morganfield looked at the dusty, battered binoculars offered to him and his expression soured. "I have a pair, thank you, Garrity," he said. He reached around and rummaged on and on through his crowded saddlebags.

Behind Morganfield, Garrity and Stokes, Maydeen and Cobb sat watching for a moment until Cobb sighed, raised a field lens from his lap and started to step his horse forward. But Maydeen stopped him with a hand on his forearm. Cobb watched him shake his head. "Sit still, Cobb," Maydeen whispered.

At length, Morganfield raised a pair of binoculars from his saddlebags and gazed down onto the valley floor. He fumbled with the adjustment on the binoculars but never got the view completely into clear focus. Finally, he winced at the glare of the sun in the lens and pulled them away from his eyes. "I see nothing out of the ordinary, Garrity," he said. "What are you talking about?"

Garrity shrugged, ready to dismiss the

matter. "He just didn't strike me as being Mexican, for some reason."

Now Maydeen and Cobb got interested. "Oh?" said Maydeen, stepping his horse forward, squeezing it in between Morganfield and Stokes. Raising a telescope to his eyes Maydeen looked out and down just in time to see a man in a poncho and sombrero walk a few feet with the three horses strung behind, then step out of sight into a stand of scrub piñon at the base of the rock wall. But then Maydeen swung the telescope back across the creek and saw Kaylee, Hollister and the others ride into sight from the bottom of the hill trail. "Forget the Mexican and his horses," he said to Morganfield and the others. "Guess who just rode into Trouble Creek." He ginned wryly. "None other than Doyle Hollister and his band of saddle tramps!"

"What?" Morganfield raised his binoculars quickly and scanned until he found Hollister and Kaylee.

"We've got them now." Maydeen nodded to Cobb and the men.

"This is most fortunate!" said Morganfield. He paused for a moment, staring down at the riders, then said, almost to himself, "She looks well, in spite of how she's been treated."

Maydeen, Cobb and the others gave one another a curious look.

Morganfield, realizing what he'd said, quickly corrected himself and spoke up in a stronger tone of voice, "That is, she certainly has managed to take care of herself considering *the life* she lives." He stared firmly at Maydeen as if expecting some support.

"Yes, Mr. M.," said Maydeen. "We knew what you meant." He backed his horse a step and said, "Let's get down there and get this thing over and done with."

"Hold it!" said Cobb, looking past Maydeen and seeing the Mexicans riding silently toward them. "We're being snuck up on!"

"Not anymore, we're not," said Ben Winton. He raised his rifle and fired a warning round, kicking up dirt only inches in front of Manuel Rivera's horse. The Mexican leader jerked his horse's reins and had to settle it.

"That's close enough," Maydeen called out, although the Mexicans had already stopped. Under his breath he said, "You sneaking sonsabitches." Fewer than twenty yards separated him and his men from Manuel and his banditos.

Manuel looked rattled without the element of surprise to his advantage. He thumbed himself on the chest, trying to get back into control. "This is my trail! I say what is *close enough!* Not you!" He settled his horse quickly and leveled one of his big Walker Colts at Maydeen. As if on cue his men raised their ancient weaponry, flanking him, blocking the thin, narrow trail, the same way they had blocked Hollister's gang, only not slipping in as close on Morganfield's men. "All of you gringo *bastardos* drop your guns and hold your hands in the air, pronto!" he demanded.

"Hey, let's *talk* about this, *amigo*," Cobb said quietly, giving Maydeen and the others time to get their horses slowly turned in the same direction, facing the Mexicans.

"We are not *amigos!*" Manuel shouted. "Drop your weapons and raise your hands or we will kill you. Look down over the edge and you will see the bones of those who did not do as I said! There, we have *talked* about it."

Beside Morganfield, Stokes and Garrity looked down over the edge. They saw the body of Manfred Poole and the countless bleached bones lying strewn about in the brush on the rocky ledges. "We's dead!" Stokes murmured to Garrity.

Morganfield managed to squeeze his horse forward through the tight-pressed riders and stop beside Maydeen. Taking charge, he whispered, "Tell him who I am. Ask if he's heard of me. Ask him to ride forward and tell us how much he wants to let us pass."

Maydeen gave Morganfield a look, but managed to conceal his anger at the rich man's taking over. Gesturing toward Morganfield he said to the Mexican leader, "This man is Laslow Morganfield. Have you ever heard of him?"

"No." The Mexican leader shrugged.

"He is a rich and powerful man. We have money to pay you," Maydeen called out, following Morganfield's orders. "How much will you charge to let us pass without having trouble?"

Manuel offered a superior grin, seeing the *Americanos* once again begin to yield to him. "What?" he said in mock surprise. "You come to *Trouble Creek* and yet you expect to have no *trouble?* Are you *loco?*" His men gave a dark chuckle behind their raised weapons.

"We can see that you are bold, dangerous men," Maydeen said, having to work at keeping sarcasm out of his voice. "We would gladly pay you money instead of fighting you. Isn't that how you do things?" He gestured a nod back toward the edge where the bones and body lay. "We don't want to end up like that poor sonsabitch."

Manuel liked that. His fortunes had improved greatly since the first band of *Americanos* rode through only a short while ago. "Yes, that is how I do things. But not this time." He nudged his horse forward a step, then another, getting bolder, learning how to get his demands met by these *Americanos*. "You see, *this time,* someone has paid us to kill all of you." He shrugged. "So I think this is what we must do today."

"Tell him whatever they paid him, it's no good," Morganfield said to Maydeen in a guarded tone. "Tell him it's all counterfeit."

Maydeen nodded, resenting Morganfield telling him what to say when they all spoke the same language back and forth. But he called out all the same, saying, "The money they paid you is counterfeit."

"Is what?" Manuel looked confused.

"It's phony, not good, *falsificación,*" Maydeen called out, finally using Spanish to inform him.

"Phony? Counterfeit?" said Manuel, taking out some of the bills from inside his shirt as he spoke. "I don't *think* so." He fanned the bills and looked them over.

"Yes, it is phony, but you can't tell by looking at it," Morganfield finally cut in, speaking for himself.

"Ah," said Manuel, looking closer at the

money. "It is not real, but you cannot tell by *looking* at it." He gave his men a sly grin. "Will it *spend?*" he asked Morganfield.

"It will *spend,* but it is il-*leg*-al," Morganfield replied, emphasizing his words slowly, as if talking to a very young child or a full-grown idiot. "You will get in *muy* trouble for spending this money in my country."

"Ah, I *see. . . .*" Manuel feigned a worried look and examined the money some more, as if checking it closer. "The money is *not* real, but no one can tell by *looking.* The money *will* spend, but not in *America.*" His grin widened as he shrugged and turned to his men with the money. "If we go to America and spend this money we will be *breaking the law.* We will get in *trouble!*" A silence fell over the Mexicans as they sat tensed with their weapons raised and pointed.

Maydeen shook his head in disgust and gave his men a signal, preparing them to fire at his command.

But then laughter broke out among the Mexicans, first started by Manuel, then taken up by the others. When the laughter stopped, Manuel wiped a thumb under his eye and said to Morganfield, "You are one funny man, you are!"

"Listen to me," Morganfield said in a last

attempt to head off a gunfight in close quarters. "We will give you real money! Legal money! Money that you can take anywhere and spend. Not worthless junk!"

"Get ready, men," Maydeen whispered, seeing it coming in spite of Morganfield's wild ramblings.

"No money is *worthless* to men who have blood in their veins!" said Manuel, tightening his Colt in his fist. "We will *take your money* when we have killed you, you gringo son of a bitch!"

Morganfield stopped talking abruptly and stiffened up right in his saddle, greatly offended. "Fuck this," he growled.

"Get back, Mr. M. It's commencing!" shouted Maydeen, seeing nothing to stop a bloodbath.

But Morganfield didn't get back. Instead he held up a metal object the size of a baseball, with a long iron stem sticking out of it. "Take this!" he commanded Maydeen, who did so without hesitation. "Now pull that rod out of it quickly!" Morganfield demanded.

Maydeen pulled it — *"Hunh?"* — and looked at the orange-blue sparks spitting out of the opening.

"Now throw it into their midst!" Morganfield bellowed. "Hurry, man! Before it explodes! It's a *hand bomb!*"

"*Jesus God!*" Maydeen yelled loudly, his eyes wide and terror filled. But immediately he kicked his horse forward and hurled the sizzling iron object toward the Mexicans.

Manuel, upon hearing the word *bomb* and seeing the hissing orange-blue sparks, turned his horse and plowed through his men.

Morganfield's men, except for Maydeen, leaped from their saddles. Maydeen only had time to bow deep down. Morganfield sat crouched a bit, but otherwise engrossed in seeing the bomb's effect, as it flew through the air in a high arc and descended on the Mexicans who had managed to turn and began to flee. Stokes and Garrity had flung themselves from their saddles at the same time and landed side by side on the rocky ground, both of them wrapping their forearms around their heads.

CHAPTER 19

Laslow Morganfield sat upright in his saddle until the very last second, when fine particles of dirt stung his face and the heat of the blast caused him to finally turn away and hunch down in his saddle. But he did not do so until he'd first seen the Mexican leader flung from his horse with a scream that could be heard through the explosion. "By *God!* That is power!" said Morganfield, easing immediately back up in his saddle and staring through the smoke and dust as he tried settling his spooked horse beneath him.

"Mr. M.? Are you all right?" Maydeen asked, also rising from a ball atop his spooked horse. The back of his suit coat was smoking and ragged from the blast. He jerked his frightened horse over to Morganfield and saw blood on his face. "You're bleeding, sir!"

"Yes, yes, I know," said Morganfield,

excited. "But my God! Did you see how these beauties work? I had no idea they were this good! For all I knew it could've blown up in your hand!"

Maydeen gave him a strange look.

"But it didn't, of course!" Morganfield said quickly, as if that fact alone should justify his action. "Stokes, Garrity! Bring me another of those little beauties! Hurry, in case the Mexicans come back!"

Rising up from the ground, Stokes and Garrity looked grimly at one another, both suddenly realizing what sort of cargo they'd been carrying in the oversize army saddlebags.

Off the side of the trail in the smoke and dust, Manuel raced along barefoot, shaken by the blast, one Walker Colt missing, the other wagging aimlessly in his hand. The back of his clothes had been ripped away, leaving most of his back side blackened, smoking and exposed. His men had already vanished down the hillside toward Trouble Creek.

Across the valley, the ranger had stopped on his way up toward the spot he'd chosen above the creek and turned his attention to the explosion coming from a place on the hillside almost straight across from him. Climbing the steep path on foot, he led

Black Pot in his right hand and the two spare horses in his left. The two spare mounts grew nervous and tugged on their reins.

"Whoa, boys," Sam said, soothing the frightened animals. "It's just some fool playing with dynamite." For a moment he searched the hillside where a plume of blue-black smoke rose from within the green piñon and the breastwork of rock. Then he turned and continued upward.

On the valley floor, from inside a long adobe structure that had once stabled French officers' horses, Doyle Hollister lay on a long wooden table while an old animal doctor examined his broken leg with a frown. "What the hell was that?" Hollister asked, rising halfway up, propping himself on an elbow at the sound of the explosion.

"Todavía mentira, todavía mentira," the old horse doctor said, trying to press Hollister back with a weathered hand.

But Hollister would have none of it. Shoving the old man's hand away, he said, "Don't tell me to *lay still,* you old turd! I'm not one of your sick donkeys!"

The old man stepped back, still wearing his impassive frown.

"Let him fix you up, Doyle," said Kaylee,

standing nearby. "Quit acting like a scared child."

"A *child?*" Hollister gave a short chuckle of disbelief and shook his head. "Did you hear what I heard, up there in the hills?"

"I heard it. . . . So what?" Kaylee said flatly.

"So, we both know *who* that is. And we both know what's going to be coming down the hillside any time now!" said Hollister.

"All the more reason for you to lay still and get this leg set, don't you think?" she said with sarcasm.

Hollister gave her a bitter stare. *"Consiga trabajar,"* he said, motioning for the old man to continue as he lay back down on the table. He said to Kaylee, "What's keeping Fudd? He should have been back here by now. I'm going to want something to drink before this ole sonsabitch jerks that bone back into place."

"Fudd's coming, Doyle," Kaylee said firmly. "Shut up and lay still, like the doctor told you."

Hollister grumbled, then quieted himself down. Staring up at the sky through the broken, half-missing thatch ceiling, Hollister relaxed, feeling the throbbing in his leg and the old man's hands touch here and there, seeking out the exact point of the

314

break. "As soon as I can ride, we're all splitting off for a while. You and I might go over to a place I know about on the ocean. We might even take a steamer out of there and head on down to South America."

"South America . . ." Kaylee only smiled at the thought, watching the old man go silently about his work.

"Yeah, that's what I'm thinking," said Hollister. "With the kind of money we've got, we can live like — *Agghii!*" he shrieked loudly, as the old man suddenly yanked with all his might on the broken leg and snapped the bone back into place.

The old horse doctor stepped back, the frown gone from his wrinkled face, replaced by a faint smile of satisfaction.

"There, now," said Kaylee, while Hollister's scream still hung in the air. "That wasn't so bad, was it?"

"I'll kill this son of a bitch!" Hollister said. Yet Kaylee and the old doctor saw that the pain of resetting the bone had diminished quickly. Hollister eased down onto the wooden table and ran his fingers back through his hair. "Jesus," he whispered, sounding relieved.

Fudd pushed aside the dusty blanket covering the doorway and stepped inside, holding a bottle of mescal in one hand and a palm full of brown powder in the other. "I must've got here just in time," he said, having heard Hollister from across the street.

"Give me that!" said Hollister, half rising, reaching out a hand toward Fudd.

"Mescal," said Kaylee, stepping in between the two, "but no dope." She took the bottle from Fudd and passed it on to Hollister's grasping hand.

"No dope," Hollister protested. "But I'm in pain!"

"No, you're not," said Kaylee, "not that much anyway. We've got trouble coming down on us. I need you to be clearheaded."

Fudd looked at the dope lying loose in his hand and said, "Trouble coming to Trouble Creek."

"Get rid of it," Kaylee said firmly. *Taking command again,* Hollister noted to himself, watching her. "Tell the men I don't want to see any more dope while we're here."

Fudd gave Hollister a look for verification. Hollister nodded his agreement. "Then it's gone," said Fudd. He clasped his hand shut, covering the brown powder. "What do you figure that explosion was up there?"

"Beats me," said Hollister. "Whatever it was, I just hope our boy, *Manuel,* and his bold banditos managed to do us some good."

"We ought to know shortly," said Fudd, gazing out and up along the hills.

Inside a small cantina whose roof lay in the same disrepair as the French officers' stables, Dallas Spraggs, Elvey Parks, and Tommy Dykes rolled dice with an effeminate-acting one-eyed bartender of German descent.

"Where's all the whores in this town?" Spraggs asked bluntly.

"That's what I want to know," Elvey Parks joined in. "Or a woman of any sort, for that matter."

"Whore or otherwise, we haven't seen a woman of any sort stick her head out the door since we rode in," said Tommy Dykes.

"Can you blame them?" Spraggs laughed.

"We have no whores in Trouble Creek," said the bartender. "There is not enough business here to interest whores." He shrugged. "There are only two women in Trouble Creek. One is a widow with a son. The other is an old crone who they claim is a *bruja* who lives off to herself." He gave a sort of tight grin. "Lucky for me, I do not indulge myself with women. I like neither the smell nor the feel of them."

"Damn," said Spraggs, "nothing like declaring yourself outright, I reckon. But that's you. That's no help to me and my pards."

"If it is any *help,* I would charge only a dollar to bathe each of you," the bartender ventured cautiously, shaking the leather dice cup easily in his hand, unsure of how his offer would be taken by these rough, trail-seasoned *Americano* gunmen.

The three looked at one another with no expression. "How much would you charge *not to?*" asked Spraggs.

The one-eyed German let the dice spill out onto the plank bar top, looking unaffected by the rejection. "I intended nothing untoward," he said, reading the dice and seeing he'd won the small amount of coins lying on the bar. "Where I come from bathing is a means of cleansing oneself not only on the outside, but the *inside* as well." He checked their blank expressions, then ventured, "It is an art form the way someone like myself lays hands on another to cleanse and at the same time bring them relaxation and perhaps even pleasure."

"You need to talk to old man Fudd," said Spraggs. "I heard it's been a long time since he's had a good *all-over* washing."

"Talk to me about what?" Fudd asked, stepping inside, followed by Kaylee, then Hollister, who limped along with the help of a long walking stick, his leg held straight and braced by four strips of wood.

"Hey! Look who's up and prowling again," said Spraggs, hoping Fudd would let the matter drop. He turned around from the bar, raising a wooden cup of mescal toward Hollister.

Hollister limped over to the bar as all three men greeted him, the other two following suit and raising their wooden cups. "Ask me what?" said Fudd, still looking for an answer.

"Nothing," said Spraggs, shrugging it off. "Just this fellow, he wants to charge us for a bath."

Hollister took a wooden cup of mescal that the one-eyed bartender hurried over and shoved into his waiting hand. *"Gracias!"* said Hollister, raising the cup as if in a toast, while the bartender hurriedly filled another and handed it to Kaylee.

"How much?" Fudd asked. "I could use a bath, if we've got time."

Spraggs, Parks and Dykes stifled a laugh. "That's what I told him," said Spraggs, having a hard time keeping the laughter out of his voice.

Fudd gave Spraggs a hard, curious stare. "What the hell does that mean?"

"Here is your drink," the bartender said

to Fudd, looking nervous.

"You don't understand, Fudd," said Parks. "He don't want to just charge you for the bath. He wants to wash you *all over.*"

Fudd jerked the wooden cup of mescal from the bartender's hand. "You ought to be ashamed of yourself!" he said. His hand went to the Colt in his holster and began to lift it slowly.

But before Fudd lifted the big Colt all the way, Dallas Spraggs looked out through the open doorway toward the steep hillside and said quickly, "Hey! Here comes Manuel's men! In a hurry!"

"Put the gun away, Fudd," Kaylee demanded, seeing the look on the old gunman's face and the deadly intent in his eyes.

"You heard her, Fudd!" Hollister said sharply, seeing the gunman wasn't going to listen to Kaylee. "Come on," he added, "it looks like we'll have plenty of shooting before long!"

Following Hollister out into the dirt street, the men watched the Mexicans hurry in and out of sight down the steep trail for a full five minutes before riding into sight and racing toward them across fifty yards of short, sparse grass along the creek. Kaylee looked up along the hill trail warily, then turned back to Hollister in time to see the Mexicans come sliding their horses to a halt. Behind them came Manuel, batting his bare heels to his horse's sides, trying hard to catch up to his men.

Hollister walked right through the other Mexicans as if they weren't there, and stood leaning his weight on his walking stick when Manuel finally came to a stop in front of him. "What are you doing down here?" Hollister asked harshly, his free hand resting on his gun butt.

"We came to warn you!" said Manuel, out of breath from having chased his horse down before making the descent down the hillside.

"Yeah?" said Hollister, looking both horse and rider up and down, smelling burned hair and seeing Manuel's ragged, blackened clothes. "It looks to me like you're all running for your lives."

"We are running!" said Manuel, outraged. "You said nothing about these men having bombs!"

"Bombs? You mean they have dynamite?" Hollister asked. He glanced away for a moment and searched upward along the hill trail.

"No! I mean bombs. Hand bombs!" said Manuel. "This man is Morganfield, the rich American. I told him I never heard of him, but I lied. I see his picture many times in American newspapers!"

Hollister looked at Kaylee. She shook her head. "I put nothing past him," she said.

"Get back up there and stop them, like I paid you to do!" Hollister shouted to the blackened Mexican leader.

"Huh-uh," said Manuel, shaking his head. "We cannot fight against bombs . . . not for this money you give to us! It is worthless!"

"Worthless?" said Hollister. "Tell me one place in Mexico that will turn that money down if you shake it in front of them!"

Manuel didn't answer; he knew Hollister was right. "All right, the money is good in Mexico. But we still cannot fight men with bombs! I give you back the money."

Hollister's Colt streaked up from his holster. Behind him the other men did the same, following his lead. "Pick your poison, bold bandito," said Hollister. "You die here or you can die up there. You took my money to do a job for me. . . . Now get back up there and get to doing it."

The Mexicans, tired, scared and confused, backed their horses, and upon Manuel's signal turned and headed back toward the hill trail.

Hollister and his men stood watching. Hollister wore a dark smile as Manuel and his men crossed the fifty yards of flatland and disappeared up the trail. "All right. Let's get moving while Morganfield's men eat these banditos for supper." He nodded across the valley toward the thin, steep trail leading upward. "I spotted that trail when we rode in. We take it, and we can stop at any point going up and pin this valley down for as long as we feel like it."

"Good thinking," said Fudd. But as the gang turned toward the horses standing along a hitch rail, Tommy Dykes' stomach exploded into his hands as a bullet from high up the hillside punched a fist-size hole through the middle of his back.

"Get the horses! Get out of here!" Fudd shouted, already crouched and running, not even bothering to turn and fire, judging the distance of the shot, which had only re-sounded after Dykes started falling forward, dead on his feet.

CHAPTER 20

When the ranger had led the horses as far as he dared risk taking them, he hitched them to a creosote bush in a small, flat clearing. Then he took the round leather rifle case from his bedroll and slipped the strap over his shoulder. Inside the case lay his big Swiss rifle, broken down into four pieces, including a long brass scope.

Moments later, as he sat assembling the rifle, he watched the Mexicans ride down from the hillside. Seeing them ride off and back up the steep hill trail only a couple of minutes later gave him pause. With the rifle almost together, he sat watching Hollister limp toward the horses. Then he saw Dykes' belly fly apart and heard the sound of the shot. *There's my shooter,* Sam told himself.

He snapped the scope onto the rifle, tightened it down and ran his shirtsleeve along the barrel. From his lofty position, Sam watched everything as it happened in the dirt street. He watched Hollister's men gather the horses and take shelter behind the cantina, leaving the empty street lying beneath a looming sheet of dust.

Speaking in a near whisper to the shooter, somewhere more than seven hundred yards away across the valley floor, Sam said, "Now, then, let's see how you feel knowing you're not the only one with a big rifle."

On the steep hillside trail, standing in the cover of a thicket of juniper, Ben Winton shook his head and chuckled. Looking at the big Austrian rifle Darman Peak had handed back to him a moment earlier, he said, "You amaze me, Peak."

"Yeah, that's good," said the young gunman, "but do I amaze *them?*" He nodded toward Morganfield proudly holding one of the bombs in his hand, and Maydeen standing a few yards away.

"Don't worry about it," said Winton. "He's glad you're with us, or you wouldn't be sitting here. You'd be storming down the trail, chasing Mexicans with Cobb and the others."

A few yards from Morganfield, Garrity and Stokes stood holding the horses. Cobb had led the rest of Morganfield's men down the steep trail to Trouble Creek to make sure no more Mexicans stood between them and Hollister.

"But you saw him and Maydeen stop me, didn't you?" Peak asked in a lowered voice. "I could have picked off the whole gang if he'd let me."

"Ah, forget it," said Winton. "They're both just as impressed as I am. Maydeen gets a bee up his ass any time his *Mr. M.* acts displeased about something. Morganfield got nervous, thinking you might hit the woman."

"What's the story on him and the woman anyway?" Peak asked.

"You don't know?" Winton asked flatly.

"Would I be asking?" Peak replied, just as flatly.

"It's his daughter," said Winton, lowering his voice and glancing around.

"Jesus," said Peak. "I thought maybe he's in love with her."

Glancing around again, Winton said, "Just between you and me . . . he *is.*"

"Whoa," said Peak. "You don't mean . . . ?" He made a gesture that Winton understood to mean two people in the throes of passion.

"Yep," said Winton in a guarded tone. "If you ever said I told you, I'd deny it. . . . Then I'd have to kill you."

Peak nodded. "I'll never tell anybody you

told me." He glanced all around. "So why is she out here robbing him, her own father?"

"Beats me," said Winton. "Who knows what goes on in a person's mind? Maybe she figures he owes her everything he's got after what's happened between them. This ain't the first time she's run off with some outlaw just to strike out against Morganfield. She ran off over a year ago, took up with Doyle Hollister. Worked her way into running a hash house in Olsen, set herself up with the town banker, then put the wheels into motion."

"Damn," said Peak. "I'm feeling like I've gotten involved in somebody's family squabble."

"That you have," said Winton. "But the pay is still good, ain't it? You can still squeeze that trigger for Laslow Morganfield, can't you? No matter what craziness he's got going on?"

Peak grinned, stroking his hand along the rifle. "I always say, if you can't kill for some rich, crazy sonsabitch, who *can* you kill for?"

"Winton! Peak! Look, they're making a run for the high trail!" Maydeen shouted as he and Morganfield ran over from where they stood in the cover of tree and rock. "Don't let them get up that rock wall!"

"What do you want from me?" Peak

shouted in reply, not wanting to draw Morganfield's disfavor again.

"Shoot them, gawdamn it!" shouted Maydeen.

But before raising the rifle to his shoulder, Peak looked to Morganfield for approval.

"Yes, go ahead, quickly!" said Morganfield. "Careful of the woman, though!"

"Yeah, the woman," Peak murmured to Winton with a knowing look. He turned, slipping down from the rock he sat on, using it now as a support for the big rifle. The others crowded around as he scanned through the scope and caught sight of the riders headed out across the small stretch of flatlands toward the thin trail leading up into the rock wall.

"Give him room, gentlemen," Winton said, feeling a bit cocky for having been the one to bring Peak into their fold. "Mr. Peak likes plenty of elbow room when he's getting ready to pick a man's eyes out."

Hunched behind the rifle, staring through the scope, Peak asked casually over his shoulder, "How many do you want dropped, Mr. Morganfield? One, two or the whole bunch — except the woman, of course."

"As many as you can," said Morganfield, looking through his binoculars, watching the riders draw closer to the covered trail.

"Don't try for Hollister yet. It's too risky."

"The one riding double with the woman?" Peak asked, just toying with Morganfield, knowing he'd started getting nervous seeing the riders move farther away.

"Yes, that's Hollister!" said Morganfield, excitement registering high in his voice. "Get on with it, man!" he shouted.

"Yes, sir." Peak grinned, staring through the scope. He placed the crosshairs on Elvey Parks' back. "Here's one for you," he said, sounding confident.

The big rifle kicked straight back against his shoulder. Across the valley floor, Elvey Parks seemed to melt sidelong off his saddle, with a red mist of blood rising up around him.

"Jesus, Doyle!" Dallas Spraggs shouted, hearing the big rifle. He looked back past Hollister and Kaylee, who rode double behind him, and saw Parks' body roll to a halt on the rocky ground. "Parks is down! They've killed him!"

"Keep riding," Kaylee shouted, pressing her horse hard behind him, "or they'll kill you too!"

No sooner had she spoken than Dallas Spraggs' horse rolled forward head over hooves as a bullet bored through the center of Spraggs' back, then down through the horse's neck. Beside Spraggs, Denton Fudd had to veer his horse sharply to keep from getting tangled in the flurry of hooves, blood and bodies.

This time Hollister looked back at the sound of the big Austrian rifle. Seeing Fudd sliding his horse to a halt, he shouted, "Don't stop, Denton! Keep going!"

"You keep going!" Fudd shouted. "I've had enough of this!" He spun his horse around, facing the high trail where he could barely see the shooter hunched down behind the rock. "All right, you coward! Here I am, you fatherless back-shooting son of a bitch!" He spread his arms wide, raving loud and long toward the tiny figures standing out in the open in a clearing along the hill trail. "Shoot me, you lousy, low-down bastards! You'll never get an easier target than this. . . ."

"I wonder what he's saying," Morganfield said, watching the raging gunman's expression through his binoculars.

"I don't know, but I expect he's next," said Peak, moving the crosshairs up to Fudd's exposed chest. "This will be my easiest shot yet. Thanks for your help, oldtimer," he mused through the scope at Fudd.

"Yes, by all means," said Morganfield,

suddenly offended at the sight of Denton Fudd raising both his middle fingers toward him in the binocular lens. "Kill this belligerent, thieving old scoundrel! I don't have to take this kind of abuse!"

Peak had already settled in for the shot. He'd laid the crosshairs in place, took a breath and held it. Then he eased his finger back on the trigger, squeezing it ever so gently yet steadily. But just as he made the shot, his rifle barrel snapped a bit to one side when the ranger's shot from across the valley nailed him above his left eyebrow, flipped him backward, and flung him, dead, at Morganfield's feet.

"What's *this?*" said Morganfield, hearing the ranger's big Swiss rifle resound from the distant rock wall. He looked down, astonished, at Darman Peak. "My God, this poor lad is dead!" He gazed over in the direction the shot had come from. "Who the hell . . . ?"

"Get back, Mr. M.!" shouted Maydeen, grabbing Morganfield, jerking him along toward cover. "We're being fired upon!"

Ben Winton reached down and grabbed the Austrian rifle before turning to run for cover. The second he wasted almost cost him his life. The ranger's second shot hit the Austrian rifle midstock, just beneath the barrel, and pitched it forward beside Peak's body. The gun was shattered beyond use. "Damn it to hell!" Winton shouted, giving up on the disabled firearm and running and diving into cover beside Maydeen and Morganfield.

"What's going on over there?" Morganfield demanded, as if Winton should somehow know. "Where is our long-distance rifle?"

"I don't know what's going on over there, Mr. Morganfield," Winton said, scanning across the valley without benefit of his telescope. "But you can forget about the rifle. It's out of commission. Whoever that is over there could've killed me just as easily as he did Peak."

"Then he's one of theirs," said Morganfield with finality on the matter.

"I don't think so, sir," said Winton. "I can't think of anybody in Hollister's bunch who shoots like that."

"Then who, gawdamn it?" Maydeen demanded.

Winton winced, and said, "I'm thinking it's that ranger Peak told us he'd killed."

From his position on the high jut of rock, through his long brass scope Sam scanned the far hill trail, seeing the men had cleared away and taken cover. He took a breath, relaxed, and looked down on the valley floor at Denton Fudd, who sat bewildered in his saddle, looking back and forth from Sam's side of the valley to where Morganfield's men lay pinned in place by this quick turn of events.

"I'll be damned," said Fudd, hardly believing his luck. He looked himself up and down as if to see if he'd been hit. Then he turned toward the ranger's side of the valley and called out loudly, "Give them hell up there!"

But in a second, Fudd's words were answered by a rifle shot kicking up dirt near his horse's hooves. Without hesitation, he turned his horse and raced upward to where Hollister and Kaylee stood behind the thick trunk of an oak tree. Hollister waved him forward.

"What the hell is going on?" Fudd asked, as soon as he slid off his saddle and pulled his horse into cover beside Hollister and Kaylee's. "Who was doing that shooting for us?"

"I have no idea," said Hollister. "Bounty hunters, maybe?" He gave Kaylee a look.

"Maybe," said Kaylee. "I don't know." She avoided his stare.

"That ranger we talked about is known to carry a big shooting iron of some sort," said

Hollister, keeping his eyes on her. "But then, it can't be the ranger. . . . He's dead."

"That's right, damn it," said Kaylee. "He's dead. Whoever that is up there, it's not the ranger. I'd stake my life on it."

"Keep that in mind," said Hollister. Then he turned to the horse and said to Fudd, "All right, let's go. We've got to get up into the rocks before Morganfield's men get collected."

"What about the shooter above us?" Fudd asked.

"He's not shooting at us," said Hollister. "That's good enough for me."

"He shot at me!" said Fudd. "That's why I came hightailing it up here!"

"I'm taking my chances with *him,*" said Hollister, nodding upward toward the rock wall. "I *know* what's waiting for me with Laslow Morganfield and his men."

Fudd thought about it, then looked at Kaylee, as if for some guidance. He didn't need to ask; she saw the question in his eyes. "I'm going up with Doyle," she said with commitment.

Fudd took a deep breath. "Yeah, me too," he said.

CHAPTER 21

A hundred yards from the base of the steep trail, Branard Cobb and the Morganfield men riding with him heard the thunder of hooves on the hillside. "Hold up," said Cobb, raising a hand, stopping the men behind him. "Anybody hear that? What is it?"

The men looked at one another curiously; of course they *heard* it.

"It's *horses,* damn it, Cobb," said Cage Thomas, sounding put out at such a question. He shook his head and chuckled. "You're not getting rattled on us, are you, over a few Mexicans?"

"Speaking of Mexicans!" Before Cobb could say another word, George Hope and Bennie Freely both pointed fingers down the trail and said, laughingly, "Look who's coming here! It's our ragged banditos!"

"Our *ragged-assed* banditos," Cage Thomas corrected them, drawing a long Remington pistol from the waistband of his dress suit. "All right, men, let's mop these boys up and have this settled before Morganfield comes riding down to us!"

"I'm in command here!" Cobb shouted, enraged by Cage Thomas' show of disrespect.

"Then you better start *commanding!*" Thomas shouted in reply. "Here they come!"

Around the turn in the trail, Manuel and his Mexicans had spotted Cobb and his men at the same time Cobb's men had seen them. They'd slowed their horses for only a second, then kicked the excited animals forward into a charge, wild-eyed. Their ancient guns were suddenly ablaze, spewing orange-blue sparks and black, smoky powder.

"Hot damn!" said Dannie Freely, taking a bullet graze across his upper arm. "These boys mean business!"

A shot nipped Cobb's earlobe and left a trickle of blood running warm down the side of his throat. "Kill them, gawdamn it," he shouted, touching his fingertips to his bleeding ear, "before they kill us!" He kicked his horse forward to meet the attack.

On the thin, steep trail, Cobb and his men met the charging Mexicans head-on, clashing horse to horse, man to man, as if inspired by or reenacting some ancient battle. A Mexican's horse reared and came down across the back of George Hope's mount, causing Hope to leap from his saddle just in time to keep from being crushed to death by the animal.

Hitting the ground, Hope raised his Colt and fired straight up through the rider's chin as the rider triggered his flintlock pistol down at him. Before the rider fell dead to the ground, Hope had the horse by its reins, ready to swing up onto the saddle. But before he could step up, the swishing sound of a machete sliced through the air and cleaved his big head from atop his broad shoulders.

Hope's severed head rolled with a frozen expression of horror into the flurry of dust, hooves and boots. His headless body remained standing for a moment, quaking violently, then sank to the ground. Blood flew.

Dannie Freely leaped from his mount onto the back of a Mexican who had fired his flintlock at his brother, Bennie, and missed. Dannie yanked the man's head sideways by his long black hair, shoved the barrel of his Colt into his ear and fired. Then he flung the man from the saddle and kept his horse. Bennie Freely, who had lost his horse, grabbed Dannie's abandoned mount, leaped into the saddle and raced back into the melee.

Manuel fought up close, his reins between his teeth, both big Walker Colts exploding in his hands, until the one in his left emptied. He let his prized Colt fall from his hand, as if knowing that after this day he never again would have use for it. Bleeding from a bullet graze across his forehead, he grabbed the reins from his teeth and charged at Cobb, shrieking like a wounded mountain leopard.

Cobb saw Manuel coming and put two bullets into his chest even as the blade of a machete chopped deep into Cobb's shoulder and stayed there. The wielder of the machete fell in a spray of blood and brain matter when Cage Thomas pulled the trigger on his Remington, less than a foot away.

A musket ball clipped Clifford Devoe's shoulder. He fell from his saddle and landed flat on his already sore and swollen face. "Oh, Jesus!" he moaned. Instead of rising and continuing the fight, he crawled off the trail and into the shelter of some low-growing vines and spiky bushes. Once hidden, he covered his throbbing nose and cheeks with both hands, hearing the raging gunfire and the screams and curses of dying men.

"I'm not going back," Devoe vowed to himself, sobbing, his voice muted by his protesting hands. He rolled back and forth in pain, tears streaming down his swollen cheeks. When he did remove his hands and open his eyes, he stared up wide-eyed in surprise at the figure standing over him, with the tip of a rifle barrel only an inch from his purplish swollen nose.

"Good God!" Devoe moaned softly in defeat. "Who the hell are you?"

"I'm the man who's going to kill you if you don't keep your mouth shut," a voice said quietly.

Devoe ventured a look back and forth, catching sight of a single horse's hooves standing nearby. "Keep my mouth shut!" said Devoe, growing emboldened by the fact that this must be one person traveling alone. "Do you know who I'm riding with?" he asked in a little louder tone of voice.

"That does it," said the voice.

"Wait! No!" Devoe pleaded, seeing the rifle turn end over end in the gloved hands until the rifle butt rose two feet from his face. "Please, no! Not in the —"

Devoe's words stopped abruptly as the rifle butt thumped soundly on his already battered jaw.

On the trail, in spite of the Mexicans having put up a fierce fight, Cobb and his men had finally turned the attacking banditos and sent them fleeing off into the trees and rocks, leaving their horses and their dead and dying behind. Turning back and forth with his cocked pistol pointed, searching for any remaining Mexicans, Cobb had seen the rise and fall of the rifle stock through the brush and fired quickly.

"Got one!" Cobb said, leaning a bit to one side, the machete blade still sunk into his shoulder. "Bennie, Dannie . . . one of yas go finish him off."

Bennie Freely finished reloading his big Colt, snapped it shut and trotted off into the brush, saying, "I've got him, Cobb! Get the blade out of your shoulder."

"Hell," said Cobb, to no one in particular, "I wish I could get it out. It's stuck in the joint." He touched a careful hand to the machete handle and grimaced in pain.

Cage Thomas walked along beside Cobb toward the wounded Mexican leader who lay clutching both hands to his shattered chest. "Well, well, look who's laying here dying," said Cobb, favoring his left side, holding his left arm tight against himself beneath the protruding machete. He reached out with the toe of his boot and kicked the remaining battered Walker Colt away from Manuel's hand.

At Manuel's side lay a grass-woven bag with its canvas strap looped over his shoulder. The packet of counterfeit bills lay partly spilled from the bag. Cage Thomas reached down, picked up the bills and handed them to Cobb, who took them in his debilitated left hand and smiled, shaking his head. Blood ran from his nipped earlobe. "How good is this money to you now, pecker head?" he asked the dying young Mexican.

"Todo el dinero . . . es sin valor," Manuel gasped in a labored tone.

"What did he say?" Cobb asked Thomas as he fanned the counterfeit money in his left hand.

Cage Thomas shrugged. "Something like 'All money is worthless'?"

"Ah, now, ain't that sad?" said Cobb, with a feigned look of sympathy on his face. "I recall hearing you say, 'No money is worthless to men with blood in their veins.' "

Manuel shook his head slowly and repeated in a fading voice, *"Todo el dinero es sin valor."*

"Yeah, well, each to his own opinion," said Cobb. He let the bills flutter down from his hand onto Manuel's bloody chest. "Spend it in hell, *mi amigo*," he said quietly. He held his pistol down at arm's length and shot him one time, straight through his forehead.

Cage Thomas chuckled and said, "That was cold, Cobb. He was dying anyway."

"So what? We're all dying," said Cobb, "if you want to look at it that way."

"Cobb, there's some sumbitch over here," said Bennie Freely. "I don't know what to do with him."

"I told you to kill the Mexican I hit over there," said Cobb. "Can't you do that?"

"Yeah, I could, except this ain't no Mexican," said Bennie.

"Lead him out here, then," said Cobb. "Let's take a look at him."

"Can't," said Bennie. "He's knocked cold by a bullet across the back of his head. Looks like he busted old Devoe a good one before you shot him though. In my whole life I never saw a nose as flat as poor ole Clifford's."

"Jesus!" said Cobb to Thomas, letting his Colt hang in his hand. "Let's go see who he's got in there."

Hollister counted himself, Kaylee and Fudd lucky when they'd ridden almost sixty yards up the trail toward the wall of rock without a shot fired at them from either direction.

342

"I don't trust it," said Fudd, looking back across the valley, then up high on the rock wall in front of them. "Whoever that was, why the hell would he be doing us a favor?"

"I don't know, Denton," said Hollister, "but there's times you have to make your move whether you trust a person or not. Whoever that is, if he turns out *wrong,* he's dead. Is there any need in me telling you that?"

Fudd's consternation settled a little; he let out a breath and even offered a slight smile. "Hell, no, it goes without saying we'll kill him. I reckon I am worrying too much."

"Well, stop," said Kaylee. She turned the horse she rode double on with Hollister and nudged it upward on the steep, narrow path. "We'll be leading these animals on foot before long," she said. "We can't stop for anything until we get clear of this hill and onto some flatland."

Hollister and Fudd looked at one another. "Don't forget, Kaylee, anybody else coming this way has to get off and lead their horses too."

"Does that mean we should dally around and let them get closer to us?" Kaylee asked, her tone turning a bit prickly. Owing to Hollister's broken leg, she slid down off the saddle and said, "Here, you need this horse more than I do. Use it as far as you can."

"Thanks," Hollister said, a bit ashamed for having to accept special treatment.

Neither Hollister nor Fudd offered any further conversation as the two horses labored their way upward, the trail having turned to a rocky path, now with hardly a noticeable bare spot on the rocky ground.

"Time to walk," Hollister said, stopping the tired horse and slipping down carefully from the saddle.

There were no longer hoofprints to follow, only a fresh scrape here and there that a seasoned tracker might find upon close observation. "Hell, I reckon that's it for me too," said Fudd, dropping from his saddle and looking back down and across the valley floor. "I hate walking, even on soft, level ground. We'll be lucky if these horses ain't walking dead by the time we reach a flat trail."

"Whoever our shooter is," said Hollister, "maybe we can kill him and take his horse."

"Now you're starting to make some sense," said Fudd, passing both Hollister and Kaylee and taking the lead, pulling his horse along briskly.

Hollister trudged upward, limping badly, using the walking stick. Starting to breathe hard, he asked Kaylee between breaths, "Do you ever stop and remind yourself that you could be taking it easy somewhere. . . ."

"Keep quiet. Save your breath," Kaylee demanded, looking around and seeing he'd begun to fall farther back behind her.

"I'm all right," said Hollister. "You don't have to worry about me!"

"Like hell I don't," said Kaylee. She slowed down and let him get close enough for her to offer her arm around him. "Come on, lean on me a little."

"Gawdamn it, I hate this," said Hollister, but he let her slip her arm around him and help him along for the next few yards before stopping on a small, flat clearing. Finding a rock large enough to lean on and take all the weight off of his leg, Hollister said, "I bet if you two went on and left me here with a rifle and plenty of ammunition, I could hold these birds off for a week if I had to."

"Don't even say it, Doyle," said Kaylee. "We're all three going to make it. Just keep reminding yourself of all the money I've got in that saddlebag and of the high stepping we're going to do with it."

Hollister didn't answer. He looked over at the ground on the other side of the rock he stood leaning against and let out a breath. "Damn it to hell," he said. His hand went

345

to the butt of his Colt but stopped there, seeing he didn't have a chance.

The ranger stepped out from behind a taller rock, his Colt pointed and cocked. "All right, this is as far as you're going. Ease the guns up from your holsters with two fingers and let them fall."

Kaylee raised her hands chest high, but Sam could see her thinking about making a move. "Don't think because you're a woman I won't shoot," he said. "I know firsthand what you're capable of doing."

Kaylee's expression changed and she eased her hands higher. "All right, you got us, Ranger. Now what?"

"Ranger?" said Hollister. *"Ranger?"* The veins in his forehead stood out. "Is this the ranger you killed, Kaylee? Is this Ranger Burrack?"

"Settle down, Hollister," Sam cautioned him. "Lean over against that rock. You're down to one good leg. Don't get yourself a bullet in it."

"I *thought* he was dead, damn it!" Kaylee shouted. "I did my part. Albright was supposed to finish him off with a lethal dose of poison! I can't help it if he chickened out on me!"

"Both of you settle down," Sam said firmly, keeping an eye on Fudd as he talked to Kaylee and Hollister. "I'm alive and I plan on staying that way. Now where's the money?" He looked straight at Kaylee.

"I don't have it," she said. "I lost it."

"It's in her saddlebags, Ranger," said Fudd, finally speaking.

Sam saw a setup coming from Fudd, but he stepped over to the saddlebags anyway, loosened the straps and flipped the cover back from them. Keeping his right hand holding the Colt, he reached in with his left, searched around and came up with a handful of loose bills. "I suppose the rest is in the other side," he said almost to himself. He dropped the flap, unhitched the bags from behind the saddle and hefted them over and held them by his side.

"That's real money," Fudd said.

"I know," said the ranger. "I've seen enough counterfeit lately that I know the difference. Kaylee here gave me an education on money and its value."

Fudd chuckled. "That's funny." Then he turned serious and said, "That's all yours you know, Ranger. Just turn and walk away. . . . Keep it all."

"And fight with Morganfield's men all the way across Mexico, the way you were going to have to do?"

"If this was all about Morganfield's

money, he would have turned his men back long before now, Ranger," said Fudd. He nodded toward Kaylee. "That's Morganfield's daughter. That's who he's after now."

Sam looked at Kaylee. "It's true," Kaylee said. "It's me he's after — my dear old dad."

Sam caught the bitter sarcasm in her voice and decided not even to ask what had happened between them to bring this on. At the bottom of all the trouble, he realized he'd been involved in some dark family matter all along.

"So I take the money and slip away while Morganfield and his men go after you?"

"Think about it, Ranger," Fudd said, wearing a crafty smile. "How many chances will a man like you get to grab on to that kind of money in your life? It's Morganfield money! I smell the sweetness of it all the way over here."

Sam nodded with no expression. "I'm still waiting to hear some guns hit the ground. I'm starting to think you people *want* me to shoot you."

Hollister reached down, raised his Colt with two fingers and started to let it fall. But recognizing it as his own, Sam said, "Maybe you'd better just hand that to me." He stepped in and took the Colt instead of letting Hollister drop it to the ground. As he shoved the Colt into his waist until he could find time to check it, he said to Kaylee, "Now it's your turn."

Kaylee sighed and dropped her .36 caliber at her feet. While she did so, Sam noticed that Denton Fudd made no effort to drop his gun.

"What about you?" Sam asked Fudd bluntly. "I see what's crossing your mind."

"Yeah, well, I've been running free too long to get used to a prison cell." He took a step to one side and spread his feet shoulder width apart.

"Denton, don't be a fool!" said Kaylee. "The chase is over. Let it go. I know the best attorneys east and west of the Mississippi. Let them handle this."

Fudd shook his head. "Attorneys? No, thanks. That's not my style, Kaylee. I'm an old-timer. I've lived hard — I'll die the same way."

"You don't have to die," Sam said, but he understood what the old outlaw meant.

"Shut up, Ranger. Who said I'm going to?" said Fudd. His hand snatched his Colt and streaked up.

The ranger's shot exploded sudden and straight. Fudd flew backward with a bullet through his heart. His right knee cocked upward for a moment, then turned limp and fell sideways onto the dirt. Sam turned quickly toward Hollister and Kaylee, covering them in case they tried anything.

The two stood with their hands raised chest high, staring at Fudd. Sam stepped forward quietly and pulled handcuffs from behind his gun belt, knowing the shot had been heard all the way across Trouble Creek.

CHAPTER 22

The ranger and Hollister piled rocks on Denton Fudd's body, covering it where it lay. Kaylee stood silently beside the horses, her hands cuffed in front of her. When the ranger and Hollister completed their task, Sam dusted his gloved hands together and asked Hollister and Kaylee, "Do either of you want to say some words before we leave?"

Hollister nodded, giving a last glance at the mound of rocks. "So long, Fudd," he said, raising his cuffed hands and touching his fingertips to his hat brim. "It didn't take much rock to cover you."

Kaylee gave both Hollister and the ranger a look of mild contempt and turned away.

"Which way, Ranger?" Hollister asked.

"Straight up out of this valley," said Sam. He lifted the bag of bank money from Kaylee's saddle horn and laid it atop his bedroll behind Black Pot's saddle.

351

"They're going to hound us every step of the way, you know," Hollister said to the ranger.

"Let them," Sam replied, "I've been hounded before. So have you." He began tying the money bag in place with strips of rawhide. But he abandoned his task and turned instinctively when three shots from a repeating rifle exploded one after another from across the valley floor.

"See? They're starting already!" said Hollister, ducking to the side, with Kaylee doing the same.

Realizing they were well out of the rifle's range, Sam turned back to Black Pot and finished tying the bag down quickly. "Those shots were only meant to get our attention."

"You're right. . . . Look at this, Ranger." Hollister said, straining his vision against the sun's glare across the valley floor. "Do you know who this is?"

Sam looked first with his naked eye and saw three figures running for cover, leaving a single hatless figure standing along the creek bank just west of the dusty street. "Not yet I don't . . . but we'll find out," Sam said idly. He reached down inside his saddlebags, took out a collapsed field lens, stretched it out and raised it to his eye. After a moment, he let out a breath, lowered the lens from his eye and said to himself in a tired voice, "Ed Thornis, what in the world are you doing down there?"

Kaylee and Hollister looked at one another. "Ed Thornis, the *blacksmith?*" Kaylee asked in disbelief.

"Yep," said Sam. "He started tracking you and the banker right after you left Olsen together." Sam paused, then said to Kaylee, "You remember Albright the banker, don't you?"

"Yes, I remember him," said Kaylee, giving Hollister another look, this one closely guarded. "He cut out on me right after we left Olsen," she lied. "I don't know what became of him."

"I know," said Sam. "The buzzards ate his belly. I found his body alongside the trail, in the middle of hoofprints you people left behind." Scanning the valley floor again, Sam spotted a rider coming across a shallow spot, a white handkerchief tied to the end of a raised stick he carried in his hand.

"Whoa, hold on," said Hollister. "Don't try hanging that on me. I didn't kill that banker." He glanced at Kaylee, then looked away.

"I'm sure Kaylee's *attorney* will prove who killed the banker," said Sam, seeming uninterested, more concerned with Ed

Thornis, who stood at the edge of Trouble Creek with his hands tied behind his back. He took one more look at the single rider carrying the flag of truce. "I suspect your father is getting ready to make me an offer most any minute," he said to Kaylee. He studied her eyes to see what he could read from them. "Do you figure he's going to want to trade Thornis for you?"

"How would I know?" said Kaylee, irritated with Sam for asking. "If that's his deal, you'd be wise to take it. My dear father doesn't like getting turned down by *anyone*."

Sam heard the tight bitterness in the young woman's voice. But he had no time to figure out what animosity existed between her and her father. "There's only one deal," he said. "Here it is. I'm taking you and the money back to Olsen. I figure Hollister here was in on your bank scheme all along, so I'm taking him too. If a judge finds either one or both of you involved in the murder of Marvin Albright, most likely you'll hang for it."

"My father's money will keep me from hanging, Ranger," said Kaylee. "He may be a no-good son of a bitch, but he won't let me hang."

Sam looked at Hollister. "Then you better

have a rich father yourself, because the only place a good attorney can see to lay the blame away from her is on you. There's something for you to think about all the way back to Olsen."

"Kaylee . . . ?" said Hollister, giving her a dark, dubious look. "He's right. That is exactly what an attorney will do — free you and leave me to swing."

"Don't talk foolish, Doyle," said Kaylee. "I promise you my father will get us both off the hook."

"She's his daughter," Sam said. "What does that make you to him?" Giving Hollister a moment to think about it, Sam looked away and watched the rider draw closer, his white handkerchief fluttering on a hot breeze.

When the rider, Ben Winton, finally made it up the steep trail and stopped five yards away, he called out to the ranger, "The rifleman you killed happened to be a good friend of mine. I'm the one who got him his job and lent him the long-distance rifle."

"You mean the rifle he killed my prisoners with . . . the one he tried to kill me with? I hope you didn't come up here looking for an apology."

Winton didn't answer. "Anyway," he said, after a tense pause, "you saw your friend Ed

Thornis standing down there. You know what we'll do to him. Mr. Morganfield proposes that if you want to see him alive again, you send these two and the bank money down in exchange for him." He nodded toward Hollister and Kaylee as he spoke.

"You mean the bank money that Ed Thornis rode all this way to recover?" Sam said wryly.

"It's Morganfield's money." Winton shrugged. "But look at it however it suits you, Ranger," he said. "The fact is, your friend is going to die. So will you before it's over, if you don't take Mr. Morganfield's offer and send them down."

"Listen close," said Sam. "Ed Thornis is not a friend of mine. He's one more citizen I'm sworn to protect. Make certain that you, Mr. Morganfield and the others know what lines you'll be crossing, harming that innocent man, because I won't bow to his wishes."

"What *lines?*" said Winton. "Hell, Ranger, this is Mexico. We're not worried about the law!"

"The law is not what I'm talking about, mister," said Sam. "The lines you'll be crossing are with *me.*" He stared hard at Winton.

The hired gunman felt the intensity of the ranger's words and presence and relented, saying, "Hey, I'm just the messenger here."

Sam continued to stare hard at him as if deciding whether or not to shoot him on the spot. Ben Winton grew more and more uncomfortable with each passing second of silence. "So . . . your answer is *no?*" he finally asked meekly.

"What was that explosion I heard up along the hill trail?" Sam asked, as if indifferent to Morganfield's offer for an exchange, and even less interested in answering Winton's question.

"What you *heard* explode was a French *hand grenade,*" he said. "It's something Mr. Morganfield and his munitions companies have been developing." His confidence began to come back to him. He offered a thin, superior smile. "You might want to think about that while you consider Mr. Morganfield's offer."

"Ride on back," said Sam. "Tell Morganfield he'll have my answer within an hour. Tell him meanwhile, if anybody lays a hand on Thornis to try to influence me, I'll start doing to all of you what I did to your sharpshooting friend. Are we clear on that?"

"We're clear," said Winton, with a breath of relief. He stepped his horse back and turned it on the narrow trail.

The ranger looked back and forth, keeping an eye on Hollister and Kaylee as he watched Winton ride down and kick his horse up into a trot across the valley floor.

"So once again my father gets what he wants," Kaylee said with a thin, critical smile.

"I didn't say I would take his offer," Sam replied, still watching Winton.

"Oh, but you will, once you think it over," said Kaylee. "And who can really blame you?" She nodded toward Trouble Creek. "He's got enough trained apes to sic on you. . . . He'll kill that poor, stupid blacksmith."

"The only thing stupid about Ed Thornis is that he fell for you," said the ranger. His gaze went from Kaylee to Hollister. "Or was that what you meant by it?"

Hollister looked down at his cuffed hands and stood in silence. "But you're right about the trained apes — your father has plenty of them," said the ranger, "not to mention the hand grenades. I suppose he must've found a way to stabilize them. They used to go off at the slightest jar." He watched Kaylee's eyes for a response. But he found nothing helpful there.

She only shrugged. "I know nothing about hand grenades, or any of his munitions business, except that he seems to own almost the *entire* industry." She gave him a bitter grin. "It's almost a sure bet that one of his companies manufactured the bullets you have in your gun."

"I loaded these myself," Sam replied.

"Oh," said Kaylee, "then you must have done so using Morganfield powder, caps and brass."

"Have it your way," Sam said. He turned, walked over to where Black Pot and the other two horses stood at rest, and seated himself on the ground, in the thin shade of a short scrub juniper.

For the next twenty minutes, he sat staring down and out across the valley floor, watching Ben Winton grown smaller and smaller and eventually disappear into the row of tiny adobe buildings on the far side of Trouble Creek. Then Sam took his Colt — the one Kaylee had given Hollister — from his waist. Sam looked it over, checked it and finally, when even the dust from Winton's horse's hooves had drifted off and settled, Sam stood up, switched the Colt to his holster and shoved the other gun into his waist. Satisfied to have his Colt back where it belonged, he said to Kaylee and Hollister, who sat ten feet away in the shade of a land-stuck boulder, "All right, let's go.

We've kept Mr. Morganfield waiting long enough."

"See?" Kaylee said to Hollister. "My father always finds a way to get what he wants. Even the ranger can't resist him."

Hollister managed a nervous smile. "I'll be damned — you were right. . . . But where does this put me?"

"I told you my father won't lay a hand on you if I tell him not to. He and I hate one another, but we both know the rules of our sick little game." She gave Sam a look, and said to him as if he were her private carriage driver, "Ranger, take my friend and me to Trouble Creek."

CHAPTER 23

"Here they come, Mr. M!" Bo Maydeen said, calling out into the open doorway of the cantina. "I have to say, I'm damned impressed! This ranger is not known for turning a prisoner loose to anybody!"

"Indeed . . ." Morganfield said smugly, rising from a battered oak table. "He's nothing but a small man with a small job, which, as I understand, he tends to take too seriously." He chuckled, stuck his cigar into his mouth and, with his men following, stepped forward out of the small cantina onto the dirt street.

Looking across Trouble Creek at the three riders appearing up out of the sand and brush, Winton said, "I sure didn't think he'd do it."

"Well, he did," said Maydeen, grinning. "Bring the blacksmith out here," he called over his shoulder to Cage Thomas and the Freely brothers, who had taken Thornis out of the sun for a few minutes while they awaited the ranger's decision.

"Come on, you lucky sonsabitch," Thomas said to Ed Thornis, pulling him to his feet. "I was hoping to tan your scrotum for a tobacco pouch."

"I had claim on your ears," Bennie Freely laughed, giving Thornis a shove. "Brother Dannie was going to dry your nuts and wear them on a watch fob."

"Hey, watch your mouth. I wasn't about to *handle* his nuts!" Dannie protested, walking beside the battered blacksmith.

"It doesn't matter now," said Cage Thomas. "The ranger is coming in to make the exchange."

"He — he is?" Thornis asked. Stepping in alongside the Freely brothers, Clifford Devoe said in a pained voice, "I hope this goes wrong, blacksmith, so I can kill you real slow."

"Get out of here, you purple-faced wretch!" Thomas said, shoving Devoe away. "You're an embarrassment!"

In the middle of the street, Morganfield looked Thornis up and down and said to Garrity and Stokes, "Get this fellow a hat and some cool water. We don't want to fry him. After all, we are *not* savages." He smiled, puffing his cigar.

On the other side of Trouble Creek, Sam watched Morganfield and his men gather in the street with Ed Thornis in their midst. He saw the black manservant come up to Thornis with a pith helmet and place it atop his head. When Stokes stepped away, Sam saw the wiry little Irishman, Garrity, raise a dipper of water to Thornis' parched, swollen lips.

Upon turning and seeing the ranger staring at them even from thirty yards away, the two backed away, turned and trotted to where their horses stood off to one side, away from the crowded hitch rail. Sam took a good look at the large army saddlebags behind the saddles.

"Well, well, Ranger!" Morganfield called out, waving the three of them in with a thick hand. "Come on in. We are both honest men. No harm will come to you. We each have something the other wants. Let's not be shy." He gave a strong, superior grin. "I've heard many commendable things about you, sir!"

"I'm not here to socialize, Morganfield," Sam called out. "I've brought down the money and these two. Let's make our swap and get done with it."

"Gets right to the point, doesn't he?" Morganfield said sidelong to Bo Maydeen, with a slight chuckle.

"Mr. M, don't spend any more time at this than you have to," said Maydeen. "This Burrack is a lawman to the bone and marrow. Make the swap and get rid of him."

Morganfield gave him a stern look. "I decide how much time we'll spend on this ranger. You be prepared to do what needs to be done when I say so." He waved a hand. "Now get these men spread out! I want to see this little place covered with guns from every direction!"

"Yes, sir," said Maydeen, taking a step aside, being clearly reminded of his place. "Thomas, Dannie and Bennie, Devoe — all four of yas, take position," he said, keeping his voice down. Turning to Branard Cobb, whose shoulder had been put into a sling after Stokes removed the machete blade from it, Maydeen said, "Cobb, stay put here with me."

"I can *handle* a gun!" Cobb whispered, sounding put out with Maydeen. "Don't make it sound like I can't."

"I know you can, gawdamn it!" said Maydeen. "That's why I want you here beside us."

"Turn Ed Thornis loose and send him walking to me," Sam called out.

"Not so fast, Ranger," Morganfield said.

"First you send my daughter and Hollister in *my* direction. When I see that my daughter isn't going to try to run away, I'll send your friend to you."

"Hell of a relationship, isn't it, Father?" Kaylee called out. "Even as you try saving me from this lawman, you have to worry about me bolting away." She gave a short, sharp little laugh and looked at the curious expression on Sam's face. "Oh, quit looking so surprised, Ranger. You've already seen how badly we hate one another."

"Hello to you too, my darling Kay," said Morganfield in a mock tone of sweetness. "I hoped you would appreciate me doing this for you, even after you and your little outlaw friends *robbed* me."

"This will change nothing between us, Father," said Kaylee. "What you've done to me can never be undone, only covered over! Would you like me to tell everyone here about it?"

"Stop, Kay, please!" Morganfield shouted. His demeanor suddenly changed. He turned to Maydeen and Cobb. "Cut the blacksmith loose — get him out of here. Let us put an end to this whole ugly mess."

Seeing Thornis walk toward the creek, rubbing his wrists after Maydeen cut a length from them, Sam backed Black Pot a step behind Hollister and Kaylee and said, "All right, move across the creek. I'm right behind you." To Hollister he said, "Are you sure you want to ride in there with Morganfield and his men? It looks to me like this daughter and father are still at war."

"Stop it, Ranger," Kaylee said firmly. "I'll handle my father. Doyle. You have my word on it."

Nudging his horse forward into the shallow creek, Hollister said, "I had your word this ranger was laying dead back in Olsen."

Kaylee smoldered in anger, but she kept quiet.

Sam watched the interaction closely and said, "On the other side of the creek, stop when I tell you to. You'll both get down and give Thornis your reins. Then start walking forward."

"What will we do for horses?" Hollister asked. "What about these cuffs?"

"I'll take my cuffs back when we get in closer," said Sam. "As far as horses, that's not my concern," he added flatly.

"My father always travels with no less than a full railcar of horses," Kaylee reassured him. They rode on quietly and stopped on the other side of Trouble Creek. When Thornis stopped no more than ten feet ahead of them, he said to Sam across bruised and swollen lips, "Ranger, I sure am glad to see you."

"Can you ride?" Sam asked right away.

"I can," Thornis replied.

"Then climb up one of these horses and lead the other," Sam instructed. "Get away from Trouble Creek and get up past that hill. Keep going."

"What about you?" Thornis asked, watching Hollister and Kaylee step down from their mounts and hand him their reins.

"Don't worry about me," said Sam. He watched Thornis seat himself on Fudd's horse, with the other's reins wrapped loosely around his hand. "Here." Sam pulled the spare Colt from his belt and pitched it to him, realizing that Morganfield must be getting anxious seeing firearms change hands. "Don't try any heroics, blacksmith," Sam warned him. "Just get out of here as fast as you can."

"But, Ranger —" Thornis started to say.

"I mean *now,*" Sam demanded, giving him a harsh stare.

"What about my money?" Morganfield called out, sounding impatient. Thornis turned the horse and put his bootheels to it.

Sam stalled his answer for a long second, until he saw Thornis' horse and the spare horse splashing quickly across the shallows. "It's coming," said Sam, raising the bag of money from his saddle horn, nudging Black Pot along behind Hollister and Kaylee. When they had gone a few steps, he gave a guarded glance back over his shoulder, and breathed a bit easier when he saw the splashing stop and the water resume its swift but easy flow as Thornis rode up out of Trouble Creek.

Sam brought Black Pot to a halt and said to Hollister and Kaylee, "Stop here." He slid down from his saddle sixty feet from where Morganfield, Cobb and Maydeen stood abreast in the dirt street.

Morganfield took a step forward, putting himself two feet closer than his hired gunmen. "You have a commendable way of doing things, Ranger," he called out, seeing Sam step down, lift the bag of money and slap the Appaloosa stallion on the rump to send him to safety.

Sam didn't reply. Instead he said to Hollister and Kaylee, "All right, closer now, real easy like."

He continued forward slowly behind Kaylee and Hollister, the bag of money hanging in his left hand, his right hand going to his big Colt and easing up and cocking it in such a natural manner that neither the gunmen nor Morganfield seemed to question. Finally, when he saw Morganfield take a step backward to the shelter of his hired gunmen, Sam brought his prisoners to a halt, saying quietly, "This is close enough."

A tense silence passed on the drift of a hot breeze. Maydeen and Cobb both stood opening and closing their gun hands almost in unison. Maydeen nodded at the cocked Colt in the ranger's hand and whispered sidelong past Morganfield to Cobb, "How the hell did he manage to do *that?*"

Cobb didn't attempt an answer.

"Here's everything on my end of the deal," Sam called out. Seeing Morganfield take that step back had shown Sam just how close trouble could get to Morganfield before the man's personal courage began to run thin. Sam dropped the bag to the dirt at his side and took out the key to his handcuffs.

But before he could unlock the cuffs from either of the two, Morganfield called out, "Huh-uh, Ranger. First *my money.*"

"Always the *rich prick,* eh, *Father?*" Kaylee called out in a dark, critical tone, as if doing so stemmed from a lifelong habit.

Sam had also seen something else as Morganfield stepped back. He'd seen a heavy bulge in his right coat pocket, about the size

Sam would expect a hand grenade to be.

"Stay out of this, darling Kay," said Morganfield. "You've done your *usual* part — you *caused* all the trouble." Behind Morganfield, Maydeen and Cobb, the other four men made no attempt to hide themselves. They stood confidently along the fronts of crumbling adobes, their rifles loosely in hand or cradled in arm. In the street between the riflemen stood Garrity's and Stokes' horses, with their bulging army saddlebags.

Sam cut into the Morganfields' bickering by reaching down, picking the bag up by its bottom and shaking it enough to cause the bound stacks of money to spill into the dirt. "Here's your money, Morganfield. Come count it if it suits you."

"Oh, it's not the amount that concerns me, but rather its *authenticity.*" He stepped forward, with Maydeen and Cobb flanking him, giving Kaylee a dark grin and a darker stare.

"You see, much to my embarrassment, my dear daughter managed to corrupt one of my printer's devils into running off a couple of million in counterfeit bills before she disappeared last year."

"I don't want to hear it," Sam said, seeing Morganfield's mood turning uglier as he spoke about his and his daughter's relationship. "Here's the money. Here's your daughter." He stepped over and kicked a stack of money to Morganfield for him to examine.

Morganfield forced his dark stare away from Kaylee and looked to Maydeen as the gunman picked up the stack of bills and handed it to him.

After a close once-over look, Morganfield said, "Yes, this is the real thing." He looked at Sam. "Will you please release my daughter?"

Without reply, Sam stepped over and unlocked the cuffs on Kaylee with his left hand, his right hand still holding his Colt poised, his gaze moving calm and cold between Cobb and Maydeen.

Kaylee stepped off to the side, rubbing her freed wrists.

"Tell me, Ranger," said Morganfield. "Are you as worn-out from dealing with these two as I am?" He stared hard with the same dark grin at Doyle Hollister. But now the expression had turned menacing.

Instead of answering Morganfield, Sam asked Hollister quietly as he reached out to uncuff him, "Are you sure you want me to leave you here?"

Hollister didn't answer. Instead he stared at Kaylee, as if relying heavily on her.

Sam stuck the key into the cuff, one wrist, then the other, and set Hollister free. "Well, Ranger," said Morganfield, "your blacksmith friend has fled Trouble Creek. I have my precious daughter back. We can now go our separate ways." He slowly raised a thick hand. "As they say down here, adios, Ranger."

Sam didn't move. Instead he shook his head and raised his Colt slowly until it pointed straight at Morganfield's middle coat button in the center of his thick chest. "I'm not buying this for a minute, Morganfield," he said. Then to Hollister, who stood rubbing his chafed wrists, Sam shouted, "Get out of here, Hollister!"

"What?" Hollister looked confused, back and forth between Kaylee and the ranger.

"He's not intending for you or me to leave Trouble Creek alive," Sam said. "This is the way they *always* end their crazy game — no outside players leave alive! Now get across that creek!"

"Jesus!" Hollister shouted. But looking into Kaylee's eyes, he saw that the ranger spoke the truth. Hollister turned and ran toward Trouble Creek.

"You son of a bitch!" Kaylee said to Sam.

"But a perceptive son of a bitch all the same," said Morganfield, backing away from

Sam, his hand going down into his coat pocket for the hand grenade. "Kill him, men! Kill them both!" he shouted. He raised his free hand in the air, giving a signal to the riflemen behind him.

Sam fired. His shot sent Morganfield staggering backward a step as Cobb and Maydeen both went for their guns. But Morganfield did not fall. He turned, catching his balance, and ran toward the horses as he jerked the hand grenade from his coat pocket, pulled the iron stem that ran through it and heaved it hard over his shoulder toward the ranger.

"Doyle, wait!" Kaylee shrieked, as if all this had been some sort of bad dream from which she'd just awakened.

Sam saw her run toward Hollister in a blaze of rifle fire as the freed outlaw splashed across the creek. But even as the sizzling hand grenade rolled over near his feet, Sam's attention had to go to Bo Maydeen, whose pistol was coming up. His second shot nailed Maydeen in the center of his chest as well.

But Maydeen didn't turn and run the way Morganfield had. Instead Maydeen flew backward in a spray of blood, as Sam turned instantly, jumped forward, grabbed the hand grenade and threw it with all his might in a high arc toward Morganfield. *Bulletproof vest* . . . Sam told himself, regarding Morganfield not falling from the gunshot at such close range.

Cobb, rattled at the sight of Maydeen going down so quickly, sent a shot slicing the air past the ranger's ear. But then he fell as Sam's third shot hit only an inch higher than the shots that had hit Morganfield and Maydeen.

"Kill them!" shouted Morganfield, still running, not seeing the high, tumbling hand grenade sailing above him, then past, leaving a thin trail of sparks and smoke.

"Oh, shit!" said Stokes. He and Garrity bolted quickly away from the horses as Morganfield came sliding up to them for more grenades. The two dived through the open window of an abandoned adobe building and lay with their arms covering their heads.

On the street, Sam dropped to the ground quickly. Yet even as he did so, he looked out across Trouble Creek and saw Kaylee and Hollister fall with a splash into the water, riddled by a hail of rifle fire.

Sam threw his forearms over his head just as the descending hand grenade thudded into the dirt in front of Laslow Morganfield. But upon hearing the initial explosion, Sam only braced harder and felt the ground beneath him slam upward against his chest as the two army saddlebags full of grenades exploded at once.

For a moment Sam lay listening to chunks of adobe, men and animals rain down around him on the dirt street. When the sound dissipated, he pulled his bandanna up over his nose and stood up in a thick cloud of dust, his Colt still in hand. He walked toward the creek, fanning dust back and forth with the faded black sombrero until he reached the water's edge, where the dust lay thinner and had already begun settling.

"There you are," he said to himself in a relieved tone, looking out across the creek, past the bodies of Kaylee and Hollister, to where Black Pot stood looking back at him from the other side. The big stallion twitched his ears and bobbed his head as if thinking the same thing. Sam made a hand sign and the stallion came trotting out into the shallows.

"Ranger! Are you all right?" shouted Ed Thornis, riding quickly back into sight, following Black Pot out into Trouble Creek.

Sam looked down and shook his head and said to himself as he waded forward in water only ankle deep, "What if I wasn't, Thornis?"

Yet Sam smiled patiently as he walked forward and met Black Pot, followed by Thornis at the spot where Kaylee and Hollister lay dead in the water. "I thought I told you to keep riding, blacksmith," Sam said.

"I couldn't do it, Ranger," said Ed. "You saved my life. How could I ride away and not know if you was dead or alive after that explosion?"

Sam gave him a tired smile, took Black Pot's dangling reins and looked down at the two bodies in the water, blood running from them in long, spreading streams along on the shallow water.

"Since you're back, you can help me do some burying," said Sam.

"What 'bout those three?" Thornis asked, gesturing toward Clifford Devoe, who stumbled around in the dirt street, ragged and bloody with his hands pressed to his ears. Through the dust, Garrity and Stokes ran forward, shoved most of the money into the open bag and started to take off running with it. But Sam raised his Colt and fired one shot that stopped them cold. "Both of you freeze right there! That's bank money. It goes back to Olsen!"

Sam and Thornis nudged their horses forward to where the two stood beside the money, their faces covered with dust. "Don't shoot!" said Garrity. "We didn't know anybody's left alive. Everybody back there is dead, except us and ole Clifford Devoe there." A few yards away Devoe, unable to hear and still stunned by the blast, turned in a wide, wobbly circle and staggered aimlessly away up the dirt street.

"Did you fellows happen to bring along any shovels?" Sam asked.

"Yes, sir," said Stokes, "we brought shovels. I didn't know why till now." He looked all around and shook his head.

"Both of you get shovels and help us bury everybody," said Thornis.

The two looked at one another. Garrity said, "To hell with all of them, Ranger. These people never meant anything to us. . . . We're Morganfield's hired help. I'd sooner see the buzzards eat him — what's left of him, that is."

"Hold on, Garrity," said Stokes, hushing him. He looked up at Sam and asked bluntly, "How much?"

"A dollar apiece?" Sam asked Thornis. "Think Olsen would mind paying to have everybody buried?"

Thornis looked down at Kaylee for a silent moment, then said, "If they don't want to pay it, I will."

Sam looked back and forth, seeing the

young boy with his fishing pole appear in the settling dust and walk along toward the deeper water past the shallows, looking back at the dead and aftermath of the explosion. The boy waved casually at Sam and kept walking. Sam smiled to himself and said to Thornis, "All right, let's get them buried, grab the money and head out of here. The sooner I'm out of Trouble Creek, the better."

"Me too," said Thornis, reaching down, taking the bag of money Garrity and Stokes handed up to him. "After you," he said to them.

Sam and the blacksmith nudged their horses forward, and followed Garrity and Stokes through the dead, the debris and the fine, settling dust.

ABOUT THE AUTHOR

Ralph Cotton has been an ironworker, a second mate on a commercial barge, a teamster, a horse trainer, and a lay minister with the Lutheran church. Visit his Web site at www.RalphCotton.com.